DEAD LIAR

RUTH NINA WELSH

RNW
PUBLISHING

Cover: Mariah Sinclair

ISBN: 978-1-0683375-1-2

For Mum & Dad

DEAD LIAR EXTRAS

Sign up for your free ***Dead Liar Extras*** - bonus scenes, author stories and more.

Details are at the end of *Dead Liar*.

CONTENTS

PROLOGUE

Killiney Bay, Ireland – 12th August 2005

Paul Arthur Tole stepped outside his floor-to-ceiling glass doors. From his hilltop mansion, he scanned the view across Killiney Bay to Sorrento Point. Ireland's very own Amalfi Coast. Home to the rich and the famous.

His company, Tole Pharmaceuticals, had given him this million-dollar view. The decision to specialise in pain-relieving drugs had proved more than fruitful. It was now a billion-dollar industry.

His phone rang.

'We have a situation, sir.'

'What?'

'There's been a data breach.'

Tole took a step back inside and moved to his desk.

'Which data?'

'Behind the Infinity Firewall.'

He took a steadying breath.

'Who?'

'A Frank O'Neill in the IT department.'

The name rang a bell.

'His wife is on the research team, sir.'

Now the pieces slotted together.

'You know what you need to do, Hale. Call me when it's done.'

'They have a child, sir. Do you want—'

'All of them.' Tole cut across him. 'Destroy everything. Don't leave a trace. And make it look good.'

There was a pause on the line.

'Is that going to be a problem?'

'No, sir. No, it won't be a problem.'

Tole hung up. Leaned back in his chair. And waited.

As the sun went down, and the mist covered the Irish Sea, he did not move from his desk.

Five hours later, the phone rang.

He picked up.

'It's done, sir, but...' The man hesitated and took a deep breath. 'The boy wasn't there.'

'You've found him?'

'No, sir. We haven't.'

Tole took a moment.

'I'm disappointed, Hale.'

Hale paused. A deep swallow on the line.

'We will find him, sir. I'll make it my personal mission to—'

Tole hung up the phone.

Turning towards his computer, he pulled up two personnel files – Frank O'Neill and Prudence O'Neill. He opened them and began searching.

One boy. Born 1992. Now 13 years of age. He scanned through both files for a recent photo. There wasn't one. And there should have been.

He tapped contacts on his phone. Hit the number. It picked up after two rings.

‘Mr Tole.’

‘Mr Keller. Regarding the opening we’ve been discussing.’

‘Yes.’

‘I’m ready to move forward with that.’

Keller didn’t miss a beat. ‘When would you like me to start?’

‘Right away.’

Paul Arthur Tole then issued two orders to Michael Keller, his new fixer and head of security.

Erase Danny Hale and his associates. And find and kill Sean O’Neill, a 13-year-old child from Rathgar, who had just become an orphan.

There was no stone to be left unturned.

No length Tole wouldn’t go to.

For some secrets have to be kept.

Whatever the cost.

NINETEEN YEARS LATER

1

East Midlands, England – 5th April 2024

Captain Jamie Shaw watched the injured soldier as he hauled himself between two parallel bars. His progress was slow and laboured. Face tense with effort and pain. Sweat pouring across his features.

As Lieutenant Timothy Dane shifted his weight to make the next torturous step, a piercing cry hit the walls of the gym, and his damaged leg collapsed beneath him. The walking harness jerked, stopping Dane's fall, and the physiotherapist moved swiftly to help him into the waiting wheelchair.

Jamie rushed across the gym. Moved between the parallel bars and faced the soldier.

She glanced towards Carla. 'Isn't the spinal chord stimulation helping?'

The physio shook her head.

Jamie knelt down in front of Timothy Dane. His eyes were as desolate as she'd ever seen them.

'How bad is it?'

She waited for his breathing to even out.

'Bad … My whole leg feels like a raw, open wound … and like someone's holding a blowtorch to it.'

'And the new medications?'

'Worse than the last.'

'You're still doing the massage and trigger point therapy?'

He nodded.

'And the relaxation, CB—'

'All of it.' He cut across her.

Dane kept swiping his arm at the sweat on his forehead, running from his hairline, his T-shirt now soaked.

'I'm on fire, Jamie.' His voice was even more desperate. 'It's like acid is running through my veins and I'm being set alight from the inside. It's relentless and…' He turned away from her.

She put her hand on his. 'Tell me?'

He turned back. 'It's been nine months. Every day is torture. Nothing's working … If this is my life now, I don't think…' His voice tailed off, eyes glistening. He bowed his head. Drowning in shame and defeat.

Pain.

It could make a strong man, a courageous man – this man – despair. Lose hope. Lose himself. Lose everything.

She had seen this too many times as an army nurse in multiple settings. Now as a case manager, coordinating the care of wounded members of the armed forces.

'Tim, there is something else I want to talk about.'

Dane struggled to pull himself upright.

'There's another treatment option. A new drug called Tolacaine has become available to us. It's just coming out of trials and being brought into clinical settings. With your level of unmanaged pain, you will be eligible for it.'

He didn't reply.

She weighed her next words.

'Although we need to be cautious … the data and peer reviews show it could be the biggest advancement in pain management for decades.'

Dane finally focused his eyes on hers. 'Do you know anyone taking it?'

Her mind went straight to Conor. *You should have let me die, Jay.* She saw him now. Coming back to life.

'I do. And they've had life-changing improvements.'

'Side-effects?'

'Very few.'

Dane was silent.

Jamie filled the space. 'I know you've tried everything, but I want you to see Dr Gild again and talk about trying this new drug.'

Timothy Dane held her eye. Then Jamie saw it. His eyes so weary from the fight, but the tantalising flicker of hope irresistible.

'OK. I'll try it.'

'Great. That's great. I'll get that moving.' Jamie squeezed his hands. 'I'll text you the appointment time next week.'

Back in the hallway, a colleague from the IT department was coming towards her. She smiled. 'What brings you down to the trenches, Mark?'

'I just wanted to check how you're doing. I know,' he hesitated. 'I know it's the anniversary today.'

Jamie looked into kind, blue eyes. She held her voice steady. 'It's good of you to remember.'

An uneasy silence followed.

Jamie was used to this now. Ever since that day, most people either ignored her loss, were incapable of offering comfort, or pressed her to move on and "build a new life".

'I should get going,' Jamie pointed to her open door.

'Of course, of course. I'll see you on Monday.'

She heard the relief in his voice.

'Yes, see you then.'

Jamie closed her office door. She fought to stay upright when all she wanted to do was fall to her knees. She reached her chair and closed her eyes. Feeling the weight of sadness inside her, and around her, which sought to crush her. But she held it together. She knew how to hold it together. Most never saw past the façade. Didn't want to see past it. To the grief bubbling like a cauldron below.

Swivelling around, she pulled forward her keyboard and wrote an email to Dr Gild about Lieutenant Dane, requesting an urgent medication review. Opening her files, she checked her notes. Digitised and updated all her patient files from today and made a dent in her emails. She worked without stopping.

Two hours later, she logged out.

Leaning back, Jamie looked at the photo sitting on her desk, feeling pain and joy in equal measure.

The image of a couple in love. Three years ago. Their sixth wedding anniversary and last holiday. A selfie in Venice. St Mark's Square.

She heard his voice as though he were in the room.

'St Mark's Basilica has a history dating back to the ninth century.'

'Really?'

'The current *campanile* – the bell tower – is a reconstruction. It was first built—'

'Fascinating,' she interrupted. Nudging him.

He tutted. Nudging her back.

He was like a walking guidebook. She smiled across at him. She loved to tease him.

They got into position.

'You need to get them both in the background,' he said.

'I know. I'm trying.'

'Wait. Not coming out of my head!'

They tussled, moved and laughed some more.

Now she had it. The perfect shot.

'Just smile for the picture, Ed.'

And he had.

His arms wrapped around her. Her face cradled in his neck. The bell tower of St Mark's above their glowing faces. The basilica shining in the November sun. Barely anyone around. The *acqua alta* flooding the square. Them in unseen wellingtons, hand-in-hand, splashing like children afterwards.

Jamie closed her eyes and rested her head in her hands.

She still found it hard to believe.

So hard to believe.

Two long years without him. And not a day that passed made it any easier.

2

It was a short, fifteen-minute drive home from the Defence Medical Rehabilitation Centre in Stanford on Soar.

Jamie had playlists created for her journey. From opera to pop, from rap to Chopin. She'd had to abandon music radio stations as unexpected songs triggered too much emotion, too many memories.

She scrolled through her phone and hit a selection of *Les nuits d'été* by Berlioz, sung by Régine Crespin.

She thought of the first time she'd heard the complete song cycle. A present from Ed, nine years ago. As newlyweds, they'd listened by firelight in their new home. Both sat mesmerised.

'Tell me how much you love me,' he said as the music ended. His fingers running through her long, straight hair. His hand trailing a path down her bare back.

She turned to face him. Saw his eyes glowing in the light of the flickering flames. Had to catch her breath. She couldn't find the words.

She leaned towards his ear. 'Let me show you,' she whispered.

Later, they played one of their silly games.

'I definitely saw you first.'

She looked at him. 'Really?' Her eyebrow arched. 'No, I think you'll find I saw you first. Talking to Becca Aldridge. Drooling.'

His eyes gleamed. Ready to up the ante. He sat forward. 'I don't think so. I saw you when you walked in. Your hair flowing, your dress too tight, your curves—'

He broke off as she hit him mid rib.

'My dress was not too tight.'

'Really?' He mimicked her arched eyebrow. 'You were the most beautiful woman in the room.'

'To you.'

'Not just to me. If you've got it…' He let the words fade as he waved his hand across her body, pulling her close, and touching every one of those curves.

The memories both saved and devastated her. Mostly saved her. Kept her going in the darkest of days. Knowing she had been so loved.

Firing up the car, she hit play. The soulful strings and soaring voice singing *Absence* flooded the speakers.

Reviens, reviens, ma bien-aimée!

Return, return my sweetest love!

She lay her head back. Let those first minutes reach deep inside. Then she turned the wheel, waved to Ned on the gate, and signalled left onto the A6006.

As the countryside passed her by, and the music enveloped her, the tension in her body and mind began to release.

Once in Loughborough, she turned off a busy Park Road and travelled up Stanley Street. The left turn into Reed Close brought her the usual mix of emotions. Their first home together, but she was now alone in it.

She moved along the close, approaching number eight,

and saw her neighbours outside their house. Seven-year-old Freya was sitting on the step with something in her arms.

As Jamie turned into her drive, she heard Freya calling.

She watched the child make her way across the shortcut they'd created between their front gardens. Her arms outstretched, carefully taking each step, her mother trailing behind.

Parking up and turning off the engine, Jamie jumped out of the car as the child reached her.

Freya held out her arms and Jamie knelt to take the plate of colourful cupcakes.

'Wow. Did you make these?'

'Mummy helped. And we used the recipe you gave us.'

Jamie felt her eyes glisten. The child she longed for but didn't have. Freya always made her think of this. Her beautiful, shining smile and those deep brown eyes full of fun and wonder.

She put the plate on the ground and the child fell into her arms. Jamie pulled back and looked into the sweet face.

'Thank you. They look so good. I love them.' She pushed unruly, corkscrew curls from Freya's eyes. 'Do you want to come in? I'll make us some juice and drinks.' Jamie looked from child to mother.

'I have ballet now,' the girl said, before Hayley could answer. Disappointment spread across her face.

'Yes, of course, it's Friday.' She smiled at Freya. 'Soon then. I'll make us a special cake.' She paused, knowing the little girl's favourite animal. 'Maybe a giraffe...'

Freya beamed.

'Bye, Jamie.' Then she was gone. Waving and darting back to her own garden.

Her mother held Jamie's eye. 'I've been thinking of you. I'll ring you later.' Hayley pulled her close for a quick hug, her braided hair pressing on Jamie's cheek, the faint smell of almond oil comforting. She handed Jamie a card then followed her daughter home.

Hayley had been her rock over the past two years. And Freya her sweet, shining star. Jamie couldn't imagine life without either of them.

3

On the dot of six o'clock, Jamie put the key into her door. Two years to the day since her world imploded. Police officers knocking at her door. A family friend giving her the worst news she could have imagined.

'Jamie, I don't know how to say this.' DC George Hanson had paused, struggling to speak. 'Earlier today…' He looked across at the officer with him. Jamie followed his gaze. Fear building inside her. The policewoman went to speak but George held up a hand and turned back to Jamie. 'Earlier today, Ed died in a car crash.'

Her world had spun. And since that day, it had never stopped spinning.

It was the timing that haunted her most. If only Ed had left work a few seconds earlier. If only he'd left a few seconds later. If only he'd taken a different route. If only. If only. If only.

She understood illness and losing people. She knew about war and its casualties. But this kind of accident, with no preparation, no warning, was new territory for her. She didn't know how anyone grappled with the shock of it. Even two years on, it was just as sharp and jagged. Just as unbelievable. Just as traumatic.

Jamie eased off her shoes in the hallway. Hung her coat between Ed's favourite ski jacket and his khaki raincoat. She saw no reason to move them. Passing through the immaculate living and dining rooms and into the kitchen, she placed the cupcakes on the worktop and opened her card.

To Jamie,
Thinking of you especially today.
The cakes were Freya's idea.
We love you so much.
Hayley & Freya xx

Freya's pictures and scrawling handwriting decorated the card. Colourful kisses scattered around her words: *I love you, Freya.*

Jamie held the card tight. Held on even tighter to her tears.

Turning around, she made a space on the fridge beside a tiger and a card with two hands crossed, wedding rings visible. She knew the words by heart. Written in black ink in Ed's curving handwriting.

My darling wife, Jamie.
I never believed I'd find a soulmate.
I never believed I'd find you.
Now it's us against the world, my love.
Your husband, Ed x

She ran fingertips over the words. *Us against the world.* And she felt the ache in her stomach and the pull in her chest which threatened to take her under. But she stopped herself from falling, from sinking. She tucked Freya's card beside Ed's and moved away.

Back in the living room, she fired up her laptop. Over the last two years, in spite of what others advised – often forcefully – she avoided going out to socialise. She didn't want to pretend happiness she didn't feel, and she had no desire to forget. To "move on" as people described it. She preferred to be at home, surrounded by memories, her husband's presence all around her. This place was her solace.

Instead, she'd been taking online tours. Travelling the world had helped with the crushing loneliness. And she needed that more than ever today. She had a tour booked for this evening, in her favourite location.

Heading upstairs, she changed out of her army uniform and smiled at the contrast in the wardrobe she didn't want to change.

The left was Ed's side. Messy. Jackets and trousers didn't match. Jumpers and T-shirts were carelessly folded. Barely altered since that day.

She imagined what people would think if they knew. If they saw. But it was her choice to live in the past. She didn't need to answer to anyone else.

Her side of the wardrobe was immaculate and precise. Her army training meant precision was everything.

Fifteen minutes later, showered and changed, she was walking down the stairs when her phone rang.

'Dad, how are you doing?'

'I'm alright sweet pea. I just wondered if you could pick something else up for later? I've run out of batteries for the remote. Can't figure out how to put the damn telly on and it's the final of Love Island at nine.'

He laughed and Jamie heard the familiar wheeze in his chest.

'Double A or Triple A?' she said.

'The smaller ones.'

'OK. No problem. I'll get them from Ketchers on the way.' She checked her watch and smiled at his ever-quirky TV schedule. 'Don't worry, you won't miss your programme. I'll be there just before half-past eight.'

'Perfect. Thank you darling. See you later.'

'Bye for now, Dad.'

Dad.

Tom McDonald was Dad in every sense of the word. She'd called him that from the moment she was engaged to his son. Ed often joked that she married him for his father.

He was her anchor. It often seemed like he was the only one who understood the depth of her sorrow. Because it was his sorrow too.

Never knowing her own father, she hadn't realised the deep longing that absence had given her. The unconditional acceptance, encouragement and strength a good father's love can give.

As a child, her mother had tried to sugar coat it.

'Where's my Daddy?'

'He left when you were just a baby.'

'Didn't he want me?'

Her mother had been silent before offering a half truth.

'It was me he didn't want, sweetheart.'

And that was enough for Jamie. She didn't ask again.

As she got older, she'd never wanted to find him. She wouldn't betray her mother in that way. But when she died, just after Jamie's seventeenth birthday, her life shattered.

Alone in the world. Adrift. The army became her family and her home.

Until she met Ed.

Then his father – the irrepressible Tom McDonald – became hers. And she began to build the family she longed for.

Back in the kitchen, Jamie had put together a quick chicken and homemade apple and pear chutney sandwich when the timer on her phone rang.

She checked the clock. Five minutes to go.

Picking up her coffee, she took the sandwiches and one of Freya's pink cupcakes into the living room. Curling up on the sofa in front of her laptop, she settled in. Her seven o'clock visit to Ireland would start any minute.

She opened the email sent at six o'clock – *One hour until your secret tour in Kerry.*

She clicked the link.

4

The screen showed a blurry countryside image with words across the centre.

David Marr, Artist
Inside The Ring:
Hidden Kerry, Day 8
Your adventure begins at 7 p.m.

The chat stream on the left showed names of people joining the tour. The comments were flying.

Jamie recognised many of the names and typed out a few 'hellos'.

The seconds counted down as she waited for her favourite guide to appear. She checked her watch. 7:02 p.m. Seconds later, the screen changed, and David Marr was live on camera.

'Hello Jane, Kay from the UK, Jim in Wisconsin, Captain Jamie, Paul in Oz and everyone else. It's great to see you all. Sorry I'm running a bit late.'

He paused for a few seconds. Eyes scanning the comments.

'Nothing that exciting, Carl. I left my brushes in the car and had to dash back for them.'

Lots of smiling emojis hit the chat.

'OK guys, it's just past seven. Let's crack on and make a start as time is of the essence today.'

He paused for a few seconds, then carried on.

'If you're new to my tours, I'm David Marr, an English artist living in Connemara, which is on the west coast of Ireland. Last week, I travelled down to the Ring of Kerry for a two-week painting tour. It's already Day 8 on the tour. So, where do you think our secret location is today?'

David's face broke into a smile as he read the comments and suggestions.

'Interesting ideas. You're in the right direction, Matt. We have travelled east since yesterday. Let me turn the camera around and show you where we are.'

Jamie watched the view switch from his face to a single-track tarmac road with banked hedgerows and varying heights of trees on either side. She smiled. It could have been any countryside location. Emojis and joking complaints filled the chat.

'Got to keep you guessing,' David laughed as he began to walk along the road.

'Now, as many of you know, The Ring of Kerry is famous in Ireland and worldwide. But I'm more interested in what's inside the Ring. The Hidden Kerry, which visitors don't often see. Each day I'm painting the places we visit. And at the end of this two-week tour, those fourteen paintings will go into an exhibition back home in Connemara.'

Jamie always appreciated David's camera work. As he walked, there was no chance of triggering vertigo or motion sickness. Unlike many other online tour guides, his hand and gimbal were steady.

As he walked further forward, a bend in the road lay ahead.

'OK. Here we go, guys. Get ready. Here comes the reveal.'

He took a few more steps and turned the corner. He angled the camera towards the ground, then began to raise it slowly, pulling up towards the horizon. It was breathtaking. Water and mountains came into view as he scanned across the scene.

'Here we are then, the next gem on our Hidden Kerry Tour. Welcome to the gorgeous Lough Acoose. If you want to know where I am, I've just added a map. It's top right of your screen.'

Jamie took in the spectacular view. Ireland was a place she'd longed to visit, but Ed had never wanted to go. She'd travelled to Northern Ireland many times – to visit Conor, her best friend and ex-army buddy – but never crossed the border.

'So it's Day 8 and the weather has been incredibly kind to us. Welcome to a Lough & Mountain Sunset Tour. We're going to walk part way around the Lough, then I'll be setting up my easel. You'll be able to watch as I paint the sun going down over those mountains, the awesome MacGillycuddy's Reeks.'

The scene was stunning. The sun radiant. Light glistened and twinkled on the calm water and across the lower part of the mountain range which encircled the Lough.

David started walking again. His camera now turned to the road ahead.

In the far distance, on the curving road, Jamie saw a figure. The first sign of life they'd seen today.

'I've got a couple of tour facts for you, as I know you love them. Lough Acoose is a freshwater lake, and it's just over half a mile long and a third of a mile wide. And in the distance,' he moved the camera away from the road and back

onto the Lough, *'you can see Carrauntoohill, Ireland's highest mountain.'*

He paused.

'Sure, Daniel. I can zoom in for you.'

With the sun sitting above the mountain range, he zoomed in and scanned across the entire panorama. Even as the lowering sun cast deep shadows, there were hues of greens and browns, stones and scattered rocks, and terraced stepped areas visible across the mountains.

Zooming back out, David began walking again and settled on the view of the road ahead.

Jamie's eyes were drawn back to the figure. It was a man. He was much closer now. She could see his head bent low, covered in a dark hat. Blue jeans and a cream woollen jumper completed his look.

He was walking at pace, left hand in his trouser pocket and right arm swinging loosely by his side. It was a rolling gait. Favouring his left leg, an unusual but definite limp from the hip.

'Yes Pam, there's a lot of walking and hiking tours around here and across the Reeks. And Amanda, you can absolutely go fishing in the Lough. You'll mainly catch brown trout and—'

But Jamie wasn't listening anymore. Her eyes were fixed on the walking man. Now around seventy feet away, his head still dipped low, face hidden, looking at the ground.

She sat forward on the sofa. Leaned further into the screen. Watched the man move closer, step by step.

Her heart began to thump in her chest.

It was impossible.

Completely impossible.

She blinked harder to clear her vision. But the man was still moving closer in a relentless rhythm.

She knew that stature.

She knew that walk.

She'd know them anywhere.

The swinging right arm and a distinctive limp that came from a fractured hip on a skiing trip in Chamonix six years ago.

The mug of coffee in her left hand crashed onto the wooden floor. Her hand reached up to her chest to try to still the powerful beat inside her ribcage.

For on-screen, walking towards the camera, right in front of her eyes, was Ed.

Her dead husband.

5

Jamie ignored the coffee seeping into her wooden floor and the broken mug around her bare feet. She crouched over her laptop, taking screenshots as she watched her husband get nearer and nearer to the lens.

She needed these pictures, or she might never believe what she'd seen. It would be hours before David uploaded this tour video to their private subscriber group. She couldn't wait that long.

As the man got within twenty feet of the camera, he still did not look up. His head now turned more to the right. Jamie saw shoulder-length brown hair and a full beard, making the skin on his face almost invisible. Then he spoke in Irish. Words she did not understand. David answered, adding more incomprehensible words.

Jamie's shock ratcheted up another notch. Doubts flooded her mind. He didn't sound like her husband. It wasn't just the language, the timbre was different. This man's voice was higher in pitch, lilting and musical. Nothing like Ed's rich, low tones.

She continued to take screenshots as the man got closer.

Then her brain slowed, one thought chasing on top of another. Fractions of a second between them.

She must have been mistaken … It wasn't Ed at all … This man was thinner … Had a beard … There must be so many other people who walk in the same way … And this man was speaking Irish … Crazy of her to think it was Ed … This is what grief does … The two-year anniversary playing tricks with her mind … Her husband was dead … She had caressed the wedding ring and chain, the only things which survived the firebomb of the crash.

Then more thoughts flashed across her mind, chasing the others away.

But she hadn't seen his body … It was too badly burnt … Beyond recognition, they'd told her … What if it hadn't been Ed at all?

In escalating shock and confusion, Jamie didn't know what to believe.

But then she saw it. Just before the man walked out of shot. His head leaning to the left.

Something unmistakable. Something which changed everything.

In that moment, she felt her entire world pivot. Because she knew, without a shadow of a doubt, that her first instinct had been correct.

The impossible was real.

This was Ed.

He was alive.

And he was walking on a deserted tarmac road in the middle of the Irish countryside.

6

The stitching on the beanie hat.

How could she have imagined, when Ed's mother knitted and embroidered a pair of golf clubs and his initials on the dark blue hat, that it would lead to this moment?

Jamie had searched for it everywhere. Distraught that it was lost. Ed's favourite beanie. Especially cherished after his mother's death five years before.

After turning the house upside down, with her father helping, Jamie had to accept the precious hat was gone. But she never stopped looking for it. Never stopped hoping it would show up.

And it had shown up.

On a dead man.

A dead liar.

She couldn't comprehend the magnitude of it.

With her husband now out of shot, she frantically hit the keyboard, typing at speed.

David, can you spin the camera around, back up the road you've just walked down? I want to see something.

She waited, desperate that he would see her comment.

As a paid subscriber to David Marr's channel, her profile

and words would show up in blue. They'd stand out from the many other comments onscreen. But there were hundreds of words and emojis flying through the chat.

She typed the message again.

Seconds passed. Long seconds. With David talking about things she could not begin to take in.

With shaking hands on the keyboard, she started typing again. *David, can you—*

'Of course, Jamie. Let me turn around.'

She watched as he turned a circle. The camera looked back up the long, curving, tarmac road David Marr had just walked down.

It was empty.

Not a man in sight.

Not a soul in sight.

Her husband had simply vanished.

7

Jamie stared at the screen. David's voice chattered in the background, his laughter now jarring.

It felt like before, when police officers sat in this very space and told her Ed had died. But this time it was amplified. There wasn't just shock and disbelief, confusion and bewilderment. There was betrayal. And anger. It wasn't molten, fiery rage. It was ice cold. As though the blood running through her veins was freezing her from the inside out. Her body like stone, her limbs leaden and lifeless.

Her mind flashed to the walking man. To her husband. She heard the Irish words. Saw his gait. The swinging arm. A partial beard. The country road. The beanie hat. All the images appeared out of order. Like snapshots of a jumbled-up montage, with each picture blurring into the next.

Then she saw something else. The face from her past. His smile, his laugh. Things she had not seen in real time for two years. And it hit her like a force. Her husband was alive. His face, his smile, his touch, were no longer gone forever. Were no longer lost to her forever.

Ed was alive.

A feeling she could only describe as ecstasy flooded

through her. Pushing heat through her body. The warmth spreading from her core, her heart, out through her limbs. It was all she'd wanted for two desperate years.

But as new images formed in her mind – of Ed, of Ireland, of her, of them – cold, hard reality hit. The truth shattering her fairytale dreams.

Her husband had chosen to leave her. A tragic road accident had not separated them. He had deliberately left her alone. Abandoned her. Left her to mourn him. Faked his own death. And he was alive and living in another country. What kind of perverse cruelty was that? What person could do that? Not someone who loved you.

She bent forward, doubled over. Her stomach cramping, chest aching, making it hard to breathe. Her heart did not know how to live with this reality. It was easier before, believing he was gone but knowing she had been loved.

Sickness rose in her stomach. Moving as fast as she could, avoiding the broken pieces of the coffee mug near her feet, she got up. Stumbled. Her legs like jelly, almost giving way beneath her. She just made it to the bathroom in time to throw up. Retching from the deepest part of herself.

When there was nothing left inside, she swilled her mouth and doused her face with cold water. Leaning on the sink, exhausted and shaky, one question forced itself into Jamie's mind.

Why?

Why would Ed do this to her?

But that wasn't enough. Other questions weaved their way in and swamped her.

Had their love meant nothing to him? Had all those years of blissful married life been a lie? Had she been mourning a man who had never really loved her? And worst of all, most painful of all, was he even alone in Ireland, or did he have a life there with someone else?

As these dark possibilities took hold, she sank to the floor. There were no wracking sobs. No wailing noises. She didn't make a sound. The trauma had rendered her mute. And as Jamie felt silent tears running down her face, she held her arms tight around herself as though, somehow, this would keep her from breaking apart.

8

Jamie sat in the still silence. Tears slowing but questions continuing on a loop inside her head.

She thought of Tom. Their father. Her anchor. She needed to tell him that his son was alive. He would be overwhelmed with joy, but as shocked as her that they'd been deceived. Mourning and suffering for nothing. She didn't know how she'd find the words.

From the photos and video, he would recognise Ed immediately. He'd know the beanie hat. Remember his wife making it. And remember them looking for it when it was lost.

'I think it's gone, sweet pea.'

'It can't be gone, Dad.'

'Maybe,' he'd paused, as though struggling to speak. 'Maybe it was with him when…' He didn't need to finish the sentence. Their eyes met, and she leant into his arms as they wept together for all they'd lost.

Jamie knew her father. He'd want to know what she'd seen right away. Keeping it from him was a betrayal. But it was only six months since his serious heart attack. She feared the shock of this news could actually kill him. She needed to wait before unleashing this grenade.

Taking a towel from the rail, she wiped her face. Her clothes were wet where unchecked tears had fallen. Pulling herself to her feet, she almost toppled over. Her head spinning. A look in the mirror shocked her. She was beyond pale, her skin opaque.

She made her way unsteadily back to the sofa. Picked up her phone and glanced at the laptop. David Marr was sitting at his easel, his paint palette beside him, his camera on the tripod behind him. The sun glowing on top of the mountain range.

'As you can see, I'm using watercolour again today. I've laid down a rough outline before I start to paint. Now I'm going to...'

Jamie reached over and hit mute. She needed to think.

A glance at her phone told her it was 7:35 p.m. Her father was expecting her soon. She knew she had to get herself together. Facing him was going to be almost impossible. They didn't keep secrets from each other, he would know something was wrong the moment he saw her. He wouldn't even need his x-ray eyes and acute antenna. She'd have to invent a cover for her fragile state. Maybe it wouldn't be so difficult to be convincing on this two-year anniversary of her husband's death.

Her mind was racing, chasing thoughts and possibilities round and around. If she couldn't tell her father, she needed to talk to someone. To tell someone what she'd seen. If she didn't, she might go mad, her brain implode.

Her first thought was Conor. Her second thought was better. George. Ed's best friend. He would be shocked, horrified and overjoyed to learn this news. But he could help her get the answers she needed. As a police officer, George had the connections. He could even get the local police in Ireland to help look for Ed.

She took a steadying breath. Tapped contacts on her phone and dialled. George picked up after just three rings.

'Jamie.'

She heard his soft, deep voice. It usually made her feel less alone, connecting her to the past and to her husband. Right now, it increased her agitation. She swallowed, preparing to speak.

'I've been thinking of you today,' he carried on. 'I was going to call by later. Sheena sends her love.'

Jamie couldn't speak. The words trapped inside her mouth.

'Jamie?'

Another long pause, then it all came pouring out.

'George, something … something crazy has happened.' Before he could answer, she rushed on. 'Ed is alive.'

There was a pause on the line. She could hear a change in George's breathing.

'What? What do you mean?'

'I've just seen him online. I was—'

He cut across her. 'I know it's the anniversary today. I've been struggling too. Are you sure that…' he broke off. 'It's impossible. Did anyone else see him? Is anyone with you?'

He didn't believe her. Of course he didn't. He wanted an extra witness for verification. What she was saying did sound like madness. She had actually seen Ed and even she'd doubted herself earlier. But she could put George's doubts to rest very quickly. He would recognise Ed from the tour footage in a heartbeat.

'No. I'm on my own. But I saw him, George. He's alive.'

'It's … unbelievable.' His voice was distant. 'I … I can't believe it.'

‘I have photos. Let me WhatsApp them to you. I’ll have a video soon too.’

‘No.’ He was abrupt. ‘No, don’t do that. I’ll come over. I want to come over and be with you. I can look at them then.’

‘We have to find him, George. Will you travel with me to—’

‘I’ll do anything you need.’ He interrupted her again. ‘Let’s talk about it when I get there.’

Jamie checked her watch.

‘I’m worried about Tom. I’m due there at half-past eight. He’s expecting me. I need to tell him, but his heart…’ she tailed off.

‘I’ll be there in time. Let’s keep this between us just now. We don’t want Tom finding out from someone else.’

She paused. Thinking. It made sense. That would be horrific. And she knew how quickly this news would spread among George’s colleagues and ex-officer friends of her father.

George talked through her silence. ‘We need to tell Tom first, but with his heart … like you say, it’s going to be a terrible shock. We can make sure it’s Ed and then tell him together.’

Jamie stayed quiet. *We can make sure it’s Ed.* He still didn’t believe her.

‘Just wait for me at home,’ George kept talking. ‘I can study the photos and videos. We’ll go to Tom and tell him together.’ He paused. ‘Then we can start looking for Ed.’

She heard something in his voice. She felt a sensation in her gut. He didn’t think they’d be finding Ed anytime soon. He was just pacifying her. But his words about her father were true. The shock would be enormous. She couldn’t imagine what it would do to him.

She took a few more seconds before deciding. She’d wait for George. Half an hour wasn’t long and her father counted

George as a friend. There was no-one better to have by her side when she broke this shocking news.

'OK. I'll wait for you. We'll go together.'

'Good. That's good.'

She heard him moving around. A door slamming. The car starting.

'I'm just leaving home. I'll be there in thirty minutes.'

Before she could answer, he'd hung up the phone.

9

Killiney Bay, Ireland – 5th April 2024

A large, glass pavilion held Paul Arthur Tole's family. The setting sun across Killiney Bay and Dalkey Island was a good background for this gathering. The photos would be outstanding.

Tole watched his wife, his three children, and seven grandchildren. He felt satisfied. Had no regrets. No stabs of conscience that he'd denied others these same moments with their family. He knew some men softened with age. Not him. There was far too much to lose.

'Grandpa! Grandpa!'

The small boy was running towards him. Wonder on his face. The bluest of eyes looking at him. The child carefully held out a flower in the palm of his hand. A delicate pink crown with bright yellow stamens.

'I found this on the ground. What is it Grandpa?'

Tole took the flower. Pulled the boy closer. Arthur was the third of his grandchildren, the one who almost made him feel paternal. His firstborn Lincoln, the boy's father, was the heir apparent. In time, Arthur would gain it all. His legacy. With the right training.

'It's just a flower.'

'I know, but what kind of flower? Flowers have names.' The boy looked impatient.

'Why does it matter?'

The child stopped, looking up at him. 'Well…' He faltered as the blue eyes pierced his.

'A flower's a flower.'

Tole dropped it to the floor and ground it beneath his feet.

Tears sprang in the boy's eyes.

Tole watched the small face look down at the crushed petals. Watched him raise his head. The child met his gaze and did not flinch. Only Arthur, and his father, had ever managed this. The boy's misty eyes cleared.

'Go back to the others. Play now.'

The child waited, as though he wanted to speak. Blue eyes fixed to blue eyes. Instead, he turned. Slowly walking back towards his cousins.

Tole cast his eyes around. His smiling wife was beckoning him towards her, their son Lincoln beside her. The photographer from Time magazine had arrived. He was setting up, preparing to capture an image of him, the man with the pre-eminent role in discovering the best drug for a generation to manage chronic pain. Tolacaine was finally making its way out into the world.

He walked a few steps. Stopped as he felt his phone vibrate. Pulled it from his pocket and saw the name in the window. Keller. His head of security.

With the music playing around him, his wife gesturing and growing more impatient, he answered the phone.

'Mr Tole.'

'Yes, Keller.'

'Regarding Sean O'Neill.' Keller paused. 'Our suspicions were correct.' He paused again. 'He is still alive.'

Tole felt his whole body tense.

He listened to Keller's quiet words. His explanations. And plans.

Depending on how much O'Neill had learned and pieced together, Tole could lose everything that mattered to him. He could be ruined. Shunned. A pariah. Even by his own family.

He took a breath. Scanned around him. It was easier to fall than anyone realised. It could happen in an instant. There was always the fight. Always the defence. The stakes so high to keep on advancing. To never go back to being nothing. Being nobody. Like his feckless parents.

'What do you want me to do, Mr Tole?'

He took in a deep breath. The rage that drove him beginning to infiltrate every cell in his body. The scent of the hunter filling his veins.

Find and kill Sean O'Neill.

He remembered the words like it was yesterday.

Nineteen years later, as his family laughed and danced beneath a sunset sky, he spoke them again.

10

County Kerry, Ireland – 5th April 2024

Ed Taylor sat watching the sun set across MacGillycuddy's Reeks. A magical sight which he never tired of. Colours were now emerging across the pale blue sky and he had his camera at the ready. It was going to be spectacular tonight.

It was a cool evening sitting out on the porch. One of his favourite times of the day, especially when it wasn't raining. He'd learned to love the rain, there was so much of it in County Kerry. Ireland's forty shades of green wasn't an exaggeration.

He'd almost grown used to the silence too and used to his own company. Tucked away from prying eyes, he had a view of the tracks and hills for miles around. No-one could get close without him knowing. His house was an unseen fortress, protected and safe.

The sound of the Hallelujah chorus pierced through the still silence.

His body went rigid. His heartbeat quickened.

Reaching into his pocket, he pulled out a burner phone

which never left his side. Placed on his bedside table every night, to ensure it was always charged. The phone, which had not made a sound for two years, was now ringing. He recognised the number in the window.

He clicked the button to answer.

'Ed?'

He felt a pain hit his chest. Hearing his best friend's voice after so long. The separation still overwhelmed him.

'What's happened?'

The reply was distorted. A poor signal.

'Say that again.'

'Jamie knows.'

Ed's hands clenched.

The words were clear this time. The distress in George's voice palpable. Was this the moment? The moment he had feared and dreaded every day for two years.

'What does she know?' Ed said.

'She knows you're alive.'

Ed felt a spinning in his head.

'How? What did she say?'

'That you're alive, that she saw you online…'

The signal dipped again.

'…has proof, photos and videos.'

Ed put a hand to his neck to feel rock hard tension, struggling to see how this was possible.

'Did she say a location?'

'I stopped her. Better if I still don't know where you are. But she knows. I'm sure of it.'

Ed paused, taking in the information, and the enormity of the ramifications.

'Has she told anyone else?'

'No. But she's on the edge of telling Tom.'

Ed felt a further stab of pain in his chest at the mention of his father.

'I'm in the car, on my way to Jamie now. I persuaded her to stay at home, to wait for me there, said we'd go to Tom together. She'll want to find you, Ed. What do you need me to do?'

'You have to stop her. Do whatever it takes. Tell her anything you need to. Just take her and my father away. Keep them safe.'

'I'll call you when I get to her. I'll be there in twenty minutes.'

Ed hung up the phone. He'd been unable to offer any pleasantries to the best friend he had not talked to for two years. His mind in shock, firing in multiple directions.

He reached into his pocket. From a notebook, he texted a new phone number to George. He took the back off the phone, retrieved the SIM card and snapped it into pieces.

He rushed inside. Pulled off his beanie hat and cream jumper and stood in front of an internal steel door which had a retinal eye scanner attached and a digital keypad.

He opened the door to his office. An oblong room with white walls and no windows. Opposite was another steel door. On the left was a long desk with a bank of computers and a black chair on castors. A tall, fireproof filing cabinet sat in the far left corner. On the right, a whiteboard covered the wall with a vast network of information. Photocopied news reports, handwritten notes, photos with vibrant red crosses struck through them, and arrows linking back and forth between the information. At the centre was a photo of Paul Arthur Tole. And at the top, Tole Pharmaceuticals was written in capitals in bold, black writing.

Ed sat at his desk. He couldn't believe this was happening. How had Jamie seen him? He checked across all his cameras and his sensors. He'd had no alerts. No triggers had gone off. His security was state-of-the art. He had surveillance covering a radius of two miles out from his house. Sensors in the ground, cameras triggered only by human presence, with delicate trip wires. All would warn of any intruder. He also had radar installed, watching the sky. He kept himself away from the world, careful with every movement he made. But George had said there were photos and video. How was this possible?

His mind went back to half an hour ago, walking along the Lough Road, the man with his camera held up on a gimbal. He'd looked like a harmless tourist. Ed had taken a risk to walk past him. Thought he'd protected himself by making sure his face was not visible, but it was too much of a coincidence.

He took a minute to visualise the scene. They'd spoken in Irish, but he knew the man was English from his accent. Ed focused his mind and searched his memory. He'd only looked at the man from a safe distance. He wore light blue denim jeans, and a dark long-sleeved shirt. There was a striking white logo covering the entire front of his top which Ed had never seen before. The word GLOBE written in capitals above an image of the earth. More writing and imagery that he could not make out was written underneath the logo.

He did a rough drawing, took a photo, and started an image search on Google. There was no match, just similar imagery and logos. He scanned through page after page, then stopped. He saw the image he was looking for. He clicked. It was an online virtual travel company. He hit the website link and read their mission statement.

Globe & Go offer virtual tours around the world. Following our success during the pandemic, our guides are pushing even further to share their experiences with you. Our aim? To take you – virtually – to every place on the globe.

He created a fake account to log in. Less than a minute later, Ed was typing "Lough Acoose" in the search bar. No results came back, but a related list showed guides and tours across Ireland.

Ed scanned the profiles.

A *Hidden Kerry Tour* was live right now. He read the summary. *Tour guide David Marr is an English artist travelling throughout Ireland…*

He read no further. He clicked the link to join the live tour.

There was the man he had seen behind an easel painting the mountain range of MacGillycuddy's Reeks. The screen was full of people chatting. Comments were flashing by, and he noticed many names had locations attached. Just a cursory glance showed him people were watching from all over the world.

Ed pulled up the volume.

'…trying to capture a scene like this and working at speed can be a challenge…'

Could Jamie have been watching this live stream? Exploring her love of Ireland. Did she see him walking along the Lough Road? He hung his head in despair. What were the chances of that happening?

Clicking away from the tour, he visited the blog of artist David Marr. He scanned through the comments. Searched post after post. Then there it was. A message from the profile "Captain Jamie." His heart cramped as though crushed in a steel vice. The profile picture was from their last trip to Venice. He had taken it. Jamie was standing in front of the Doge's Palace.

After two years of seclusion, with a perfect disappearance, he had been found.

Head in his hands, he thought of all he'd done, all he'd lost to keep those he loved safe. All he'd done over two decades to honour his first mother and father, his birth parents, Prudence and Frank O'Neill. To continue their work and get justice for them. To unearth the truth of why they were murdered. Why all their lives had been shattered.

He couldn't believe it. Couldn't believe this million-to-one random chance of being discovered. Especially now, when he was so close to the truth. So close to putting the last pieces of the puzzle together to get the answers he had sacrificed everything for.

Fear rippled through his body.

He knew his wife. She wouldn't stop until she found him.

But she had no idea of the danger she was in.

No idea of the danger Tom, his beloved adoptive father, was in.

And no idea of the danger Ed himself was now in.

11

Jamie checked her watch. The minutes felt like hours. She'd been wandering around the kitchen, gathering things together for her father, but she was going around in circles. Trying to get a grip on herself. On her emotions.

She thought of the war zones she'd been in. Of Iraq. Afghanistan. How she'd been able to cope with anything. Nursing soldiers who came in with life-changing injuries. Dealing with danger. Always on alert. Her mind sharp and her skills sharper.

She needed some of that focus, that control, right now. But nothing she'd ever experienced could prepare her for a dead husband returning to life. It was like an emotional tsunami, volcano and earthquake all rolled into one.

'How much do you love me?'

She heard those words now like a taunt. Saw her husband's face and felt physical pain through her chest. Her limbs heavy. Her mind a fog.

Ed had left her. Deliberately left her. Faked his own death. How much had he really loved her?

Through all the confusion and the unanswered questions, there was one thing she did know. One thing she was sure of.

After she saw George and her father, whatever either of them said or tried to persuade her to do, she was going to Ireland. She would track Ed down herself. She needed answers. However bad those answers were. For as much as she tried to hold on to the crushing revelation of his betrayal and deception, the desperation to see him, lay eyes on him and touch him, was visceral. It was taking her over. Those emotions had a will of their own and they were driving her forward.

She glanced at her watch again. George was still fifteen minutes away. Jamie started pulling her own things together for the trip she intended to make.

Upstairs in the front bedroom, she paused at the window and looked out around the close she called home. Nick Grant pulled into the drive opposite, his children playing in the front room. Mrs Thornton had her curtains open, her TV flashing colours high above the fireplace.

Everything was the same as yesterday and yet everything had changed. It was impossible to grasp. She closed the blind. Closed out the normal world. She wasn't a part of that anymore.

At her wardrobe, she looked through her clothes and dressed for her journey. She put several thin layers on underneath a thick black hoodie and found her most comfortable trainers for walking. She paired them with warm socks.

Reaching up, she pulled her emergency go bag from the shelf. The army had taught her to prepare for swift exits. She opened her backpack to check its contents. She had her passport, a bundle of cash, an unused credit card, a pay-as-you-go phone with extra SIM card, a fully charged battery pack, charging leads and essential toiletries. She tucked in extra underwear and she was ready.

Backpack on her shoulder, she moved along the landing. The back bedroom door was open, the light from the hallway shining a path to her father's washed and ironed clothes. As she walked forwards and bent to pick up the laundry bag, she glimpsed the sky. The sun had set, leaving behind a radiant mix of oranges and reds, flashing in patterns across the horizon.

She stepped towards the window, looked over the back garden, and thought of her husband. Could Ed see the sun setting? Would the sun set later or earlier for him? Would he have his camera poised to add this evening's view to his collection? Her mind was ready to continue on another damaging loop of questions when movement distracted her. Something in her peripheral vision.

Glancing down from the far horizon, her eyes adjusted to the dimming light. She saw shadows from the line of trees which edged her path.

Moving shadows.

She felt a drop in her chest.

She squinted and focused again.

Her eyes had not deceived her. Two men were creeping along the edge of her garden towards the house.

Her heart rate rose second on second. The men were just eighty feet from her back door.

Jamie jolted back from the window. Stood to the left side and peered around again. She could see the men move stealthily. Not looking up, but intent on moving forwards, using the border of trees and shrubs in her garden as some form of cover.

Jamie felt an adrenaline surge. Strength jolted through her body. She had no idea who they were, she just knew she needed to move. And move fast.

She dropped the bag of clothes, ran downstairs, and grabbed her coat and keys from the hooks in the hallway. She would be in her car in seconds. She just needed her computer.

In the front room, she leant to pick up her laptop from the table. As she unplugged it from the charging lead, her eyes flashed to the front window. Through the angled venetian blinds, she saw a black, four-wheel-drive crawl past Hayley and Freya's house, stop in front of her drive, and block her car in.

The passenger door opened.

A tall, well-groomed man, wearing a dark suit and striped tie, stepped out. She glimpsed the gun and holster before he buttoned up his jacket.

He started walking up her driveway.

She darted back into the hall, shoved the laptop inside the padded compartment in her backpack and put the keys into her pocket.

She heard a noise at the back door. Heard a long creak as it opened. There was no banging. No thud of a break in.

They had keys.

The alarm began to beep. It was quickly silenced.

They had the alarm code.

Trapped inside, from the back and from the front, there was only one way Jamie could go.

Up.

12

Missing the first step, Jamie took the carpeted stairs, quick and soft. Reaching the top, she heard the men below in her kitchen. Their low voices travelling through the house. She heard a knock at the front door.

Tiptoeing across the landing, she reached the open and exposed wooden staircase to the loft. This was hazardous. The wood expanded and contracted, with differences in temperature, making the stairs creak at random times when walked on.

Jamie took each step, slowly, her heart now beating to a fierce rhythm.

She felt a large creak underneath her as she made it to the halfway point of the staircase. The sound seemed to reverberate throughout the entire upstairs space.

Pausing, she heard the loose board creak on the first step of the lower stairs. She couldn't wait any longer.

Moving quickly, she reached the top of the staircase and slid around the open door into her home office and library. Light from the hallway partially lit the room. Enough light for what she needed to do.

In the loft space, sloped eaves held one Velux window

looking onto the back of the house. An easy chair in the corner and a large desk taking centre stage. Books covered each wall. The angles of the room, and the shorter side of the eaves, meant all the wooden ash shelves had been handmade. Not a joint was out of place. This was one of Ed's projects, something he'd insisted on doing.

Her husband's words came to her through the mists of memory.

'If anything ever happens, someone gets into the house, you feel in danger, you come up here.'

Jamie had looked around the loft space as Ed stood watching her.

'What do I do next?'

He pushed aside a group of hardback books, flicked a hidden catch, and pulled the bookcase towards him. 'You go in here and call the police. Then you wait until it's safe to come out.'

She bent forward and saw the depths his fear had taken him.

He had created a small, hidden space under the eaves. Like a priest hole, from the time of Catholic persecution. He shone a torch inside and showed her the bolt which needed to close to ensure the unit anchored back in place once you were inside.

He looked at her and pointed at the open gap. 'Try it.'

She shook her head. Stepping back. She didn't want to crawl into the dark, tight space. It looked suffocating. And it felt like a step too far, even for Ed's obsession.

Standing here now, what had previously seemed crazy, felt lifesaving. She wished she'd been inside, had some memory to call on. But she had never opened it, even after Ed's death. She hoped the hinges had not seized.

She heard noise in the hallway below. She needed to move now.

Hands trembling, Jamie pulled forward the bookcase. It glided. She took it slowly as every minuscule sound was magnified by the still silence around her. Once pulled forward, the shelves pivoted on a hidden hinge. There was a small creak as the hinge bent backwards, but it opened fully.

The dark space under the eaves appeared in front of her.

Jamie heard a creak on the loft stairs. She could feel her heart pounding on her rib cage. She pushed her coat and backpack into the space. Crawled in and pulled the bookshelf back into place, inch by careful inch. As she felt for the bolt, she slid it into position.

With just seconds to spare, she was safe. Invisible. Her hiding place pitch black.

Footsteps were pacing the wooden floor. The boards creaking as he walked. She was sure he would hear her heavy breathing and her pounding heartbeat through the walls of the room.

She heard books being moved. Tapping noises. She held her breath. Listening. There were clicks from the ball bearing office toy on her desk as he moved things around. She heard her desk drawers opening. A metal clang. Banging. Maybe the filing cabinet being struck? She visualised him prising it open. Then there was a ringing dial tone.

'She's not upstairs.'

The voice was English. Cultured. It sounded incongruous in this situation.

She heard another voice. The phone was on speaker, but she couldn't make out the words or the accent.

'Well she's not here now. There's nothing on the desk, nothing in the drawers. Just an external hard drive in the filing cabinet.'

The response was too faint for her to hear.

'Yes. I have it.'

The man moved across the room and she heard his steps on the creaking staircase.

Her heart was now at a cardiac arrest level. She felt light-headed. It was suffocating in this space. The sweat running down her face, her multiple layers of clothes sticking to her.

She understood the fear reflex, the automatic instinct of the body, and she knew how to control it. Army training and drills had seen to that.

She closed her mouth and slowed her breathing. Not the deep breaths many advised. The opposite. Shallow breaths with the mouth closed. Holding for a count of four on the fourth breath, then repeating.

It was hard to focus on controlling her breathing, lying tucked in the eaves. This pitch black, thin space without standing height, and the angled ceiling sloping above her, felt as tight as she'd imagined it would be. There was no discernible air. The ventilation holes along the fascia did nothing to mitigate this.

Jamie had lost count of how many times she'd witnessed her husband's obsession with security. He'd told her, when he was a young child, his best friend had lost his parents in a home invasion. A burglary gone wrong. It had affected him deeply. He'd even have nightmares. The marks of childhood trauma are indelible and Ed had a gentle soul. She loved him all the more for it. She accepted all of it. There were worse things to be obsessed about. Being secure and safe wasn't one of them.

She heard movement below the loft room, in her bedroom. All that separated her was a plasterboard ceiling, joists, and the wooden floor she was lying on. She must not move.

She heard drawers opening. Objects being moved. And continual pacing. Relying on sound, she pieced together what he was doing. But she wanted more. She needed her phone.

He started banging. It sounded like drawers being upended. The noise her cover, she took a risk. She eased the phone from her pocket.

Turning it on, the light blinded her after the black darkness. She then followed Ed's emergency procedure. Checked her phone was on silent, turned off GPS tracking, enabled her Virtual Private Network, and ensured she was using data instead of the Wi-Fi network.

As the light bounced around the small space, she saw a small black bag to the side of her. Something Ed must have left behind.

His voice came back to her. 'Get safe, then ring the police.'

She would. But first, there was something she needed to do.

13

Check Ed's security cameras.

Ed had installed hidden cameras all around the house – inside and out. When activated, each camera would save the footage onto hard copy SD cards. This footage could then all be downloaded to any cloud server.

She'd thought it excessive but accepted her husband's need to feel secure. She had deleted the app and the password from her phone soon after Ed had died. She saw no need for it. A part of her felt a release from the burden of needing to feel secure. Of removing that anxiety her husband felt – which had sometimes felt contagious. But she had not disconnected the hardware. She hadn't even thought of it. Now she wanted to use it. Wanted to see who these men were and what they were doing in her home.

Jamie downloaded the app. It seemed to take forever. Then she clicked and created a new password. In seconds, she was in. She switched on the system and waited.

Pictures flooded her bright screen from each camera around the house. A red recording button was flashing on each picture.

She studied the images.

One man was sitting in the car across her driveway. Two men were in her living room, pulling open drawers and cupboards. The tall man who'd left the car was in her bedroom pulling clothes from her wardrobe. She watched him reach up. He accessed the top shelf with ease, sweeping across it with his hand. He must be well over six feet tall.

She waited for a perfect image and took a screenshot. Then she watched him locate the small safe attached to the wall inside the wardrobe. Within minutes, the safe was open, and he was flicking through the contents – cash, jewellery, and other important documents. He put back the cash and jewellery and took the documents. No ordinary burglar. He was searching for something specific.

Jamie looked back at the living room images. There was something about one of the men. He was short and stocky, carrying a little extra weight around his middle, and he was now looking straight at the hidden camera.

She hit screenshot and took a breath in. She recognised him. She struggled to recall his name but knew where she'd seen him. With her father, at a police function, some months after Ed had died.

She fixed on the moment George had introduced them.

'We've just moved from Belfast,' the officer's wife said. The husband's hand had shaken hers. Moving towards her father, who was in his old police uniform, his hand outstretched, the officer spoke. She focused on the introduction and tried to remember the name. It was an Irish name. It was right there on the edge of her mind. Then it came to her. *Denis O'Malley.* This time, unlike last time, Chief Inspector Denis O'Malley was not in uniform.

The other man in her living room was broad and thickset. The build of a bouncer with a wall of muscle. As he reached up to a shelf and pulled down books and magazines, she saw a gun underneath his jacket. As he turned, she captured a perfect image of his face and huge neck.

They worked quickly and methodically through her house as she watched.

Her mind flashed to George. She checked the time. 8:15 p.m. He should be here by now. He would be driving up any second. She needed to warn him. Her finger hesitated on the phone.

'Just wait for me at home. You must wait for me.'

George had been so insistent. Forceful even. He was concerned for her. Wanted to see her. To help her.

Then she remembered more from the police function. Chief Inspector Denis O'Malley was not just George's colleague. Their wives talked of evenings they'd shared. Mentioned each other's children by name. Places they'd been together. They were all close friends.

Had George persuaded her to wait here to send these men on ahead of him? He said he'd be thirty minutes. He should be here by now. Why wasn't he?

Ring the police. Ed's order echoed through her brain. But how could she? She couldn't trust them. Not now.

She thought she heard movement below in the hallway. Watching the cameras, she saw the tall man walk into the living room. The police officer spoke to him, then lifted a mobile phone to his ear.

Jamie put the volume up on her phone. With all the men downstairs, out of earshot of the loft, this now felt safe. They would not hear anything.

The camera picked up O'Malley's words crystal clear.

'No, she's not here.'

Shaking his head, his arms gesturing around him, he turned in circles and walked back to the kitchen.

'I know it's a big problem,' he spoke rapidly into the phone, with his strong Belfast accent. 'You don't need to tell me it's a big problem.' His agitation continued. He looked under pressure.

Jamie saw a message banner come up on her phone.

George.

You still waiting at home? Running late. Crash on the A6, traffic backed up.

The timing. Was it George on the other end of that phone with O'Malley, trying to find out where she was?

Eyes fixed on the images, she watched the three men together in the kitchen. She took another screen shot. Saw her external drive and documents placed into a briefcase.

'The location tracking on her phone still shows she's in this area.' The tall man was speaking, a phone in his hand. 'She hasn't got her GPS on, so we can't pinpoint her location. George just texted her. He's running late.'

Jamie felt chills rippling through her body. Fear. They were monitoring her phone. Could see her messages. Maybe hear her calls. Could they tell she was watching the cameras? She didn't think so. The men would surely have mentioned that by now. She steadied her breathing and kept watching the cameras.

O'Malley walked to the fridge, flicking through her precious cards. Throwing some onto the floor. He gave the tall man one of them. The tiger. He turned it over.

'It's from the kid next door. They're not there. They go out on Friday evenings.'

Jamie struggled to breathe. They knew Hayley and Freya. Had been watching them as well as her.

A cold sweat crept across her body. The crushing heat from before now gone. Her body chilled.

The officer placed two cards in the briefcase.

'Evans.' He beckoned the tall man towards him. 'We need to get moving. What are you thinking?' O'Malley had lowered his voice.

'She's due to visit the father at eight thirty. She must have gone early. We need to check what he knows. I suggest a team move to that location.' Evans spoke quietly, but she could hear his perfectly enunciated words.

The police officer, sweat now prickling on his forehead, paused again.

'I've met the father. He'll recognise me. I'll stay here. We need to get this right. You know where these orders are coming from. If we don't find her, we might as well—'

Evans interrupted. 'We will find her. It's only a matter of time. There's nowhere she can hide that we won't find her.'

O'Malley headed back to the bouncer. 'Smith. We'll wait here. Evans and Brooks are going to the…' He held up a hand and pulled his phone back out from his trouser pocket. He moved away from both men and into the utility room off the kitchen. His words now whispered, not audible to her.

Evans and Brooks are going to the…

Father. She was sure of the end of that sentence.

Her hands were now shaking. Fear spreading through her body. Her father was a brave man. Ex-police. An amateur boxer. In his prime, he wouldn't be beaten. Not even by two of them. Now he was frail, with no way to defend himself. But she knew he'd try. He wouldn't let these men cross his threshold without a fight. But they would swipe him away and crush him like a fly.

She thought again of George. How he'd talked about going with her to Tom. Insisted she wait. Insisted he go with her. It was hard to believe he was working with these men who had invaded her home. George and his wife, Sheena, had been her lifeline over these years. Ed and George were like brothers. But had George stayed close to her for more than friendship? If these men had been listening to her phone, maybe they'd been watching her too. Her mind struggled to unravel all the threads. So much had happened, was happening, so much she couldn't understand or believe. In this moment, she wasn't sure of anything. Of anyone. And that meant she wasn't at all sure she could trust George.

She focused on her options.

She could text or ring her father. Tell him to leave the house. But the men were monitoring her phone. They'd see the message. Would it mean they could also pinpoint her location in the loft? She didn't know. She couldn't risk it.

She could give herself up to the men. She knew what her father would say to that. *Never surrender, Jamie.*

She could stay hidden. Not an option with her father in danger.

She could leave the loft. Her only choice.

Ed had planned this cramped space for safety. To wait things out. But she couldn't stay here any longer.

There was only one viable way out. The Velux window. It terrified her. Clinging on to multiple, steep, pitched roofs in near darkness. Heights had been her nemesis during her basic training. Vertigo her companion. But there was no choice. This was the only way to get to her father.

She pictured the descending roof pitches and extensions at the back of the three-story house and the drop from each. The heartbeat she had quietened was rising again. Beat on beat.

If the men went by car to her father's house, they would hit the temporary diversion and traffic lights around Park Road. On a busy evening, it would take nearer to ten minutes. She could walk there, across the field and through the jetty, in five minutes. Even quicker if she ran. She just needed to tackle her descent. And tackle it quickly.

Jamie looked one last time at the camera footage. The men called Smith and Evans were standing motionless in the kitchen. O'Malley was still on his phone, in the utility room, in heated conversation. The driver had not moved from his car at the front of her house.

She needed to go now. The horror of her situation stark.

Four men were here for her. Four men. What did they want with her? What did they want with her father?

And then it hit her. It was so clear. So obvious.

They weren't here for her. Or her father. They were just links in the chain.

They were here for Ed.

They were here to find her husband.

14

Jamie pushed the bookcase forward. Crawled out, dragging her backpack and coat behind her. She reached back into the space, retrieving the small package Ed had left behind and tucked it deep inside her pack.

The air in the main room was a relief after the stale air under the eaves. She breathed it in. Got to her feet with a struggle. Just a few minutes trapped in that coffin-like space and she was stiff. Stretching back, she clicked her shoulders and neck on both sides. Pushed the bookcase closed and pulled on her coat and backpack.

She opened the catch on the Velux window. It was pitch black outside. Distant house lights twinkled but not close enough to break the darkness. Lights from her kitchen and living room offered some residual light, but not enough to see where she was going. She had a head torch in her pack, but she couldn't risk using it.

She fully opened the Velux window. Breathed in the cool night air and heaved herself up and over the window. The manoeuvre was treacherous, landing on sloping tiles, her pack moving, affecting her balance. She gripped the window edge to gain stability. Crawled backwards a few feet. And felt for the edge of the roof.

The height difference was minimal to the pitched roof of the large two-storey extension below. Hanging backwards over the roof's edge, twenty-five feet above level ground, she navigated the gutter, her feet tentatively finding tiles.

In the darkness, she inched her way up towards the ridge of the main extension. Then started her move sideways, crab-like, across the pitched roof on hands and knees. Her rubber-soled trainers were giving good grip until her right foot slid from under her. Moss. She'd let maintenance slip. That was always Ed's job. She was unbalanced and almost cried out. Clinging on with her hands to the ridge tiles and her left foot. Her fingers burning as the skin grated on harsh tiles.

She was breathing heavily. Felt a dizzy, heady feeling. Vertigo. The world was spinning. She heard her Sergeant's voice when she was thirty feet up on a high wire. *Don't look down, Shaw. Focus.*

Jamie took in a shaky breath. Focused. Steadied herself. Edged her right leg back up and found better purchase. She closed her mouth to control her breathing. And slowly she moved.

She approached the edge of this roof, knowing the drop was much bigger to the flat roof of the smaller one-story extension. The extension housing the utility room and bathroom, where O'Malley had disappeared for his private calls.

Her eyes were now adjusting to the darkness. Some light reflected up from the utility room window, helping to guide her. But this was the hardest part of the descent. There was no grip to be found on the brickwork, just the long aerial pole to stabilise her. And she was not at all sure it would hold her weight or be long enough. She slid, clinging to the pole, inching down, but she could not feel the roof below. She dangled from the pole, her arms now fully stretched, and she finally felt solid ground beneath her feet. She touched down on the torch-on roof.

She waited. Her hand pushed at the sweat running from her hairline, stinging her eyes. Then she moved across the flat, one-story extension. Careful with each step, ensuring it did not creak. Knowing O'Malley could be below.

She was nearly there. The last drop was short and easy. A window on the end wall of her house would give her a foothold. As she balanced with her hands on the roof edge, and one foot on the window ledge, she heard a long creak. The back door opening. She froze in place.

'They've already left.'

O'Malley. His loud voice cut through the silent night.

She heard footsteps pacing. The security lights clicked on, flooding the entire side of her house. Just a few steps further and he would see her.

Her grip was faltering, her already sore fingers struggling to hold her weight. Burning in her hands and forearms. The pack pulling her backwards, threatening to unbalance her as she hung helplessly.

'I've got men at the train and bus station. We're all over the CCTV.'

He was moving as he spoke.

'She hasn't got a hope. We've got eyes everywhere across this town and beyond.'

Another pause.

'I've got an alert set up. If she uses her passport, it'll be flagged.'

Silence.

'What do you mean?'

Jamie's body was tiring. Trying to hold on. Trying to listen. Piecing it together.

'Don't worry, O'Neill won't be going…'

The back door closed.

As she let herself drop to the small wall which divided part of her semi-detached property from Hayley's and Freya's, she needed to remember this name. Wondered how it related to the nightmare she was in.

One more jump and her feet hit level ground. She leaned on the wall, stabilising herself, breathless and lightheaded. But she could not pause for long. She took a few deep breaths to the base of her lungs. Felt the oxygen flood her system, her brain equalising. She was ready to move.

Running beside the edge of the small wall in her garden, she reached the playing field. Now she was sprinting across the open space towards her father's close. Making the most of the shortcut. Hoping she was fast enough to get her father away from his house. Knowing the roof descent had taken longer than she'd hoped.

She pulled her phone from her pocket. This phone was on borrowed time, they were tracking it. But her father only had this number. He wouldn't be able to reach her if she got rid of it. She had to risk ringing him now she was on the move.

She dialled her father.

Midway across the field, still running, she was three minutes away.

No answer on his mobile.

She tapped the screen again. Re-dialling. Still no answer.

She slowed, searched, hit his landline number.

Picked up speed again.

Heard the engaged tone.

She was at the edge of the field. Two minutes away.

She hit the mobile number again, travelling down the jetty which connected the field next to her father's house. Slowed her pace to account for passing walkers.

One minute away.

She was now on Burton Street. Taking a left onto Park Street, she was at the junction of her father's road.

It was a small close, all detached houses, just ten in a horseshoe formation. She moved past the street sign – Alice Gardens – and around the curve in the road.

She jumped backwards. Pressed herself against the wall. There was a black four-wheel-drive parked outside the neighbour's house. There was no-one in the front seats. She scanned to the left. Two men were almost at her father's door.

She was too late.

She wanted to scream. To cry out. Run across the road to save him. But she knew she couldn't. Her father wouldn't want that. And she couldn't win a frontal attack against these men. She couldn't save her father in that way. She was so close, but not close enough.

The man she knew as Evans held something up to the spy hole. Her father opened the door. She cursed his friendliness. How many times had she told him not to do that?

She saw her father in the porch light. Smiling. Watched as Evans pressed the door open and pushed him backwards. Saw him stumble into the stairs, try to hit back, then disappear out of view.

The hallway light went off.

It was all she could do not to run to him. To pound on the door.

She put a hand on the wall to stop herself from falling. Forcing herself to hold back. It was against all her instincts. An agony she had never experienced.

Seconds later, she watched Evans draw her father's front room curtains.

15

Jamie felt another surge of adrenaline hit her body. She ran across the close and quietly clicked open her father's side gate. He never locked it, however much she begged him. Moving along the narrow path at the side of the house, she stood next to the French doors which opened onto the back garden.

With her back to the wall, she crept to the edge of the glass doors, inch by inch. She peered around the corner. And what she saw made her heart stop and her mind fracture.

In the front living room, the two men were tying her father to a chair. They towered over him. He looked so frail. Blood was falling from his chin, his lip cut. Evans was holding him and Brooks securing the ties. A holster with a gun also hung from Brooks' shoulder.

The guilt she felt as she watched, unable to intervene, was crushing. But she knew she couldn't beat them, not two men with weapons. She had a play of her own. To use it, she had to watch and wait.

Brooks hit her father across the face. Jamie felt the blow as though it had struck her.

In that second, Evans turned around and looked at the

French doors. It was as if he'd felt her there. His instincts sharp. She pulled back, pressed herself against the wall and slid back around the corner, ducking down beneath the line of recycling bins. She heard the French door open. A pause. A crunch into the gravel as he moved around. The security light blinding. As she held her breath, the door clicked, locked, and she heard the bang of the indoor shutters closing.

Her heart pounded. Her body shook. He had been just ten feet away from her.

She raced along the side of the house, to the bottom of the garden, hiding behind the log cabin summerhouse. It was pitch dark, but she had the light from her phone, and it was enough.

She tapped the security app icon on her phone. Ed had wanted his father safe, too. Had pressed him into allowing the security installations. Like her, their father had never used it. Had only allowed it to pacify Ed. But now, it was finally useful.

Logging back into her account, and clicking the icon for her father's home, the pictures came up clear. Her heart wrenched again as she saw him strapped to the chair. Brooks shouting close to his face.

'Where is Ed? Where is he?'

Her father looked bewildered. Shocked. His usual strength absent. He didn't know what was happening. Confusion and distress written across his face.

Brooks launched an open palm at his jaw.

She thought of his heart. She was terrified for him. For his life.

'Where is your daughter-in-law? Where is Jamie?'

He didn't answer. Another blow hit his stomach. He bent forward in agony.

She couldn't take anymore. What she'd seen had to be enough. She hit dial to her father's mobile.

She watched Evans move towards the sofa, pick up the phone and take it to her father. Evans whispered something in his ear. Laid the phone in front of him and hit a button. Her father's voice came on the line. On speakerphone.

'Hi Dad. How are you doing?'

'I'm good, sweet pea, really good.'

He sounded bright. No-one else would have known he was in trouble, but she could hear a shake in his voice. She kept her own voice level.

'I got delayed. Remember I had to get that coffee cake for you?'

He didn't miss a beat.

'I remember.'

'I might not get back to you tonight. There's somewhere I need to go. An old friend I need to see. Will you be…' her voice faltered. 'Will you be OK?'

She watched Brooks put pressure on her father's wrist. Saw his face contort. Evans whispered in his ear. He shook his head.

'Don't come, Jam—'

He pushed out the words with all the strength he had before Brooks muffled her father's mouth.

Evans picked up the phone.

'Jamie?'

The Queen's English voice she'd first heard in the loft came across the phone. Still on speaker. Her father listening to every word.

She didn't reply.

'We just need a location.'

'My father doesn't know anything.'

'I realise that.'

'So what are you doing there?'

'Leverage.'

She paused.

‘And if I don’t tell you?’

‘We’ll hurt him. Then we’ll kill him.’

His voice was matter of fact. The threat strange coming from this voice. She held the pause. Her father was shaking his head. Looking directly at the hidden camera. He hoped she was watching.

She was ready to make her move.

‘Evans…’

She paused, ready to say more, but didn’t need to. She watched the shock on his face. He was quick. Realisation dawned. He looked all around him.

‘No point looking around you. It’s too late.’

She clicked on WhatsApp and sent a picture through to her father’s phone. The three men assembled in her kitchen. Their faces crystal clear.

‘My husband was very security conscious. I’m surprised you didn’t realise that.’

Evans was silent. Looking across at Brooks.

‘He wanted to keep his family safe.’ She paused. ‘Untie my father.’

She spoke with force. Fear for her father. Anger at this treatment of a frail old man. Using him as a bargaining chip in a game he knew nothing about. These men, whoever they were, were monsters.

The men stood, not moving.

‘It’s never good to threaten to murder someone on camera. If anything happens to him, this footage will find its way to police officers who are not on your pay roll.’

She watched the men look at each other. Evans nodded to Brooks, who untied her father.

‘You’re going to be OK, Dad.’

‘I know, sweet pea.’

She texted a picture through of the two men and her father tied up.

Evan's calm demeanour vanished. Angry at his situation. He pulled out his own phone from his trouser pocket. Checked it. Maybe tracking her again or messaging the others.

'Jamie. You can't win here.' His voice harsher now. 'You don't know who you're up against.'

'Why don't you tell me?'

Silence.

She'd done as much as she could to help her father. She just hoped it was enough.

'I'll be back soon, Dad. I…' her voice wavered. She pulled herself back. 'I love you.' She said it with strength. With power.

'I know, my darling. I know.' But there was no strength in his voice. She heard resignation. It frightened her. Then he looked directly at the camera. 'Don't look back. Don't look back, Jamie.' His eyes pleading with her.

It took everything she had to do it. She hit the red icon on her phone.

She needed to run. But there was something even more important she had to do. Consolidate her bargaining chip.

Jamie opened up her backpack. Yanked out the laptop and watched it power up. Turned off Wi-Fi, used her phone on data as a hot spot, and installed the home security app.

Her fingers moved fast on the keys. The security images from the app showed the men and her father were still in the living room. Evans on the phone. Her father sitting, looking lost and alone. Her mind wanted to spiral, but she needed to focus. This was all she had that could help to protect him. She downloaded the footage from his cameras into her Dropbox account. As she reached towards her pack, a banner appeared across her phone.

George.

'Almost there, traffic hell, where are you?'

She swiped the screen to get the message out of her view.

Almost immediately, another message appeared. This time from Sheena.

'Jamie, please call me. I need to talk to you.'

Before Jamie could swipe away the message, the screen changed. An incoming call. From Sheena.

She hit the red button. As she looked at her laptop, the surrounding area lit up. She glanced across and saw a reflection. The garden security lights were back on, including the one at the cabin behind her.

She looked back at the screen. To the cameras.

Evans was outside in the garden. Standing at the back door, on the phone. He stepped onto the path.

She heard the crunch of gravel as he moved further down the garden path. She'd made a horrible mistake staying here. She looked around at her feet for something to defend herself with if he rounded the corner. There was nothing. She closed the laptop and turned off her phone. Held her breath. He'd paused on the path. A loud whistle sounded. More crunching on gravel and a door slam.

Her heart was thumping so hard her chest muscles ached. Her fingers trembled as she opened up the laptop to see Evans back inside the house.

She needed to work faster.

She checked back at the cameras in her own home. A quick glance showed O'Malley searching in the kitchen. He was close to finding one camera and its SD card. Evans had been in touch. Smith was upstairs in the box room, searching through Ed's things.

Jamie pulled her backpack nearer. Tugged on a small zipper inside the main compartment. Her fingers cold and shaking. She tugged again and it opened. She pulled out a USB. In seconds, she had the memory stick in place and the footage downloaded.

Ed's life as a tech expert, and gifted hacker, had changed everything she did online. It was automatic to her now. She knew cloud accounts were vulnerable. If these people hunting her had been watching her, maybe they'd compromised all her accounts. She heard Ed's words. *Always have two physical backups of your files in different locations.* She pocketed the memory stick in a zipped part of her cargo trousers. For now, this one hard copy, in one location, had to be enough.

She could now go off the grid. No more messages from George. Or Sheena. No more tracking of her phone and location from the men following her.

She hit factory reset on her laptop to remove all her details and did the same on her phone and deleted her eSIM.

Standing up, she dropped the laptop and phone into the water butt.

She was ready to leave. To leave her father behind. It took all of her strength. She felt physically pulled back up to the house. But her army training overruled her emotions. The only way she could protect her father was to save herself. To get away. Get to Ed. And figure out who these people were and what they wanted.

Hauling herself up and over the low fence at the bottom of the garden, she started running down the alley, ready to circle back around to reach the playing field. Pushing on, she picked up her pace. Finding a rhythm.

She heard her father's voice echoing in her head. Saw his pleading eyes as he looked at her through the camera lens.

And she did what he told her to do.

She didn't look back.

16

Jamie's body felt leaden. She had done what she could, but her father was still in the hands of men with guns. She wasn't foolish enough to think her threats would carry much weight.

Her mind was spinning. What had Ed got himself involved in? Who were these people chasing her? Threatening her father. Hunting her husband.

Running fast on the grass playing field, she stumbled and fell. Her hands grazed across stones in the grass, the field uneven. Pulling herself up, she knew she needed to focus. She had to get out of this area. Make her way towards Ed.

O'Malley had said the trains and buses were being monitored. Flying wasn't an option – her passport would be flagged immediately. With the wait time at airports, the men would be there before she took her flight. And there was CCTV everywhere. O'Malley's words had confirmed that her hunters were connected to all these networks. Maybe more of them were officers of the law. She could only wonder how far their reach went.

She made her way back onto Park Road. Only a handful of people were walking on the pavement. She moved with her head down, hood up. The temporary traffic lights were up ahead, and she needed to cross. She stood next to a woman with her child. The boy was grabbing at his mother. Pointing at the traffic lights. Impatient for the little green man. The lights went to red. Cars on both sides pulled to a stop. She looked up, ready to move, and her eyes met the man in the car on her right, stopped at the crossing.

It was George.

He didn't register her at first, but as she looked away and started walking, she heard a horn beeping.

'Jamie! Jamie!'

She ran the rest of the way across the crossing, hearing him shout her name. She heard a car rev. He would follow her. She needed to go in the opposite direction. He was stuck on Park Road and she would disappear by the time he could turn off.

She ran as though the world were on her heels. Keeping her head down, she backtracked, turned left and kept running. The backpack now lighter, another adrenaline spurt. She took a right and headed to the end of Garton Road. Away from the prying eyes of private and public cameras. Hidden from any searching cars.

Her breath coming in gasps, she tucked herself against a brick wall, tight in the corner beneath a large evergreen tree, close to backyards and garages. One streetlight, across the way, offered some light.

She was sweating, her body shaking.

Breathless, she got down on her haunches. But she couldn't sustain that. Her legs gave way beneath her and she collapsed onto the hard, cold pavement.

17

Jamie needed to calm her body. Her heart was hammering.

She needed to calm her brain. It was spinning.

She closed her eyes.

Focused.

Breathed.

Three minutes later, she opened her eyes. Her heart still thumping, but her mind sharper.

She had to move from here. She knew there was someone watching her on every corner of this town. From every camera. Facial recognition was everywhere. Her husband's constant talk of our Orwellian society was now an actual danger to her.

Jamie opened up her backpack. Dug deep. Pulled out the pay-as-you-go burner phone, with an unused physical SIM card and prepaid minutes. Unregistered to her, it was untraceable. She turned it on. It had charge but was running low. The battery pack came to her rescue. She plugged it in. Checking GPS was off, and she was on the 4G network, she connected to the internet.

If she wasn't going by air, there was only one other way

left to get to Ireland. By sea. It was the last thing she wanted to do, but it was her only choice.

She checked online. There were two ferry routes worth considering. Fishguard to Rosslare and Holyhead to Dublin.

Fishguard to Rosslare left for Ireland at 11:35 p.m. and 1 a.m. She wouldn't make either of those times, and the route west across Wales was long and torturous. She'd travelled it before when going to St David's Bay.

Holyhead to Dublin was better. There were two ferry companies and several times. The earliest was leaving port at 2:10 a.m. If she missed that, the next was half an hour later.

An idea had formed while she'd been running, passing a stationary taxi. It was as good a plan as she could come up with. Taking multiple taxis to get her to the ferry port. Avoiding all transport networks and CCTV wherever possible. It would make her more difficult to track.

She checked her watch. It was close to nine o'clock. Entering details on the AA route search told her it was a three-and-a-half-hour drive to Holyhead Port. She had a good chance of making that early ferry. A little more research and she had her first stop-off point to change taxis.

Checking on Google, she found a service. Dialled the number.

'Hi there. I'm on Royland Road at Turner & Smith's. Can I have a pickup? I'd like to pay with cash, please.'

'We don't take cash. It's contactless. Payment by card in advance.'

She hung up.

Contactless. Everything was going this way. The pandemic had made this buyer behaviour more acceptable, even necessary. It was also convenient. But it meant someone could track and trace every move you made. Being invisible was almost impossible nowadays.

She called another firm. They accepted cash. The pick-up was arranged. They would arrive in fifteen minutes.

Jamie closed up her backpack and struggled to her feet. Her legs felt weak, her trousers damp and cold from sitting on the hard concrete. She slung her pack over her shoulder. Pushed her phone into her pocket, with its portable charger, and started walking.

She turned right, head down, making her way towards Royland Road. She crossed and veered behind a brick pillar at the entrance to the accountant's private car park.

As she waited, hidden from view of the pavement and road, and from George and the hunters, she leant against the wall to steady herself, the chill wind whipping around her.

The wait felt long. Listening to the hum of passing traffic and occasional blasts of music from passing cars. Checking her watch every minute.

Finally, her phone vibrated. A banner message came across the screen.

'Your taxi is arriving.'

She heard the car pull up, the engine running. Keeping her head down, she stepped forward. The driver rolled the window down.

'Davis. Holliday Inn, Stoke-on-Trent?' A foreign accent. Maybe Polish.

'Yes.'

He leaned across and opened the front door. She pushed it closed. 'Thank you. I'll go in the back.'

She opened the door behind the passenger seat, pushed in her backpack and sat down. Her head still bowed.

The clicking of the indicator stopped as the taxi drove off.

Jamie saw her father's bloody face flash in front of her. She was leaving him behind. Her hand moved to her chest, to the physical ache inside her heart. *Don't look back, Jamie.* She blinked away tears. Brushed over her pocket and felt the memory stick. The men had less leverage over her now they couldn't contact her by phone. She had to hope it was enough.

Jamie pressed herself back into the leather seat. The ebb and flow of a football match coming through the radio. Her body cold, bruised and broken. Her mind a jumbled mess of emotions and thoughts.

'Is bothering you?'

The voice jarred her from her thoughts. They were paused at traffic lights. The driver looking round at her, pointing to the radio.

'It's fine. All good.'

'Thank you. Good. It's my team.'

She attempted a smile as the driver turned back around, the car moving forward.

She watched through the side window as houses flashed by. Within minutes they were outside the town limits, the motorway approaching. Driving away from those chasing her.

She exhaled a long breath. Checked her watch. 9:20 p.m.

For the first time in two hours, she could breathe a little easier.

18

The minutes felt like hours. George should have rung by now.

Ed had plans, contingencies, for this eventuality. A protocol to follow. As soon as he was compromised, he had to run. But his world had turned upside down. Everything had changed now Jamie knew he was alive.

He looked through the living room window. The stunning sunset sky had left behind a band of orange and pink across the horizon. Darkness was closing in. He scanned the distant mountains, the dense area of forest, the fields of gorse and bracken. His mind thinking of only one thing. Jamie.

He'd hidden himself away from the world for two years. Living alone and in solitude. But this had made it impossible to keep the promise he made to himself when he disappeared – that he wouldn't track Jamie or follow her life. He knew it was an invasion to do it. Unhealthy. Dangerous. But in loneliness. In love. He'd weakened.

He'd texted George every month on a separate burner phone to check in. To make sure Jamie and his father were OK.

When his father had a heart attack, he was so close to breaking cover. There wasn't a day that went by that he didn't want to go home and wrap his arms around them. Rest in Jamie's embrace. Feel her head against his chest.

Instead, he trapped himself in his office and buried himself in his work. He did it one day after the next. One foot in front of the other. An existence more than a life.

He regularly searched the internet for 'Captain Jamie Shaw Loughborough'. He saw her praised in army news magazines. Watched how the Centre where they'd both worked – him in IT, her as a practice nurse, now a case manager – was developing state-of-the-art rehabilitation facilities. Her role increasing.

She deserved it all. It gave him confidence that he'd been right not to tell her anything, right to leave her behind and let her live a real life and fulfil her potential.

He would have followed her on social media, but he couldn't access any of her accounts. He'd taught her well. She had everything set to private and knew every person she allowed to access her information. He could have hacked her, but that was a step too far. It was the one step he wouldn't take.

As time passed, he realised it was for the best that he didn't know these more personal details about her life. He would have pored over every word and picture. Seen posts with her out, visiting places, with friends, maybe with another man. The pain would have eaten him alive.

The Hallelujah chorus rang out, blasting through his thoughts.

George.

He picked up.

'I haven't got her.'

His stomach dropped.

'What happened?'

'Delays. A crash on the A6. It was bumper to bumper. And there are temporary works on Park Road backing up the traffic. But I saw her. I was sitting at the lights. She walked onto the crossing right in front of me. She recognised me. Then she ran.'

'What do you mean, she ran? She couldn't have known it was you.'

'She did know. She knew it was me. She looked straight at me. I called. Shouted. She didn't look back.'

'It doesn't make sense. Have you been to our house?'

'I'm heading there now. On Stanley Street.'

Ed was silent. Waiting for information that might help him figure out what had happened.

'Just turning into Reed Close.'

Ed travelled the street in his memory as though it were yesterday. Passing Mrs Ethel on the corner, waving from her garden. Hayley and Freya next door. Nick opposite, always looking to talk, always bemoaning his lot in life. He felt the loss of it all, all that normality and ordinariness.

George was talking again.

'I'm parked further up the close. Jamie's car is in the drive. The blinds are closed flat.'

'She never closes the blinds.'

'I know.'

He heard the tension in George's voice.

'There's someone in the box room. The lights are on and I can see a shadow moving.'

Ed was quiet. He knew George had told Jamie to stay at home. If someone broke into the house, she must have been there when they came. They may have been listening to her, maybe bugging the house. Most likely, they were hacking her phone. The consequences of this for him hit instantly.

Did Jamie hide in the loft the way he'd told her to? Did she see the package he'd left there? The one he'd been unable to retrieve. The things he was told to destroy but couldn't. It would have been like losing all he had left of his parents. Of their life before.

Jamie had got away from the house, that much he knew. But why was she running from George? His mind was firing thoughts in every direction.

George was talking and he needed to concentrate.

'…going to go to the end of the close. I'll cut through the alley and check around back.'

'Do you think—'

'Hold on, Ed. Change of plan. There's a four-wheel drive pulling up at the house. A tall guy getting out. Going to the door and…'

George stopped talking.

'What's wrong?'

Silence.

'George?' Ed's voice was rising in volume.

'I know why she ran from me.' George took a long pause. 'She thinks I sent these men to the house.'

'I don't understand.'

'I know the man who just opened the door. He's on the force. A colleague. A friend.' George paused again. 'Jamie has met him. If she saw him, if he came for her, she knows we're friends…' George tailed off. 'And I'd told her to stay in the house. Insisted … She thinks I'm involved in what's happening. That's why she ran.'

Ed had it pieced together in an instant, but he was struggling to accept what it meant. He let George keep giving him the information he needed.

'The officer at the door is Denis O'Malley. There are three other men. The tall guy at the door, one in the box room, and the driver. There may be someone else in the back of the four-wheel drive. I can see a shadow, but the windows are tinted.'

Ed had already moved into his office. And he was typing the officer's name into his research files.'

'O'Malley works out of Loughborough station. He's a Chief Inspector.'

'Did he start after I left?'

George paused. 'A few months after. He came from Belfast. Our families are friends, our children go out together. This is,' he broke off. 'This is bad, Ed. How did they get here so fast?'

Ed took a long pause and bent his head into his hands.

He had made a terrible, terrible misjudgement. And he knew exactly how this had happened.

19

‘They never believed I was dead.’

George was silent.

‘They’ve been tracking Jamie ever since they found the firewall breach. They put someone in place for just this moment.’

‘Ed, I’m…’ George broke off. ‘I’m so sorry I didn’t get to her.’

Ed felt dawning horror creeping through his body. All he’d done, all he’d lost, and he hadn’t kept his family safe at all. Tole and his men were one step ahead of him. He was a fool to think he’d tricked them.

And now it was so much worse. Jamie had no defence or knowledge against these people. She didn’t know what she was up against.

Jamie knew his location. And these men knew that. There was nothing they wouldn’t threaten or do to get her to reveal that information.

As George talked, Ed gripped the phone as though his sanity depended on it.

‘I can’t believe I didn’t get to her in time. I should have jumped out of the car at the lights. I should have—’

'You did all you could to keep us safe, George. You and Sheena risked everything for me. To protect Jamie and my father. No-one could have done more. I'll never forget it.'

He had to steady himself. He needed to keep his mind on track. 'Let's focus on now. Jamie is out there on her own. Have you tried to ring her? Track her phone?'

'It's not trackable now.'

Jamie had more than likely ditched her phone. That was a positive and a negative. Now she couldn't be tracked, but she was also unreachable on that number.

Ed thought of making contact by email. But he couldn't risk it. They'd have hacked Jamie's online world and email accounts. He knew she had a burner phone with another SIM card. She always kept it in her pack. He just hoped she'd use it wisely. Hoped she'd remember the information he'd bored her with endlessly.

He stood and paced the room. Hands raking through his hair. He'd made a catastrophic error and underestimated his opponent. That they would watch Jamie for this long, this intently, and get to her this fast, hadn't occurred to him. It was a failing on his part. He'd exposed her to a terrible level of danger.

'Ed?'

'I'm here. Sorry.'

'I need to know what you…' George broke off.

'What? What's wrong?'

'Ed…' George's voice was quiet as death. 'It's your father in the back of the car.'

He felt the full horror now. Both the people he loved most in the world were in grave danger.

One captured.

One hunted.

Anger railed inside him at Paul Arthur Tole. The man at the heart of this. The man being fêted by the world for his company's groundbreaking research on pain management. The world who didn't know who he truly was. Didn't know the secrets he was hiding.

He thought of his tender, frail father. In the hands of Tole's minions. He knew how they'd use him. He had heard stories, seen images, spoken to many eyewitnesses. All too afraid to speak up. Threatened into silence.

George's voice brought him back.

'Ed, are you there? Ed? What do you want me to do?'

He took a breath to calm himself. Levelled his voice. 'Nothing, George. You do nothing.' He couldn't risk another family, people he loved, in danger because of him. 'I want you to get out of there. Get somewhere safe with Sheena and the girls.'

George didn't reply.

Ed could feel the battle in his friend.

'You can't help. There's too many of them. And Jamie is in the wind. She's coming to me, George. She's already got away from four of them and made herself untraceable. She knows what she's doing. She'll find her way here, then I can protect her and help my father. I want you to take care of your own family now. You've done enough for me. I'll never be able to repay that.'

'I could go higher up the chain, contact the superintendent?'

'No. We don't know who to trust. And they will be watching you. Please, I want you to go home.'

'But if you need me—'

'I'll call if I need to.' Ed took a breath. 'There is one thing.' He broke off. He didn't know how to ask. It wasn't the right time, but he wouldn't get another chance. And he had to know.

He'd spent all this time trying not to think about it. Never asked about it once in his messages with George. But he needed to know now. Now Jamie was coming to him. He needed to be prepared.

It had been two years. He left her so she could be safe. Secure. Could build a new life. Had she? How much of a life had she built without him? Was she with someone else?

'Ed, talk to me. What do you need?'

'Jamie, is she…' Ed couldn't find the words. Couldn't speak them out loud. 'Has she found…'

His friend, always on his wavelength, knew what he was thinking.

'She lives for you, Ed. She's never stopped.'

He wasn't sure what he should feel. Pleased Jamie was still his or appalled that she'd stayed living a shadow existence. All he knew was relief swept through him, then a flash of joy that she hadn't left him behind.

'I just needed to know.'

'I understand.' George paused. 'But you need to move location now, Ed.'

He knew George was right. He should move. Shouldn't let Jamie find him. He had to consider how much of her online life had been compromised and what that meant for him. But he was tired. So tired. He thought he knew the toll these two years had taken on him, but it was far worse than he realised.

'I can't George.' His voice was quiet. 'I have to see her.'

George took a few moments. 'I know.'

The silence was heavy between them. George broke it first.

'If you need me, remember, I'm still here.'

'Go to your family, George. Go now. Stay safe. And thank you for everything.'

The dial tone sounded as Ed hung up the phone, cutting off his dearest, loyal friend. Ed removed and broke the SIM card. And for the first time in two years, he didn't send a new contact number. George now had no way of reaching him. Did not even know where in the world he was.

The despair was a weight. Crushing and painful. This was all on him. All that was happening was down to the decisions he'd made. The decision to pursue the truth.

It had started out as justice for his parents, to right terrible wrongs, but it was so much bigger now. He stood, turned back to the wall behind him and moved towards it. Touching the photo of his dead parents, he looked at the clippings, the links, the array of photos representing financial investigations, disappearances, threats and murders. And at the heart of it all was Paul Arthur Tole and Tole Pharmaceuticals.

He thought of all this search had cost him. All he'd sacrificed. But even knowing that, he couldn't stop. Wouldn't stop. Someone has to be willing to risk everything. To get justice for the innocent. And to bring the powerful to a reckoning.

He didn't imagine he'd ever have to explain to Jamie what he'd done and why. He put aside those days and times of doubt, fearing he hadn't done the right thing. Jamie would understand. He was sure of it. She'd see he'd done what was best for them all.

He could feel she was on her way to him. But whatever it cost him, he couldn't run from her again.

She lives for you, Ed.

He closed his eyes to stop the pounding in his head. The hope in his heart.

Because there hadn't been an hour out of any day, for two whole years, that he hadn't lived for her too.

20

Jamie had her head back, sitting on the squeaky leather seat. Feeling safer in the steel cocoon. Breathing in the mixed bouquet of smoke, sweat, heady perfumes and pungent air freshener. The rhythm of the car soothing. The ebb and flow of the football commentators' voices anchoring her.

She already had her next taxi booked but had more research to do. It had been years since her last brush with a trip on the water – she didn't travel on any kind of boat by choice and wasn't at all sure of the protocols. Looking back at her phone, she searched the government travel portal.

As a UK citizen, she didn't need a passport to travel by ferry to Ireland. It was part of a Common Travel Area. But they would check her ID at the ferry port. She needed photographic ID. She could use her driver's licence.

Jamie looked up from the screen. Rested her head back, her eyes closing. This wasn't good news.

From what she'd heard O'Malley say, about the reach these people had, showing her ID could be as bad as showing her passport. The passenger list would surely flag her name. Her ID would be registered at the port and the hunters would be alerted. She needed to prepare for that possibility.

Something else triggered in her mind. Hayley and Freya. She should have rung Hayley earlier, but it was the last thing on her mind.

They were due to talk later. Hayley would be ringing, then she'd be texting. When met with silence, she'd be banging on Jamie's back door, worried on this second anniversary of Ed's death. She'd go into her house, using the keys she had for emergencies, see the house turned over, Jamie gone, but her car still in the driveway. Hayley would think of the threats of violence and internet trolling Jamie had received after her recent magazine interview. She'd call the police and they'd issue a search. That wouldn't be good.

Jamie needed to get in touch. But she couldn't risk using her new phone number, knowing their house was being watched. Maybe Hayley's phone was also being bugged. She'd email.

As her hands moved to log into the Gmail app, she stopped. Ed's voice ringing in her head.

'There's an IP address in the header of every email which reveals your geographic location. How do you not know this stuff?'

She'd looked at him. 'Why would I know it? Do you know how many ligaments hold the knee together and their names?'

'Touché.'

And they'd laughed.

She needed her Virtual Private Network on. It would cloak her IP address and location. She could download the app to this new phone and use 'Forget Password' to access her passwords on her Dropbox account.

Then it dawned on her. All her important accounts used two-factor authentication. Two-factor authentication to her phone. The phone drowning in a water butt in her father's garden.

Jamie wanted to bang her head on the side window. She couldn't use any of these accounts. And she also wouldn't be able to access the live tour footage on the Lough Road, or see her own photos to find the exact spot she had seen Ed. A rookie error of huge proportions.

Her brain was spinning. She was way out of her depth. She closed her eyes, fighting for stability, for clarity. Under pressure, what other errors was she making?

These men chasing her were powerful.

She thought of O'Malley's words – *She hasn't got a hope.*

Of Evans – *You don't know who you're up against.* The threats against her father – *We'll hurt him, then we'll kill him.*

Could she risk going to Ireland and lead them to her husband? Was she making the worst of all decisions for her own selfish reasons?

She tried to think of an alternative. She could go into hiding herself, but for how long? She didn't have the preparation for that. They would find her and beat Ed's location out of her, or drug it out of her. Or use her father against her.

There was no other option, she needed to find Ed.

She closed her eyes and used every technique she knew to calm her overloaded mind.

Twenty minutes on, she'd made no progress. There was no let-up. An avalanche of questions spun inside her mind. And they all centred on one thing. The death – the disappearance – of her husband.

21

Why?

Why would Ed fake his own death and abandon his entire life and those he loved? Those she believed he loved.

She thought of disappearances she'd heard of. They were often about money. Insurance scams. But she'd lost no money and Ed's insurance payouts had come to her. He'd gained nothing from his own death. It wasn't about money. She was sure of that.

Her husband was in danger. If men carrying guns would threaten to kill their father to know his location, then Ed was highly important to someone.

Had he disappeared two years ago to protect himself? To hide from the people now looking for him and the people now chasing her. It seemed a logical conclusion.

Then more questions rained down on her. What had Ed done? Or what did he know? And why couldn't he tell her? Didn't he trust her? Unless he was too ashamed to tell her? Had he done something terrible? She dismissed that thought out of hand. She'd never met a man with a stronger moral compass. Steeped in justice. The elderly men and women scammed out of their life savings could vouch for that. Ed's small charity had worked tirelessly to help and support them.

Another loop spun.

How?

How had Ed faked his death? Who had helped him? He couldn't have done this alone. Who else knew her husband was still alive?

Her mind went back to that terrible time. Searching for clues. And she thought about things in a new way. Things she'd had no reason to be suspicious of before.

It was George who had visited her at home with another police officer to break the news. Jamie wanted to know every detail. Needed to know, to believe it was real.

'How did it happen?'

George held her ice cold hand. 'We're not sure. We just know Ed's car left the road and crashed into a tree and exploded and Ed…' He broke off, unable to keep going, his voice breaking.

'What time?'

George gathered himself together. 'Reports started to come in at 2:45 p.m.'

She took this in. She'd been at home. Had no premonition of danger.

'Was anyone else involved?'

George shook his head. 'We think he may have swerved to miss an animal in his path. There had been reports of deer in the area and also,' he paused. 'Reports that Ed had been seen earlier driving above the speed limit.'

She couldn't believe that. He wouldn't even go thirty-one miles an hour in a thirty zone.

'Which area was it? Where was he?'

'On the Rempstone Road.'

She puzzled for a moment. Getting her bearings. A

country road, north of their work at the Defence Medical Rehabilitation Centre. 'Why was he there? He should have been going south. He was coming home.'

'I don't know, Jamie.' He seemed distraught. She could feel his hands shaking as they held hers.

And later, there were the explanations by George's wife Sheena – the pathologist who handled Ed's post-mortem – about having a closed coffin.

'There's no easy way to say this, Jamie. The fireball of the crash was intense.' Sheena paused, struggling to speak, putting her hand out to clasp Jamie's. 'Ed's body is too burnt for you to see him.' Her voice had cracked. It was genuine emotion. Why would Jamie have questioned it?

Sheena's statement at the inquest had reported Ed's body could only be identified by his dental records, alongside his gold wedding ring and necklace, which had survived the fire.

Jamie grasped the chain around her neck and rolled the ring between her fingers. She'd worn them every day in memoriam. She dropped her hand. Now that felt like a mockery.

In the months that followed Ed's crash, she'd driven the Rempstone Road so many times. Pausing at the exact spot. Wondering if fate would take her too. Wishing it. Feeling guilty for thinking it. For wanting the easy way out.

George and Sheena had been her and Ed's closest friends. They had stayed close by her, unlike most other couples who had abandoned her with the death of her husband. Had they known this entire two years that Ed was still alive and told her this shocking story of his death? Watched her suffering, knowing it was all a lie? It was too horrifying to contemplate. But she forced herself to contemplate it. And she concluded that the two of them, had they wanted to, could have helped Ed fabricate this story and fake his own death.

The thing she couldn't reconcile was George. If he'd helped Ed disappear, kept his secret, why was he sending men with guns after her now? It didn't make any sense.

Her mind was overwhelmed. Not just from thinking, but from reliving traumatic events. Events which had all been a lie. She didn't think she would ever recover from that betrayal. Nothing Ed could tell her could justify his lies and deceptions. Nothing could justify what he'd done to her. She felt that deep in her gut. It was unforgivable.

But despite all of that, a mix of emotions tormented her. Her stomach turning, churning, desperate to see him. Her body burning at the thought of touching him. Him touching her. Seconds later, her mind railing in anger and despair at the betrayal he'd visited on her. And then the fear. Fear of what she would find when she faced him. Him sitting in a quaint cottage in Ireland with someone else and the baby they couldn't have. Her forgotten. Dismissed.

Jamie knew she was plaguing herself with thoughts on unanswerable questions. She needed to get to Ed and get the answers. However bad they were.

She focused her mind back on the most pressing issue. Men waiting for her at Dublin Port. The more miles she travelled, the more certain she was of it.

Jamie tapped her phone and began to research the layout of the port. She could change clothes to exit the port in Dublin. She might get through the terminal without being recognised. But then she needed transport. She scrolled through multiple images. There were taxi ranks outside the terminal building, but the hunters would have eyes on those. And the nearby bus and train station were also impossible for her to use. She couldn't travel on any kind of public transport, the cameras would track her. Like O'Malley said, their eyes were everywhere.

Jamie began another search. *Car hire Dublin Port.* She

scrolled until she saw *YourCars*. She clicked and scanned the page. A car could be waiting five minutes' walk from the port. She just needed to upload her driver's licence and a selfie. The glimmer of hope vanished. She closed the tab and rested her phone back in her lap. If she booked that service, the hunters would surely be waiting for her at that car when she arrived.

She leaned back. Watched the lights flashing past the side window. The rain falling, causing the night-time view to blur. To seem distant and otherworldly.

She saw the sign ahead, heard the clicking indicator as the car turned off the motorway towards the Holiday Inn.

Minutes later she was standing, hoodie up, at the edge of the car park. Hidden from the very visible security cameras.

A text came up on her phone.

'We're running ten minutes late. We apologise.'

She zipped up her down jacket. The wind chill increasing as the temperature dropped.

Jamie calculated her timings. She was still on track for the earlier ferry. This pause for the taxi gave her time to make a final decision.

She knew, whichever way she looked at it, she was in trouble. She didn't want to pull anyone else into this dangerous whirlpool, but she needed help.

There was only one person she was willing to call. Someone she trusted, who had the skills, and was in the right location. A year ago, she wouldn't have even considered it. But he was doing so much better. The new medication and regimen offering him his best life since rehab.

She decided. She was going to pull in that favour from the desert death zone that had been Afghanistan.

'You ever need me, you ever want me, I'm here for you. Always.'

Words spoken by her best friend. Decorated army sniper, Sergeant Conor Daly. Her chosen family.

She pulled out her phone and typed.

Conor, it's Jay. I'm in trouble. Can you call me.

Ten seconds later her phone rang.

22

She tapped the green icon.

'What's wrong?'

To hear his voice, even one sharp with concern, gave her instant calm. Instant strength.

'I need your help.'

'What's happened?'

'I'm coming to Dublin Port.'

'Dublin Airport?'

'No, the ferry port?'

'The ferry port?'

It was no wonder his voice rose. Her mind flashed to their first meeting. A raging sea, several army battalions being transported on the ship, and her up on deck, dying in a quiet corner. Trying to get some air into her lungs, her stomach heaving.

She'd heard a voice.

'You doing OK?'

'Ummm.' She looked up. Gripping the bench, knuckles white, hoping it would save her. 'I've been better.'

'You look like you're gonna throw up.'

The sea pitched. Her stomach lurched. And to her horror,

she did just that. Threw up with projectile force. Across the deck … and across his shoes.

She was mortified. Her hand went to her mouth, tissues wiping away at her lips. She grabbed her bottle of water to swill her mouth.

'I'm … so …' She couldn't get the words out. Her eyes met his. He was smiling. Slate-blue eyes. Soft eyes. 'This is … embarrassing. I'm … I'm not good on the sea.'

'Really?'

His Irish accent was broad. Northern Ireland, she thought. He put his hand out to her, to guide her away from the mess.

She took it. And felt it instantly. It wasn't attraction. It was something else. Something rarer. Deeper. A feeling of safety. Of belonging.

Conor's voice bought her back to reality.

'Jay? Jay!'

He was shouting down the phone.

'Sorry. What was I saying?'

'That you've chosen the car crash of a ferry to travel to Ireland.'

'Right … It's a long story.'

'It must be.' He paused. 'And why the new phone number?'

'Like I said, long story.'

'I'm getting that. Tell me what you need.'

'I need a car. And a lookout.'

'OK. Looking out for what?'

She took a breath. 'There are men following me.'

'Who?' His voice changed. No levity now. 'Because of the article?'

It was a natural assumption. Vicious letters and online threats had followed her interview in *Soldier* magazine talking about her work at the DMRC, the role of nurses in the army, and her personal time in war zones. Threats the police were still investigating.

'No. Not because of that. I don't know who they are. I think there may be more at the port in Dublin. Waiting for me.'

Conor stayed silent. She knew that tactic well. It always surprised her how hard it was not to leap into the space with an explanation. She kept things tight.

'I can't tell you more.'

'Can't or won't?'

'Both. I need you to trust me. Can you do that?'

There was an even longer silence. He finally spoke. 'What kind of men are we talking?'

'Ones in suits carrying holstered guns. Glocks.'

He paused, taking that in. 'You're coming as a foot passenger?'

'Yes. I'll get a ticket at the terminal in Holyhead.'

'You're not booking it ahead?'

'No. I … I don't want to use my card.'

Another pause. She could feel him putting the pieces of information together.

'What time are you docking?'

'Depends which ferry I can make. Around five thirty or six in the morning. I've researched the terminal. I can change clothes. Make it look good. I might get out unseen, but it would be safer with a lookout. And I still need a vehicle to get away.'

'We'll talk more about getting out of the terminal later. What sort of vehicle do you need?'

She thought of some of the narrow tracks she'd seen in the Irish countryside on her online tours. 'A 4x4 would be ideal.'

He paused. 'Jay, what in the hell—'

She cut across him.

'There's something else. Hayley will be wondering where I am. There could still be men at the house.'

'Men at the house?'

His voice was even sharper.

She needed to be more careful. She'd just opened up another whole can of worms.

'I think—'

'Did someone hurt you?' He cut across her.

'I'm OK.'

'Jay—'

'Conor, I'm not hurt,' she interrupted him. 'Can you just text Hayley and say I've had an emergency and I've gone up north. I'll be in touch with her soon. Something like that. I'll text you her number.'

'I can do that but—'

'I'll ring you when I know which ferry I'm going to make. It'll be this number. I had to ditch my phone. Don't forget to tell Hayley that.'

'You want me to give her this new number?'

'No,' she shouted down the phone.

A couple getting out of their car nearby turned her way.

She held up a hand to them.

'No.' She took a breath. This was harder than she expected. She wasn't used to filtering around him. 'Don't give her this number.'

She carried on quickly. 'You always said I should call if I needed you.' Her voice wavered. He would hear that. He heard everything. He saw everything.

Conor took another pause. She could hear his breathing. Deeper breaths. Feel his brain working. Deciding which path to take.

'Always. Anything for you, Jay. Anything. Anytime. You know that.'

Soft voice. Calm.

She breathed out. She was desperate to see him. To feel the strength and safety he always gave her. Even if it was just for a short time.

'Thank you, Con.' She swallowed. Her throat dry. 'I'll … I'll be in touch again soon.'

Then she hung up the phone. Before he could press her for more information. Before she weakened and told him everything. And before her voice broke completely.

23

Ed was in his office, sitting in front of several computers, browser windows open, trying to focus on Chief Inspector Denis O'Malley and any links to the Tole network.

He was struggling, his mind refusing to focus. Thinking of Jamie. Terrified for her. That she'd get to him safely. But more than that, he was worrying about seeing her.

After his initial euphoria, reality was creeping in. How would he explain all the secrets he'd been hiding? Who he really was. What he'd been doing all these years right under her nose. He was a fool to think she'd forgive him for what he'd done. The lies and the deceit. Honesty was her litmus test for all relationships.

He forced himself to focus. To get back to what he knew he could control. Back to his screens and the research he was doing on the police officer George had recognised.

It was a new name to him. It had not cropped up in his own research. Checking Denis O'Malley's personnel file – via Loughborough police station – was an easy hack. He read his work history through, and three things jumped out at him.

Belfast. 2005. Morden.

O'Malley was a police officer at Morden station in

Belfast at the time of Zoe Bridges' death. He hadn't taken part in the investigation, but he would have known the officers in charge of the case. And he would have been able to look at the evidence they'd found. Maybe manipulate it. Or maybe he'd even been involved in the actual incident.

Ed leaned back. Spun his chair. The photo of 28-year-old Zoe Bridges was on his whiteboard with a thick red cross drawn over her smiling face. Right next to his parents, with their own devastating red cross.

He'd first heard the name Zoe in whispered late night talks by his parents. He now had a digital file devoted to her. He turned back to his desk and clicked to open it, revisiting his research.

Zoe Bridges had worked as an archivist at Tole Pharmaceuticals, digitising paper files from decades of research projects. His mother, Prudence O'Neill, a senior researcher at Tole Pharmaceuticals, had noted down conversations with Zoe in early March 2005.

Something is very wrong here, Prue. I've found things I shouldn't have seen. I'm investigating. You need to know about it.

Later in March, on a weekend break, Zoe was walking on the Falls Road in Belfast. A car mounted the pavement and mowed her down. She died instantly. The car fled the scene and the hit-and-run driver was never found. No vehicle was ever traced.

Ed clicked on the interview given by Zoe's parents to the *Irish Times.* Scanned across it and noted his own highlights. It heavily criticised the Police investigative work. It was "shabby at best, inept at worst." The officers had "shown little interest" in Zoe's case and in finding the negligent driver.

He looked over O'Malley's personnel file. It showed a speedy rise up the ranks. Ed had already dug into his online footprint and tracked his complex financial affairs. The Chief Inspector owned multiple properties. Properties far outside the reach of even a high-ranking police officer. Denis O'Malley's move to the small-town Loughborough police station now made more sense. He'd been sent there to monitor and track his best friend George and his wife.

Ed turned back to the open browser windows. He now had even more of a connection between Paul Arthur Tole and Zoe Bridges, via Denis O'Malley. Tole's reach was far, and it was wide. The many red crosses through the pictures on his whiteboard bore witness to that.

Over the years, the press had regularly devoted headlines to the alleged links between organised crime and Paul Arthur Tole. A court case involving fraud, financial irregularities and money laundering had held the nation gripped. But the case collapsed. Tole's solicitor stood on the court steps, his client by his side. Cameras flashing from the waiting press, making headline news.

'Today, justice has been done. The witch-hunt from the media and vicious competitors seeking to ruin Mr Tole's reputation and selfless work have been unsuccessful.'

Ed had looked on in despair. He knew about the people in Tole's back pocket. From police, to lawyers, to government officials, to those in the criminal underworld. The key witnesses who did not give testimony at the trial, others who changed their stories, documents which went missing, some which were miraculously altered.

Claiming to be a journalist, he had spoken to Lisa Stoke, the lead prosecutor.

'Leave it alone,' she'd said to him. 'You don't know who you're dealing with.'

'What do you mean?'

'I can't say more. But if you value your life and the lives of those you love, stop digging into Paul Arthur Tole.'

She hung up the phone.

He'd heard pure fear in her voice. He could imagine what was behind it. Someone she loved being threatened. Or even her own life. He was sure that was the reason she'd moved herself and her family away from Ireland.

He thought of his father. Now in the hands of men willing to do Tole's bidding. He thought of Jamie. In danger. Hunted and alone. And then himself. In isolation. Cut off from all those he loved. All because of one man.

And it forced him to question again, as he did on a near daily basis, why he had persisted in this search for the truth about his parents' death. He could have listened to the words – obeyed the words – his mother had written in the letter hidden deep in his loft. *Destroy everything in this package.*

His eyes scanned across the whiteboard. Information created over ten years of investigating. He wished he could have been the kind of person who could forget. Could let things go. Could live his life without looking back. But he couldn't. Justice and truth were hard-wired into his DNA. It had cost his parents their lives.

Would Jamie understand? Could she?

She lives for you, Ed.

Would that still be true now he'd deceived her? Betrayed her. And would it still be true when he told her everything?

24

In her second taxi, heading for Chester West Holiday Inn on the A55, Jamie's journey was going awry. Delays on the M6. It gave her even longer to regret calling Conor. She was berating herself for asking for his help. For risking a relapse in his health and for risking his volatility.

Hearing Conor's sharp words, his even sharper voice, reminded her of what he was willing to do to protect her. The soldier Conor hospitalised in Iraq when he wouldn't take Jamie's 'No' for an answer, as he pinned her against a wall outside the soldier's mess.

'I was handling it,' she'd said to Conor afterwards.

But his eyes, fierce with anger, dismissed her words. 'You shouldn't have to.'

He'd risked his commission for her on that day. His role in the army that he lived for more than his own life. But not more than hers.

She wanted to ring back, say she'd changed her mind. But he'd see through that. He'd still be waiting at the port. It was too late to go back on what she'd done.

Jamie closed her eyes. Desperate for sleep and a break from her whirling mind. But sleep wouldn't come.

She pulled out her phone to text Conor an update.

Delays en route. Won't make earlier ferry. Still hoping to make the 2:40 Irish Ferries. Where are you?

Her phone rang a minute later.

'I'm still at home. The car's arranged. I'm picking it up later.'

'Are you going to be OK to drive? I shouldn't have called you.'

'You should have. I'm good. I can take breaks if I need to.'

'Make sure you do.'

'Yes, Nurse.'

'I'm serious.'

'I know you are. And I will.' He paused, shuffling noises in the background. 'You had any sleep?'

'Not yet. I'm trying.'

'Try harder!'

He said it in a raised voice. She smiled. One of their army jokes. A drill sergeant they knew. Words he'd bellow at every recruit.

'I'll try again now.'

'Good. Talk in a while.'

Conor hung up the phone.

She made another attempt to relax each muscle group of her body. Visualise a calm place. Slow her breathing. Counting each breath.

She must have finally slept because she jolted awake from a vivid dream. Conor's unconscious face seared into her brain. Her chest tight. Struggling to breathe. Trying to remember where she was. What she was doing in this car. Her heart pounding. Her mind full of the visions. The noise. The smell. It didn't take much to get her back there. To the hell that had been Afghanistan.

25

They were in Helmand Province. It was 2014. Only a few months left on deployment. They were all shipping home. Afghanistan was being returned to its own people, an Afghan army, and a Taliban ready to resurge.

They were travelling in the burning heat. The wind throwing sand like dust in the air, affecting visibility. The escort truck was ahead. Two soldiers in the front seats, Conor in the back. She was in the car behind, sitting on the back seat, sorting through the medical bag with Dr Seela Salma driving.

She felt the car slow and looked up. An old woman was ahead, limping along the road. As the advance truck got level with her, she turned. In a split second, the world changed. The truck exploded. Debris flying. Bodies in the air. Flames shooting up as their own vehicle flipped, landing on its roof.

Her body slammed and jerked back. Head hitting the door. Stunning her. The seatbelt dug into her flesh and her shoulder, with the force of the car spinning. Her hands struggled with the belt. It was caught. She tugged. Tugged. Clicking it open. Freeing herself and crashing down onto the upturned roof. Then she was scrabbling for the medical bag, pushing things inside. Checking her weapon was still in its holster. Calling out.

'Seela! Seela!'

'I'm OK, Jamie. I'm OK. But I'm wedged in.'

'Call it in, Seela. I'll go to the others,' Jamie shouted as she edged across the roof of the car, ramming her feet against the twisted door to get it open. It gave way on the third crash and she was out, stumbling onto the ground, almost falling. She stabilised herself. Then she was running with the open medical bag over her shoulder. Her heart hammering, her body shaking, only adrenaline pushing her forward.

Twenty feet ahead, smoke in the air, the smell of burning flesh and carnage all around. Blood matted on the sand with tissue and limbs.

Through the smoke, she scanned the three men lying on the ground. Her eyes searched for Conor. She rushed to him. Blood was pulsing from a wound two inches above his right knee. His femoral artery severed. Two to five minutes without treatment and he would bleed out. More than two minutes of that was gone. Jamie registered his other leg, twisted viciously at the hip and a compound fracture at the knee, the bone visible.

'You're going to be OK. Conor. Conor look at me. Talk to me.'

'Jay, Jay, I'm…' His voice slurred, his eyes closing. Blood pouring out of his body. The spurts coming with each rapid beat of his heart.

'Stay with me, Conor.'

Placing her knee across the top of his thigh, she bore down on it to exert pressure and help slow the bleeding. Pulling open the medical bag she grabbed a combat tourniquet, flicking it to open. Reaching down, she pulled the tourniquet over Conor's foot, up his leg, three inches past the bleed, threading through the buckle and pulling it tight. She began turning the windlass. One turn, two, three. The blood flow slowed. Another turn and it stopped. She secured the strap over the windlass and adhered the Velcro. Checking her watch and grabbing a pen from the side of her bag, she wrote 14:43 on the white space.

'Con. Conor.' She touched his face. Slapping it. His eyes opened. 'Stay with me.' Glassy eyes. They closed again.

Glancing around, through the haze of smoke and dust, she saw Ben to her left. It was Davy laid out on her right. The driver. His face gone. One arm and one leg no longer on his body. He had taken the full blast of the explosion.

She heard murmuring.

She yelled out. 'Ben. Can you hear me?'

'Shaw…'

His voice was weak. A whispered plea. Hard to hear. Harder still not to go to him. But she couldn't leave Conor. His pulse was racing. His trousers saturated. He'd lost so much blood. The sand around him black with it, wet and matted. His face beyond pale.

She pulled out the IV fluid bag, her fingers trembling as she tried to push in the cannula. It took four attempts, his veins collapsing from the blood loss. Up on her feet, she pressed the bag, pushing the fluid through as fast as she could.

'Ben. Talk to me.' She shouted.

'Sha…'

Barely a whisper across the desert.

With dust pricking her eyes, smoke from the burning vehicle drifting across her sight line, she saw part of Ben's left leg was gone.

'Get your pack, Ben. Get your CAT!' Her voice trying to raise him, bring him back to consciousness. 'Use your tourniquet on your left leg!' She shouted.

Silence.

Even if Seela had got through, the helicopter was still six minutes away.

As the last fluid drained from the IV bag, Jamie knelt back down. She needed to check Conor's upper body. His breathing was changing. His breaths shorter. Shallower. She pulled open the layers of his outer pack and saw blood soaking the inside. She sliced open his saturated clothes. A piece of metal was protruding from his left lung. A tension pneumothorax. Air trapped in the plural cavity. She opened the medical bag and rifled through. Dug deeper and found what she needed. She felt for the second rib at the intercostal, took in a breath, steadied her hand, and pushed in the syringe. The hiss of air leaked out and Conor's breathing changed instantly. She taped the protruding needle in place.

'You're gonna be OK, Conor. You're OK.' She gripped his hand and felt his pulse. It was still racing. He was unconscious. 'Hold on Conor.' She touched his face. Lips to his ear. 'I'll be back. I've got to help Ben.'

She pulled herself away from Conor. It took physical will to leave his side.

She knelt beside Ben. His left leg was crushed, his right leg missing beneath the knee. His left arm twisted, and his right trapped underneath him. Blood soaked his clothes and the sand around him. No matter the training, with his injuries, he had no way of using his medical pack. Pulling out another tourniquet, she tied it above the right knee. He'd lose the knee joint. It was shredded. Mud and tissue jammed up into the wound.

She took his racing pulse. He was now slumped and unconscious.

'You're good, Ben. You're good. You're going to be fine. They're coming. Help is coming. Hang on.'

She heard the helicopter. It was close. Much closer than she expected.

She reached into her bag for another cannula, another IV, and she searched for a vein.

'Shaw! Shaw!'

Dr Seela Salma screamed out across the battlefield of burning sand. Jamie swung around. Two Taliban fighters were approaching Seela's car from over the rise. Guns up. The follow up to the suicide bomber.

Jamie pulled out her Glock. Steadied herself. Aimed. And shot. She hit an arm. Second shot. To the heart. The man closest to the car went down.

The second Taliban fighter had moved his assault rifle, it was now pointed directly at her. She went to the ground. Bursts of fire fizzing around her. She was pinned down. Then she heard shouts. Her name. More shots fired. Soldiers were approaching the area. Moving to Seela and coming towards her.

In a blur of seconds, the scene filled with uniforms and medics. Someone grasped hold of her. It was Keeley, a friend and colleague. She touched her face and head, but Jamie pushed her away, trying to get back to Conor.

In minutes, the men were loaded on stretchers, and they were moving towards the waiting Chinook. Its pulsing sound and blades threw up acres of blinding sand. The noise echoing through the desert. The choking sand stuck in her eyes and mouth as she followed the stretchers, her breaths coming in gasps, looking at the horror scene around her.

Her eyes turned towards the rise, near the upturned car, to the man she'd shot. She was here to save lives, not take them. Her hands began to shake, her body trembling. Stumbling forward, she went down, landing on her knees on the hot, soft sand. Then hands grasped her, pulling her back up, back onto her feet.

On the flight back to Camp Bastien, Conor opened his eyes. Saw her. Closed them again. Ben crashed twice. Davy

Grade lay covered to the side. They didn't leave a brother in arms behind. Even when he was dead.

Conor and Ben were both taken straight into surgery. As she waited for news, she feared the effect of Conor's injuries. For now, and for his future. But when the surgeon emerged, and she knew he was alive, that was all that mattered to her. All she cared about.

Ben didn't make it. He died on the table. Things might have been different if she'd gone to him first. She knew she'd made a choice. She'd chosen Conor.

Jamie had nightmares about that moment more than any other in all the horrors she'd seen over a decade as an army nurse. Dreamt she was the one injured, laying on the dirt, who did not get chosen first. Her murmuring, calling for help. Her hand held out and someone walking past her. Leaving her gasping for air. Leaving her to die.

She had to live with that. Live with Ben's wife and two small boys without him. There was no reparation she could ever make. She accepted it for what it was. Conor was her family. She was always going to put him first. Later, she wondered if losing Ed was her punishment. An eye for an eye. One husband for another.

In the darkness of the taxi, Jamie realised tears were running down her cheeks. Tears for Conor, always for Conor, and the life he lost on that day. The years of rehab that couldn't get his hip, fractured knee, and wrecked ligaments back to strength. The fragments of shrapnel in his lower spine, that she'd not known were there, causing damage to all three branches of his pudendal nerve. The affects brutal and increasing in severity over time. Affecting everything below the waist. Turning bodily functions and pleasure into searing pain. Making sitting down its own kind of hell, causing flares of agony which made him unrecognisable to her.

Please, Jay. Go.

The first time she'd ever seen him weep, crying out in pain as she bathed him. Begging for another nurse to take her place. His eyes burning with shame.

He was discharged from the army, his purpose in the world lost, his career gone. The army was all he'd ever known. Sometimes the visible wounds are not the worst.

She swiped at the tears. Remembering the lowest moment of all.

You should have let me die, Jay.

His eyes empty. His life a wreck. The physical pain and disability destroying any meaning he could find in his life.

It seemed that every dark thought she'd ever had was playing in her conscious and unconscious mind. She needed to pull herself back from the past. Only the lost and the broken stayed there.

Jamie watched the hazy car lights coming towards her. The wipers beating back and forth to an even rhythm, the rain now in torrents, a lorry ahead throwing up spray. She turned her eyes away from the windscreen. Head leaning on her coat on the side window. Eyes closed to stop the headlights from blinding her. And she started that journey. Dragging herself back, one foot in front of the other through deep, dark quicksand. Dragging herself back into the present.

26

'Foot passenger to Dublin, please. I'd like to pay in cash.'

Jamie had her wallet in her hand. Eyes focused on the blonde woman on reception with her white Irish Ferries logo sitting proud on her top.

'Your ID, please.'

She pushed her driving license across the counter and saw the camera lens at the reception desk in the port of Holyhead trained on her. It was pointless trying to hide. There was nothing else she could do now. She was committed. A cold rock sat in her stomach. Was her image racing through the network, alerting whoever was searching for her? Were they scrambling to get men to wait for her at the port in Dublin? It was like willingly walking towards a traffic collision. Still, she did it.

Once in the departure lounge, the two-dozen or so people travelling on foot were lost in the large domed ceiling, with its long rows of red and blue seats back-to-back.

She scanned around the space. A group of eight passengers travelling together – three women and five men – interested her. They were varying ages, around twenties to forties, and all wearing hippy-style, boho fashion.

She moved to sit closer to them and she could overhear every part of their lively conversations. One man on the edge of the group stayed silent, a guitar leaning on the empty chair next to him. The others were all talking about a festival in Galway.

'Can't wait to see Forward Path.'

'Me too. I missed them last year.'

'And the campsite facilities look great.'

'It's got to be better than last year!'

Laughter hit the group.

Jamie pulled out her phone and googled *Galway Hippy Festival 2024.* A new Spring festival, celebrating 1960s music, was taking place over this weekend in Kinvara**.** The famous Irish band Forward Path was headlining the event. This was their destination.

She sensed movement ahead of her and looked up from her phone. Everyone was getting up onto their feet, moving towards an open door at the far side of the departure lounge. The bus to take them on board the ferry was waiting. She took a few photos of the group. Tapped Conor's number and forwarded them to him, following it with the festival's website link and a text message. *Eight travelling. Going here. Meeting friends inside the terminal at Dublin. They're our cover. Jay*

She made her way forward, keeping a distance behind the others. Knowing she would be visible to the security cameras. She reached the shuttle bus, the last of the foot passengers, and took a step up. One literal step closer to Ireland. Closer to Ed. Closer to the answers she needed.

As she moved forward, a sensation gripped her tight around the chest. She steadied herself on a glass partition. It was as though someone was standing behind her, arms squeezing around her middle, pulling her back. She pushed against the vice-like restriction. Forcing herself to move forward.

She slid into a window seat, her heart pounding. It wasn't like any fear response she'd ever experienced. It felt like a warning.

She lay her face on the cool glass scattered with rain drops. Murky darkness outside. She watched the lights of passing lorries waiting in line to go on board the ferry as they drove towards the cargo deck.

As the bus came to a stop, the passengers began walking down the aisle, passing beside her, but she couldn't move.

Sickness rose from her stomach, her head started to spin, her lungs felt tight. It was panic. Something inside her wanted to run. Get off the ferry and not stop. Forget her questions. Go back to yesterday when everything made sense. But she knew she couldn't do that. There was no going back.

'Are you ready to dismount?'

An impatient male voice.

She looked up. The driver was standing at the open door. She looked around, there was no-one else left on the bus.

Decision time.

It was never in doubt.

She stood on shaky legs, walked forward, and stepped off the bus. She avoided the sign for the lift and passed through an open door. A sign ahead told her she was on *Deck 6. The Ruby Stairs.*

She pushed upward with each heavy step on the bright red stairs. Clinging on to the cool, steel handrail. Dragging herself forward. Climbing up and up towards the shops on Deck 9. Committed to her path. Wherever it led. And whatever it meant for her.

27

It had barely been twenty minutes and Jamie's stomach was lurching with every swell of the boat. And even though she had no food in her stomach, she still retched up every drop of the water she'd drunk.

After going around the shop, getting the clothes she needed, and speaking to Conor from the Club lounge confirming their plan for exiting the terminal, she'd settled into her cabin.

As they were leaving port, the words coming through the ship's intercom had given her hope:

'Our expected time of arrival in Dublin is five to six. There are some south-westerly winds, but we're expecting a smooth crossing.'

She'd chosen a berth with no window, hoping this would help her forget she was on the water.

It didn't.

Rough or smooth, window or not, the motion of the boat wrecked her. It was clear why she'd sworn never to go on a boat again. But here she was, lying prone and still. Trying to ride the waves inside her stomach and overcome the feeling of deathly nausea.

She pulled her backpack towards her and took out her medication. She'd already taken two seasickness tablets before she travelled. She checked the packet. It wasn't time for another dose for six hours. She took two more tablets from the foil strip, swigging them back with the smallest amount of water she could manage. Then she curled into a ball and tried to roll with the waves.

Half an hour later, the rolling continued but the tablets were taking the edge off. She stumbled towards the shower and regretted it instantly. Movement was the enemy, stillness the only answer to equilibrium. She lurched back to bed. Checked her watch. There were still two and a half hours left to reach Dublin port. It felt like a lifetime. She pulled out her charger, battery pack and phone, and plugged them in. Then she lay back down, weak and exhausted. Closed her eyes. Hoping the double dose of cinnarizine would knock her out.

She woke with a start. Her heart thumping. Brain fuzzy. She was being chased by George, her father, and Officer Denis O'Malley. They were all working together against her. Her mind was a mess of confusion. She tried to steady her heartbeat. Swiped at the sweat lying in beads on her forehead.

Checking her phone, Jamie saw she'd been asleep for almost an hour. The sickness was now less severe, but it still felt ready to surge again at any moment.

She pulled herself up and propped the pillows behind her. She needed to swap out her things from her backpack. She had a large, beige tote bag she'd bought in the shop and a duty-free carrier bag. Both would help to complete her new look for exiting the port

Jamie poured everything from her backpack onto the bed. Picked the things she needed and put them aside. Then she saw the package she'd brought out from the loft, the one Ed must have stowed there.

Sitting forward, cross-legged on the bed, she pulled the small, black, leather case towards her.

She turned it over in her hands.

Hesitated.

Then she pulled open the zip and emptied out the contents.

28

There was a phone with four SIM cards, a charging lead, and several white envelopes. The phone was dead. Jamie reached across for her own phone, now fully charged, swapped over the leads, and set the new phone to charge.

She looked at the envelopes and felt a heavy beat in her chest. She started with the thin, square one. It held a silver disc with a DVD logo across it. She turned it over. Nothing was written on either side. She'd have to buy an external drive if she wanted to play it.

Next, she held the bulky envelope. A glance inside showed papers and passports. She paused. The only people who had multiple passports were criminals or undercover agents. She almost put them back. Ignorance a blessing. But she had to look. She couldn't stop now.

She opened the first passport. Not her husband. A woman called Prudence O'Neill. The name leapt out at her. O'Neill. The name Officer O'Malley had said while she was hanging precariously from the roof. The second passport was Frank O'Neill. The third, a young boy, Sean O'Neill. She checked the dates on each passport. All expired in 2013.

Jamie looked at the faces. The young boy was about

eleven or twelve. It was clear as day to her. The child had her husband's eyes and the distinctive nose of the woman called Prudence. And the adult Ed she knew bore a striking resemblance to Frank, even down to the kinks in his brown hair. She had no doubt about it. This was Ed and his birth parents.

Jamie stayed fixed on the images. She'd never seen a photo of Ed as a child. And she'd never seen a photo of his parents. Turning the pages on the passports she read Prudence was born in Keswick in England. Frank in Bandon in Ireland. And Sean was born in Rathgar, Ireland.

There were two more passports. She opened them. Penny Taylor and John Taylor. She checked the pictures. They were the same as the adults on the O'Neill passports. She searched through. The boy's second passport was not there. Then it all clicked into place. It wasn't there because her husband, Ed Taylor, had been using it all these years.

Her brain pounded. A whole different history of her husband was unfolding before her eyes.

She laid out the papers. There were birth certificates and driver's licenses for the adults – the O'Neills and the Taylor's. And a birth certificate for the young Sean O'Neill but not for a young Edward Taylor.

She pulled forward her phone from the side cabinet. Turned the brightness down, her head now starting to throb viciously. Sweat peppering her forehead, nausea rising and the words jumping on the page. But she had to keep going.

She put the names in the search bar of her phone. 'Penny John Taylor car crash.' Only one search record. She clicked. It was the online clipping Ed had shown her years ago of his parents' death, with the headline – ***Couple die in head on collision.*** She remembered thinking, when Ed had died in a car crash, that there was some kind of morbid symmetry. His death matching his birth parents. There were no other articles or mentions of them online. And no photos.

Next, she put the names 'Prudence Frank Sean O'Neill' in the search bar. Many more results appeared. Her eyes went to a headline:

Punishment killing of drug-dealing Rathgar couple. Where is Sean O'Neill?

She clicked on the link. Checked the date. It was written in 2020 by a journalist for the *Irish Times,* Fay Dunlow.

Fifteen years ago today, the upmarket town of Rathgar, once home to our greatest writer James Joyce, was at the heart of another brutal attempt to control the flow of illegal drugs into Dublin.

Paramilitaries had received a tip off about a couple working at a nearby Pharmaceutical Company. Frank and Prudence O'Neill were illegally making heroin and selling it onto the streets of Dublin and its suburbs. The O'Neill's had known connections to Perry O'Keefe's notorious criminal gang. Their deaths on 12 August 2005, with bullets to both legs, and their house set on fire, were clear signs of punishment killings. A brutal example of continuing paramilitary involvement in controlling the supply of drugs to rival dealers on the streets of Dublin.

The O'Neill's employer, Paul Arthur Tole, multi-millionaire owner of Tole Pharmaceuticals, had been approached for comment at the time of their deaths. 'They were good workers. We are all in shock to learn of their secret life.'

Mr Tole is not new to the pages of the Irish Times. Investigations into fraud and money laundering have plagued him. Although currently all charges have been dismissed, rumours continue of his alleged links to organised crime.

The disappearance of thirteen-year-old Sean O'Neill remains an unsolved mystery to this day. He vanished without a trace. Stories abound of what happened to him. Many speculate that he died, was trafficked by crime bosses, or escaped and is living in witness protection. People in Rathgar still speak his name in whispers. The words, 'Where is Sean O'Neill?' able to provoke a spirited discussion in any pub in town.

An old, grainy photo of the O'Neill family sat beside the article.

Jamie pulled up from her phone. Leaned back. Her heart pounding. Head cracking open with sharp stabs of pain, trying to piece this all together.

Drug dealers.

Could Ed be connected to this world? It seemed impossible. And yet it would explain why men with guns were hunting him, chasing her, and threatening their father. Had Ed lived a double life and continued his parent's involvement in drugs? Had he angered some kind of cartel?

She found it impossible to believe. If Ed was involved in anything like this, she needed another serious recalibration of everything she'd ever known about her husband.

Her mind in turmoil, she picked up the last white envelope. It was slim. *Sean* was handwritten across the front in blue ink. It wasn't hers to read. She turned it over. It was open. She couldn't stop herself. For as much as there was to know, and as bad as it was, she had to know it.

29

16th July 2005

My darling son Sean,

If you are reading this then we have failed you. Our worst fears have been realised. Forgive me, forgive us for leaving you like this.

Know that we love you with all our hearts. The day we first laid eyes on you our lives changed forever. You have brought us boundless joy. We're so proud of you.

You'll read a lot of different things now. Just remember, whatever is said, whatever story is told, you know us. We are on the side of truth and on the side of right. Never question that.

Now I'm going to ask the impossible of you. I want you to destroy everything in this package. This letter, the disc, and all the other papers and passports. I don't want you to look back, my beautiful boy. We have been at the mercy of dangerous people and now you are too. We don't want anything to happen to you. Somehow you have to find a way to live as though this never happened. Just try to carry the best of us with you and all the memories of our good times together.

I know you, my son. I know this will be hard, but I beg you to do it. You will lose everything if you don't and that is beyond what either your father or me can bear.

I've trusted Uncle Perry with getting you out of the country and to a new home. You will be safe there and loved.

But remember, you must never tell anyone of us and of our life in Ireland. Never. The reach of Paul Arthur Tole is vast.

We love you my beautiful boy. Never forget that. We will be watching over you. Your guardian angels.

Carry us in your heart, Sean. And know that you are, and always will be, our greatest joy.

Your loving Ma and Da.

Jamie felt tears brimming in her eyes. She pulled her head up. Couldn't believe what she'd just read. It was like clicking pieces of a puzzle together. So many things falling into place.

Ed's obsession with security. The cameras. The little safe room in the loft. She saw it all through eyes of new knowledge. His fears were nothing to do with a childhood friend and a home invasion. He had built the safe room for his own security. He always knew people were looking for him. His nightmares, which she'd seen him struggle with, were not for a school friend but for himself. For all he'd been through, his parents murdered, his fear of being found.

The story Ed had told her of his birth parents, Penny and John Taylor, was all a lie. The car crash when he was ten, his upbringing in Northamptonshire, and his time in foster care did not happen. Ed had escaped from Ireland at the age of thirteen, the year Tom and Grace McDonald had adopted him.

She flashed to the Lough Road and Ed's knowledge of

Irish and his accent. Another piece fell into place. He'd lived in Ireland until he was thirteen. His father, Frank, was Irish and his mother was English.

There was also his unwillingness to go to Ireland. His excuses about visiting Conor in Northern Ireland, even when Conor was too sick to travel. His fear of being found was too grave to travel to any part of the island of Ireland. And yet he was there now. Why?

Then Jamie thought of his lack of history, of stories about his parents, the absence of photos, documents, and childhood treasures. It all made sense now. Lost in the house fire. Or kept secret.

This one letter filled a gap of knowledge she'd never realised needed filling.

She looked back at the letter.

…whatever is said, whatever story is told, you know us. We are on the side of truth and on the side of right. Never question that.

Not drug dealers.

Not what the newspaper articles said.

His mother had requested he destroy everything in this package. But the disc, papers and passports were sitting here in front of her. She knew why. Her husband's hatred of injustice. He couldn't let lies about his parents' death go unanswered.

Jamie looked at the letter again. *The reach of Paul Arthur Tole is vast.* Ed's mother believed Tole was a dangerous man. Lined up against them. And against her son. Someone to be feared. She put the letter down. It was hard to believe. Tole was a hero. His relentless quest to bring Tolacaine to market was changing lives. And he'd been exonerated of financial fraud and money laundering. How could he be connected to murder? And why?

Then another question hit her right in the solar plexus.

Had her father known about Ed and his history? How could he have adopted Ed without knowing of his past? Had she been lied to by her father, too?

Her stomach ached. Her brain ached. Her heart ached.

Jamie leant back on the pillow. Her head pounding, the skin on her scalp sore and tingling. She closed her eyes, trying to assimilate all she'd read.

Her husband had lied to her every day since they'd met. Deliberately deceived her. Covered up his true self. Even his real name. But in this moment, something else eclipsed all of that. Jamie saw an orphaned boy of thirteen in fear of his life. Saw that boy leaving behind his murdered parents, coming by stealth to a foreign country, unable to ever speak of his family or his home.

Her heart broke for this boy and for the man who carried this weight.

Her heart broke for her husband.

And that made her wonder something. Wonder if Ed had ever thought he could trust her. If, in spite of what his mother had begged, he'd ever wanted to share his true history with her. His true self with her.

How much do you love me?

Ed's words echoed inside her painful, throbbing head. And her reply came silently and unbidden.

How much did I ever really know you?

30

Ed had been watching his computer for hours. It was a good sign that he hadn't found Jamie. Hadn't seen her image flag up on his tracking software on any kind of public transport. He had alerts set up at airports, but he was sure she wouldn't travel by plane, there was too much waiting time ahead of the flight. She'd come by ferry. It was her best option, however little she'd want to do it. Preparing for that possibility, he had browser windows open at Fishguard, Liverpool, Holyhead and Cairnryan Ports.

The ping of his own facial and body recognition software alerted him. He turned to his right and there she was. Walking through the doors to the port terminal of Holyhead. Her head was down, in the shade of her hoodie, but he'd know that walk anywhere. He closed all the other search windows on his computer and focused. He had already gained access to the cameras inside the terminal and on the perimeter. CCTV was everywhere and appallingly easy to hack into.

Dressed in black, top to toe, his heart contracted at the glimpse of her. Her stance, her walk, her movements. The first time he'd seen her in real life for two years. A moment he never thought would happen.

As she stood at the reception desk to buy her ticket, her eyes met the camera, and he held his breath. She was looking straight at him. As beautiful as he'd ever seen her. Barely changed. Her hair a little shorter. Her face thinner. But behind the eyes, it hit him like a force. Fragility. Something he wasn't used to seeing.

'Foot passenger to Dublin, please. I'd like to pay in cash.'

His heartbeat ticked up, hearing her voice. New words for the first time in two years. He watched as she showed her ID and paid for her ticket. He heard the click of computer keys and saw her pick up the boarding pass. Then beeps sounded across his computers. Loud and insistent.

He turned.

At this moment, it was over. Her ID flagged. Tracking software doing its job. The network buzzing. Actions being taken.

The next event was inevitable. Tole's men would be waiting for Jamie when she reached Dublin Port.

Like him, they'd be watching the CCTV now. Viewing Jamie through the obvious cameras mounted high up on walls. The less visible ones in the ceiling, ensuring a 360-degree view. If he could hack in so easily, so could they.

The feeling of helplessness seeing this unfold, unable to do anything, knowing what was coming, was past anything he'd ever experienced. And most of all, knowing that she was putting herself in danger because of him, to find him, left him drowning in guilt.

Did Jamie realise men would be waiting for her at the port? If only she could have pulled Conor into this. But Conor wasn't strong enough, or well enough, to help her. He couldn't even travel to meet her.

Ed tried to keep his mind on solid ground. Jamie had made it this far alone. She could make it the rest of the way. But then his mind shifted again. Getting away from the port was a huge challenge. He had no idea how she'd do that. How she'd get away from Tole's men who would be circling in on her arrival.

He knew Tole would throw everything at him this time. He'd been lost to his network for nineteen years. Now Jamie was drawing them towards him. He was as prepared for that outcome as he could be. His defences were robust, his back-up plans on top of back-up plans were good. He just hoped they were good enough.

He looked back at the screens and watched Jamie sitting in the departure lounge checking her phone. Then she was standing and taking photos. Hanging back behind the others.

He thought she'd try to mingle, to lose herself among the other people. Instead, she was a very visible solitary figure in black walking towards the shuttle bus. The last of the foot passengers. He was sure this was deliberate. Because he knew his wife. And he knew she would have a plan.

He tracked some of her movements on the ship and inside the duty-free shop. His last glimpse saw her walking down a red-carpeted corridor, disappearing around a corner which he knew led to a cabin door.

Ed leaned back and closed his eyes. He thought of Jamie alone inside that cabin. Wondered what she was thinking and feeling. The loneliness. The fear. Wondering at his betrayal. The questions she must have.

It triggered memories he'd tried so hard to forget. His journey in the opposite direction, from Dublin to Holyhead, at the age of thirteen. Frightened. Alone. Having lost everything.

31

He could still see his mother's face, pale against black curls, as she'd looked at him on the day his world ended. As she gave him the small black package with trembling hands. His scuffed brown suitcase sitting on the floor at the bottom of the stairs.

'You go ahead to Uncle Perry. We'll be right behind you. I'm just waiting for your Da.'

He looked at her. 'I don't understand.'

'Remember when we talked a few weeks ago? Something was happening at work. We said you might need to be brave?'

'I remember.'

'This is that moment, Sean. I need you to be brave. I need you to do exactly what I say.' Her hands gripped his arms. 'No deviation. You go now and we'll follow.'

He hesitated. He heard what she said, felt her urgency, but he didn't want to leave her.

'I'll wait with you, Ma. We can all go together.'

She shook her head. 'No. You go. Keep these things safe.' She pressed his hands around the package. Her hands shaking even harder. 'All our documents are inside and our work. We're relying on you, Sean.'

He could still feel the imprint of her lips on his forehead – the last time he ever felt them. He could still feel the crush of his bones as she held him – the last time she ever held him.

He'd been so afraid, standing there. In his mind, he knew something was terribly wrong.

Things had been strange for a while. The late-night work, his parents' poring over documents and hiding things. Not leaving papers out as they usually did with their research and work. They'd never been secretive before, but in the last five months something had changed.

He'd overheard snippets of conversations. *An eavesdropper never hears anything good.* That's what his mother used to say. Still, he'd listened.

Something was going wrong at work. At Tole Pharmaceuticals. They spoke of leaving. Then spoke of needing to stay. If they didn't do it, who would? He'd heard the name Zoe. He knew she was dead because his mother had been to her funeral. But Zoe had found something important. He couldn't piece it all together, what it meant, but he knew it didn't sound good.

And he remembered hearing something else. Two weeks before the madness hit. The door was open a crack, it was past midnight, and he was meant to be asleep long ago. He heard his mother talking to his father.

'I don't think you should do that. It's too risky. How can you get a disc out of there with the security they have?'

'I already did, darling.'

There was a long gap of silence. Sean held his breath. Not wanting to be discovered, but wanting to hear more.

'How much did you get?'

'All of it. The whole folder. And a cache of financial documents not declared to the courts. But they're all encrypted. Enter the wrong code and the files will be useless.'

There was more muttering. Then his father carried on.

'Now I know it's possible, I'll give it a couple of weeks and try for the encryption key. I know it's there. Behind the Infinity Firewall.'

'Then we all go?' His mother said.

'Yes. Then we all go. Perry's got our new identities. We hide out. We decrypt it. Then we can finally expose what's happening.'

Sean heard movement and stepped away from the door. Padded softly back to his room. Trying to make sense of it. He couldn't. He only truly made sense of it later, with his parents dead and the black zipped package in his possession.

Later, he'd plague himself with thoughts that he could have saved them. Could have told someone he thought they were in trouble. He'd watched his mother grow more anxious and his father more solemn. His mother now questioned every movement he made when just going out to meet his friends. And no more video games after school with his father, he was too busy, head in his computer even after long days at work. And then that strange conversation about being brave. Sean saw all of it but didn't know what he could do.

And now it had come to this. Pushing him out into the street with a small suitcase and a package of documents.

She'd told him to go fast, and he had. He'd run all the way. To find Uncle Perry on the doorstep pulling him inside. He'd heard things at school about the O'Keefe's and their criminal connections. A family to be feared. His uncle an important man at the head of the family. *But they don't hurt anyone who doesn't deserve it.* That was the mantra running around. Sean didn't know the truth of it. He just knew that Uncle Perry was kind and solid. Always interested in what he was doing. And always encouraging him. *Work hard Seany, you can change the world, there's nothing you can't do.* His hand slapping him on the back. The closest Uncle Perry ever came to physical affection. Unlike Aunt Kathleen, Uncle Perry didn't do hugs.

Once inside the house, Sean was led through to the back door to a waiting car. Then on to another house, one he'd never seen before. Here he had waited. Waited for his parents to come. The television on in the living room, minutes passing into hours as he flicked through the channels. Uncle Perry in the next room talking on the phone, sometimes shouting, sometimes whispering.

With drinks beside him, and sandwiches brought to him lying half eaten on the table, he waited. But no-one came. The feeling in his stomach, the knots of fear twisting as time passed. And that feeling that something was badly wrong kept growing.

Exhaustion finally overtook him, and he slept sprawled out on the leather sofa. The TV playing in the background. Darkness falling outside.

Until Uncle Perry woke him.

Shaking him.

32

'We need to go, Sean.'

It took him a minute to realise where he was. 'Go where?' Then it all rushed back. Why he was in this strange place. He pushed himself up 'Are they here?'

Uncle Perry crouched down beside him.

'They're not coming, Sean. They're … not coming.'

His usual strong face had a strange look. His voice faltering.

Sean struggled to take in the words. It made no sense. They'd come later. That's what he thought he meant.

But that wasn't what Uncle Perry meant.

Speaking in a rare soft voice, Uncle Perry made him open the package his mother had given him and find a new passport and birth certificate.

'Your name is Edward now. Edward Taylor. You can use Ed for short.' Uncle Perry gave him a weak smile. For once, all his bluster was gone, like a burst balloon.

His uncle then handed him another piece of paper. His hand shaking.

'You have to read this and memorise it,' he said. 'This is your story now.'

Sean read the words and tried to take them in. It all felt completely unreal. Like a nightmare he couldn't wake up from.

And as he travelled by car with Uncle Perry, to the ship which would take him over the water to England, he was told the rest. That his parents were dead. That there was a bounty on his head. Half of the criminal underworld was looking for him. Searching for him everywhere. And even though his parents were heroes, Uncle Perry's voice had broken as he said those words, he needed to forget everything he'd ever known about his life in Ireland. His mother had set up a safe place for him in England. He'd be cared for and loved there.

When Uncle Perry stood opposite him at the doors of the departure lounge, his face drawn, eyes glistening, he repeated those unbelievable words, gripping his arms so tight Sean could feel pain.

'Remember, my boy. Sean O'Neill no longer exists.'

And then he put a coin in his hand and pressed his fingers around it. The one he'd played with when he was a small child. The lucky coin Uncle Perry always carried with him.

'Heads or tails?' his uncle used to say, flipping the coin.

It took him a while to realise it was always heads. One day, he'd snuck a look at the British two-pound coin and saw two Queen's heads on it. One on each side.

As he lay alone, holding the coin tight in his hand, in that cramped cabin travelling across the Irish sea, he shook from head to foot. Reading his mother's letter over and over again. Trying to understand it all. But he couldn't take any of it in. Couldn't believe his parents were gone and he was in danger. That he had a new name, would have a new home, and that he was now in hiding. It was unbelievable.

Even later, when in England, searching out news reports of his parents' death, he didn't believe they were dead. The articles were full of lies, so maybe their deaths were lies too.

They'd come back for him. He was sure of it. That's what the passports of John and Penny Taylor were for. He wasn't destroying anything. He'd keep their documents safe, and the disc, ready for his parents' return. They were all going to escape. *Then we all go. We hide out. We decrypt it.* He'd understood that much from those overheard, whispered words.

He wasn't sure when the moment came that he finally believed his parents were gone. But as that belief came, it morphed into a need for answers. And against all his mother's wishes, he took out the DVD from that small black package and inserted it into an external drive connected to his laptop. And his search began.

His search for knowledge. His search for truth. His search for justice.

33

Sitting at his desk, Ed felt cold chills running down his spine. *Someone is walking over my grave.* Another of his mother's sayings. A threat and a warning. His mind a turmoil of memory. Of darkness.

For the last two years, since he'd been back in Ireland, he'd had more dreams. Many more nightmares. Even hearing the Irish accent and language triggered memories. It took him right back to that boy of thirteen. He'd been waking, soaking in sweat. In terror. Trapped in flames. Suffocating. The kind of nightmares he hadn't had since Tom and Grace took him in.

Grace's soft hand on his forehead when he screamed in the darkness. Both of them rushing to his side. Calming him. Soothing him.

'What's the dream about, Eddie?'

Grace stroking his face. Holding his hand tight. Tom by his other side. Him shaking his head. He couldn't tell her. Couldn't tell anyone anything. They'd been his instructions. And that part he'd stuck to. He hadn't told a soul.

After the first few years it hadn't been that difficult to keep his story to himself. It was almost as though his other life had never existed. Other than George, he'd steered clear of close friendships and serious relationships. He always knew there was a barrier inside him. A wall. It seemed instinctive. A defence to stop him revealing himself. He knew that to ensure he stayed safe, he needed to travel through life alone. His emotions always in check.

But then came that moment. A works party for his new job as an IT specialist at the Defence Medical Rehabilitation Centre. He saw her.

'Ed, meet Captain Jamie Shaw.'

Mark Draper had introduced them. Just five simple words. And in that one moment, he was gone. His entire world changed. Their eyes had locked, he'd held her outstretched hand, fallen into her deep blue eyes, and felt ripples throughout his entire body. The rapid heartbeat he'd only ever associated with fear felt entirely different. Something he'd only ever read about in books, but never believed he could feel.

All his caution, all those earlier decisions, all his lack of connection, were blown out of the water. He couldn't stop himself. There was no fighting it, as hard as he tried. And as he watched Jamie, he got to know her, to trust her, and for the first time in all those years he ached to share all of himself with someone. To tell her everything. To no longer feel unknown. No longer feel alone. He trusted her with his life. He knew she would never betray him. But telling her could put her in danger. That was his biggest fear. That something would happen to her because of him.

So he continued to carry the burden of his secrets. He didn't say a word. He lied by omission constantly and cleverly. And now that was all coming home to roost. All those years of deceit. Of masking. Of not being true.

He looked around this small room. The whiteboard, with all its pictures and notes, a physical manifestation of trauma and loss. His own and so many others. He thought of all the painstaking work he'd done and why he'd done it. And he realised that, in this moment, he cared about none of it.

All he cared about was whether or not Jamie would ever forgive him for betraying her trust in such a seismic way.

34

The alarm on Jamie's phone sliced through her thoughts. 5:05 a.m. Fifty minutes until they docked. She swiped off the alert and sat further forward. Felt a vicious twinge at her neck from the awkward resting position she'd been in. She saw the small black case and its contents spread around her. The weight of knowledge pressed in on her. The Ed she thought she knew forever changed. Her mind struggling to take on this new reality.

Gathering up the contents, she handled them with care. It was hard to believe such a small package could contain that level of incendiary information.

She reached over to the bedside cabinet. Ed's phone was now charged. She checked it, hoping for some clues. There was nothing. No numbers. No contacts. No messages.

She tapped her cargo trousers. Pulled out the USB containing the footage of her father being threatened by Evans. Placed it alongside Ed's phone and the white envelopes and pushed it all inside the black case. Zipped everything back up and tucked the package deep into her tote bag.

Jamie got to her feet, the desperate sickness gone,

replaced by weakness and exhaustion. After a quick shower, she studied her new clothes, purchased from the on-board shop when she got on the ferry. She pulled on pre-faded, flared denim jeans. Then a loose, colourful blouse, over a cream camisole top, which floated down to her knees. Next, she pulled her long brown hair back, held it with decorative clips, leaving a small section which she plaited, hanging close to her face, pulling a few extra strands out to hang beside it. She wore no makeup. She didn't need it. Her fresh-faced paleness enhanced the look.

She checked the mirror. It was convincing. The outfit and hair made her look ten years younger. Early twenties rather than thirties. She took a full-length photo of her reflection ready to send to Conor.

Jamie folded all her own black clothes and pushed them into her backpack. She placed that into the carrier bag from the shop, laying some packages of duty-free perfume on top.

She pulled the cream woollen jumper around her shoulders, picked up her tote bag and carrier bag and opened the door. She looked around the room one last time, then started off down the corridor.

A minute later she was outside on the deck of the Ulysses. The wind, cold air and hanging moisture hit her face. She welcomed it. The smell invigorating. It would help blow away the lethargy. She leaned against the steel rail, damp with sea spray, the air whipping through her thin blouse. The land mass of Ireland was a shadow ahead. Lights sparkling in the distance.

She took in a sharp breath and bent forward. Gripped the cold, wet railing. The constriction around her chest was back. The pain cutting the air in her lungs. Her husband was on that island. She swayed. Moved back to a seated area on deck and steadied herself. Pulling out her phone, she called Conor.

After confirming their exit plans, she was back inside.

Her legs almost giving way on the stairs into the Club Lounge. Conor's words ringing in her ears.

'I saw three of them in suits drive up. They've separated. There's one in the terminal building. One outside keeping watch near the taxi rank. And the other is across the road, scanning the car park.'

Three men were waiting for her at Dublin Port. The hunters' reach was far, and it was wide.

She queued at the counter and looked across at the cooked breakfast a couple were half-way through. The smell of bacon, eggs and fried everything triggered her nausea. She turned away from it. Her empty stomach starting to contract. A step too far for her delicate recovery. She chose coffee, soup and a bread roll. Picking up the tray, struggling to balance it with her tote bag and carrier bag, she sensed someone close beside her.

'Can I help you with that?'

She turned. Recognised him from the terminal building in his bright paisley top. This could make her search a lot easier.

She smiled at him. 'Sure. That would be great.'

He took the tray from her hands. 'Where do you want to sit?' he said.

Jamie glanced around. Before she answered, he spoke again.

'Looks like you're going to Galway?'

She laughed. 'You, too?'

He pushed back floppy hair from his eyes, his smile engaging.

'Do you want to join us?' He pointed at his group of friends.

Jamie glanced across the room then held his eye. 'I'd like that. Thanks.'

She followed him into the far corner where the group sat.

'Hi there.' She glanced across at each face. Gave her most

winning smile. 'I guess we're all going to the Galway Festival.'

They laughed and made a space for her on the leather corner seat. Right at the heart of them.

The voices chattered around her. Telling her their names, asking where she came from. She answered, deflecting from herself, showing interest in all they said.

Rose, the sweetest one among them, was desperate to get into port, she was meeting her boyfriend. 'Snap.' Jamie had said. This fake affinity instantly bonding them.

Jamie relaxed back as the voices laughed around her and the stories unravelled. They were trusting people. She was already in. She had her cover. And she was hiding in plain sight.

35

Jamie stayed among her new friends as they made their way through the walkway connecting the ship to land. And after they got their luggage from the carousel, she stayed in the heart of them, moving towards the exit.

She clutched her tote bag tighter. Thought of the multiple passports sitting inside under different names. If she was stopped, it would be the end of this journey.

Rose was chattering beside her. She tried to follow what she was saying, but her mind, her eyes, were elsewhere.

A solo backpacker up ahead had been pulled aside. His bag was being searched. She kept walking, gripping Rose's arm, trying not to make eye contact with the customs officers. Her heart knew the danger, it was beating faster. She walked past them. No-one stopped her.

She moved forward with Rose into the exit terminal. Up ahead she saw Conor in stone-washed jeans, a bright shirt, and a baseball cap. He was in deep conversation, blending with the waiting group, but looking in her direction. The relief she felt was immediate.

Rose yelled out next to her, disentangled her arm, and ran across the space. A young man started running and Conor moved in his wake. He timed it perfectly. As the two youngsters collided, Conor took Jamie in his arms and moved forward to kiss her. She turned her face just in time. His lips hitting her cheek.

She clung onto him. Whispered into his ear. 'What are you doing?'

'I'm making it real.'

He pulled her close to him. His chest solid and strong.

'Being a hippy suits you,' he said, taking the carrier bag from her.

She turned her face to his, leaning into him. Feeling the ease. The safety. 'Don't get used to it.'

She saw the smile flicker at his lips. But his eyes were alert, scanning the space.

He whispered in her ear. 'Keep smiling and move to the left.'

She could feel her heart still pounding. The doors were up ahead. The rest of the festival group milling around them, Rose and her boyfriend striding forwards.

She glimpsed the man in the blue suit out of the corner of her eye. Scanning the space. He looked directly at her. Then past her. They walked within four feet of him, but his eyes were trained on the customs exit doors.

Outside on the pavement, they were past the second suited man. Eyes not on this group. Glancing at his phone, then up again. His focus on each taxi that drove up and those getting inside.

Conor leaned into her. His arm tight around her waist. 'There's just one more in the car park.'

It was still dark out. Streetlights lit some of the pavements around the port. The low light helped to conceal them as the group travelled across the crossing. Noisy and joyful. Conor and Jamie were at the heart of them, mingling. The perfect cover.

Jamie looked at the area ahead and saw a solitary, standing figure. The blue-suited man's eyes scanned across their group as they moved towards him. He gave no reaction.

Then they were past him and the group came to a stop at a white minibus. Conor guided her around to the far side of the vehicle, shielding her from view of the car park. He leaned towards her. 'We need to go now.'

'Rose,' she touched her new friend's arm. Rose turned around. 'I'm really sorry, we have to get going. We're on a crazy deadline.' Jamie said.

'I can't wait to see you later in the week.' Rose pulled her in for a hug.

'Me too. See you then.'

Jamie broke free of the uninhibited embrace and waved goodbye to the others who were busy loading luggage into the van. A couple of them raised their hands.

Then Conor propelled her forwards and walked further to the left. They weaved in and out of parked cars, then empty lorries, eventually coming to a stop beside a black Toyota Land Cruiser. Conor turned back around and casually surveyed the scene. He dropped his arm from her waist.

'We're safe.'

36

Jamie set her bag down, turned towards Conor and pulled him in for a real hug. He moved her to the side of him and gave her a long hold, tight and strong.

She wanted to stay there but knew she couldn't. She pulled back.

'That was … intense.'

'Nothing you couldn't handle.' He held out the car key. Dropped it into her outstretched hand.

'Not without your help.'

He shrugged. 'I live to serve.' Then he smiled. Broad and reaching his eyes. It was like the sun coming out. It didn't happen often enough.

She put a hand on his chest. Patted it. 'You're looking really good.' He was. Even better than her last visit six months ago. Healthier. Stronger. With much more muscle bulk. Nowhere near his soldier days, but a world away from when he was at his most desperately ill.

'You, on the other hand, look like crap, Jay. You're still green.'

'Thanks for the pep talk.'

'You know me, always ready to give someone a boost.'

Jamie arched her eyebrows.

'Sorry I can't spend more time here. I should … I need to … get moving.' She pointed to the car. Opened the back door and put her bags inside. She took a step nearer to the driver's door.

Conor followed her.

'Where are we going?'

She looked back at him. Six feet two inches of iron will. This was going to be difficult. But she stood her ground and kept to the script.

'A car and a lookout, remember? That's what I said. That's what I meant.' She softened her words with a smile. 'Thank you for both. I'm going to be alright now. Don't you be worrying.' She tried for light-hearted, tapping him on the arm, not sure she'd succeeded.

'Right. Yeh. That's not gonna happen. If you're into something you don't want me involved in, you already need me.'

She searched for the right words.

'You've done enough. I'm not pulling you any further into this. You're just getting your life back, I'd never forgive myself if…' She didn't finish the sentence. Tried a new one. 'Look, I … I have to get going. I'll tell you everything when I can. And I'll be back up to see you as soon as I can.'

She moved to open the door. He stepped in front of her.

'Do you really think I'm letting you go without me?'

'Conor, please.'

'You saved my life in multiple ways, multiple times. You're in trouble. I'm ready. I'm willing. And I'm more than able to start repaying that debt.'

She was struggling not to give way. To tell him everything.

He leaned on the car, blocking the door. 'I mean, I can stand here all day.'

This time, the smile didn't make it to his eyes.

'Conor…'

'Let's get in the car. You tell me where to drive. And you start talking. From the beginning.'

He looked at her, his eyes now sharp and steady. Jamie knew the look well. Had seen it in battle – at war and at home. There was no way she was getting into this car without him.

She couldn't help it. It was selfish. But she was relieved. To have him by her side. Have his skills. And not just that, but to talk to someone. To get this crazy jumbled mess out of her head. She didn't fight that hard to stop him. Ignoring the voice in her head that told her this was a bad idea.

'You don't know what you're getting yourself into,' she said.

'We've been in the depths of hell in a war zone together, how bad can this be?'

She pulled herself upright. Took a deep breath and looked him straight in the eye.

'Ed is alive.'

He didn't move a muscle, but his eyes blinked once.

'I think you need to repeat that, Jay.'

'Ed is alive. He's alive, Conor.'

He took in a breath. Exhaled slow. Held out his palm for the car key. Hit the key fob and unlocked the doors.

'Get in the car, Jamie.'

His voice allowed for no further discussion. By the time she'd walked around the back of the car, he was settled in the driver's seat.

She pulled on her seatbelt as he fired the engine.

'Where are we going?'

She paused. 'Towards Killarney.'

The car started to move.

'From the beginning, Jay. Everything.'

37

Ed was scanning multiple cameras. His eyes switching back and forth. It was still an hour until the ferry docked and it was hard to see anything in the darkness. He was relying on lighting around the port.

He focused on a black Subaru. Its licence plate had flagged in his system. On the brightly lit road into Dublin Port, he saw the car slow. A man in dark jeans and a black hoodie got out.

The car moved on and pulled into the car park across from the terminal building. Three men in suits left the vehicle. One stayed close to the car, another posted himself outside the terminal doors, the third went inside.

Ed studied all the port's CCTV. He couldn't find the fourth man anywhere. He'd disappeared like a ghost.

He checked the men through his facial recognition software and cross-referenced with his database. They were Michael Keller's men. Tole's men.

He'd had some respite while Jamie was on the ship. When he knew she was safe. But seeing these men, his chest was tight, and his stomach churned. Four men were here for

Jamie. It would take a miracle for her to evade them all and get away from the port.

He checked his watch. Thirty minutes to docking. He went back to his search. Scoured the restaurants, all of decks nine and ten. She was nowhere. But if he couldn't find her, maybe the hunters wouldn't either.

He went back into the Club Lounge, scanning again. The hippy travellers were tucked in a quiet corner. Nine of them. He spun around to another screen, reversed his recorded footage. Eight were travelling together last time. He watched, but the cameras weren't helping, the group was in a partial blind spot. Then one woman stood up, her back to the camera. She lifted her hand to her head, tucking a piece of long hair behind her ear in a gesture he knew so well. And he saw it. The flash of a wedding band. She was still wearing it. His stomach turned over. He'd found Jamie. And her plan became clearer.

As she came into the terminal building, she was tight among the crowd. Blending in to perfection. A young woman beside Jamie started running, a young man was running towards her. Then the man wearing a baseball cap was moving forwards and taking Jamie in his arms. Pulling her tight towards him. Moving to kiss her. Ed cursed the camera. His view was momentarily obscured by other passengers.

His hand moved to his chest. It was a physical pain.

The man in the baseball cap took Jamie's carrier bag and pulled her beside him. Ed watched as they crossed the space. Glued together. Looking at each other. Whispering. Smiling. Their body language was clear. They were close. Very close.

It hit him like a ten-ton truck. Jamie wasn't alone anymore.

Ed tried to calm his heart. Calm his mind. He needed to focus. His eyes stayed on the cameras. This man had skills. He'd seen him earlier with the group, his back always to the cameras or his head down, the cap obscuring his face. He'd thought him part of the welcoming group, someone used to hiding from CCTV. Not that unusual in certain circles. He had blended with them seamlessly. Ed had not known his significance. Had not known he was here for Jamie.

They moved closer towards the exit. Ed was holding his breath. They were within four feet of the suited man. As they passed him, walking through the open glass doors, the light and angle of the ceiling camera caught something. He took a screenshot and zoomed in. Tattoos on the man's hands. His mind did a triple take. It was impossible. He looked again at the designs. And he was sure. It really was him. Conor was Jamie's miracle.

Ed turned back to the live feed. Watched the small, joyful group pass the second man beside the taxi and continue on into the car park.

He kept searching but lost track of Jamie and Conor then. He couldn't track which vehicle they were using. If he couldn't find them, and see the vehicle they were travelling in, it was likely Keller's men wouldn't either.

He leaned back, taking in what he'd seen. He knew his heart was thumping. But it wasn't fear. Jamie was clear and free. He was feeling an altogether different emotion.

He looked at the image of the tattoo he knew by heart. The intricate weaving on the back of the hand which stretched up the arm, holding the initials of each friend Conor had lost in battle. *Lest we forget* lying further up his fully tattooed left arm.

He had watched Conor almost run towards Jamie. He was unrecognisable from the last time he'd seen him four years ago. That he was even here was impossible. When Jamie had last visited Conor in Northern Ireland, she'd come home distraught at his deterioration. Conor was living out of his bed in torturous pain, barely able to walk, needing sticks to get from his bed to stumble around his house. His muscles wasting, his strength ebbing daily. He only left home for medical visits and the relapse these forays resulted in was shocking. Ed wondered what had happened over these last two years to produce this result. Had one of those thankless surgeries and treatments Conor had spent fortunes on, and travelled across Europe for, finally worked?

Relief flooded through him that Jamie wasn't alone. That she had someone with her who could protect her and who would do anything to keep her safe. And he was pleased for Conor that he was doing so much better. But the twinge was still there, more like a jagged edge of steel now. The way he'd touched Jamie, gone to kiss her, ate into his gut. Their behaviour together was different from anything he'd seen before.

She lives for you, Ed. George had been wrong. Jamie hadn't told him everything about her life. She hadn't told him about a new relationship with an old friend.

Ed tried to steady the heart beating inside his chest. Tried to still the thoughts rushing through his head. But as hard as he tried, he couldn't stop himself from seeing the reality in front of him.

Without him there, with Jamie vulnerable and alone, had Conor finally got what he had always wanted?

38

Ed had experienced naked hostility from Conor when he first started dating Jamie. He recognised it for what it was. Jealousy. He could see, the way only men see in other men, that he was in love with her. He hid it well. Very well. Hid it from her. But Ed could see it like a beacon.

He tried to stifle his own jealousy. He didn't need to feel threatened. Jamie and Conor had been best friends for years. If they hadn't got together by now, it was likely they never would. They'd spoken about it.

'So … you and Conor, has there ever been…'

She shook her head.

'No. It's not like that with us.'

He'd watched her, ready to probe the words.

'How is it between you?'

'He's family to me. It's like…' she broke off as though searching for the words. 'I can't explain. He's…'

'Like a brother?'

'No.' She shook her head vigorously. 'It's like he's part of me.'

Ed managed not to flinch. It was something to take on. A rival who wasn't a sexual rival but was embedded in her heart. It felt even more powerful. She must have seen the look.

'You don't have to worry.' Her hand went to his face. 'You never have to worry about Conor.'

He put his hand over hers. He believed her. And it was enough for him. He wanted to be with her and he accepted Conor as part of the deal. A strange triangle of sorts.

He'd never tried to come between them. Ed saw how protective Conor was of Jamie. That was a good thing. She had no blood family. He was her family. That didn't need to change. But he felt the discomfort. It was always there. An edge between them, even though Jamie didn't see it. It was made worse by the army bonds and experiences they shared that he was not part of. And the army language all of their own that he wasn't privy to.

Ed thought back to the first time he'd met Conor. Jamie had been pacing the room with nerves.

'What's wrong?'

'It's nothing, I'm just…' she paused. 'I really want you to get on. It's making me nervous.'

She tried to laugh it off but hadn't succeeded. He wasn't sure which one of them the nerves were for. The moment he was alone with Conor he knew the nerves had been for him.

'Jay is the best person I know. Don't mess her around. Don't hurt her. You'll have me to deal with if you do.'

People say words like that all the time. They don't act on them. But Ed saw the eyes fixed on him. And even though the man in front of him no longer had the physique from the army pictures he'd seen, and his body was physically weakened by injury and disability, Ed felt the weight of every word. He saw the soldier in front of him. The sniper. Saw an intensity he'd never seen before. And he believed him.

His eyes had met Conor's. 'You don't need to worry.' He paused. 'She's everything I've ever wanted. I'll never hurt her.' And he pinned Conor with his own look. 'And now I've found her, I'm never letting her go.'

Conor had held the look. In that moment something passed between them. Unspoken. Never spoken about. Conor's eyes had glazed, as though looking through him, into the distance. Then he focused back, and Ed saw a look of such sadness he took a breath in. The look was gone as quickly as it came. He wondered if he'd imagined it. Then Conor nodded. And Ed knew it was a start, he had passed the first test.

Over time, a friendship of sorts built. But it was really all for Jamie. They had little in common, except her.

He thought of those words now. *I'll never hurt her.* How he'd failed so badly. How he'd hurt Jamie beyond measure. Whatever he did in his life, however he tried to make up for it, that could never be changed. It was a stain on his soul that couldn't be removed.

He brought himself back. Jamie was on Irish soil. Just a few hours away from him. It was hard to deal with the feelings raging through his mind and body, but he had to prepare. Prepare to leave here. For he now knew it would inevitably come to that.

He checked every camera on his screens. All his security was working. His radar on. He stood up from behind his desk and pulled forward his backpack. Checked his Glock was in place and extra magazines. He opened his fireproof filing cabinet and retrieved all the drives that he needed. Added all his personal documents with Callum Marshall printed across them – the name he'd used since he'd disappeared.

Next, he went outside. The sun was rising, the birds singing in the woodland surrounding him, the smell drifting up from the damp grass of the overnight rain. He looked at the beauty. The calm majesty. In spite of everything, he'd miss it here. He'd never felt safer, more cocooned, than he had these last two years.

He moved inside the garage attached to his cottage. Checked the Honda 600 motorbike and his Land Rover. Both started, both fuel gauges showed close to full, their tyres good. Everything in order as he knew it would be.

Back inside the house, he made himself a strong coffee and a doorstep ham sandwich. Then he sat and leaned back. Arms crossed.

The minutes passed.

The drink and food lay untouched on the coffee table in front of him.

All he could do was wait. Wait for the screech of an alarm to go off on his property telling him someone had arrived.

39

Sitting in the passenger seat of the Toyota Land Cruiser, Jamie did just what Conor asked. She told him everything.

As the car made its winding way along the route, light breaking through the darkness, mizzling rain on the windscreen, she started from the beginning. From the moment she had seen Ed on screen. To the men hunting her. George's betrayal. Her father's capture. The package on the ferry uncovering Ed's past. All she had done to stay safe. And everything she thought she'd figured out.

Conor listened intently. Didn't interrupt once. Expressed no shock. No emotion. It was all about the facts. He was in soldier mode. Analytical. And that's what she needed. A counterpoint to her emotion.

When she finished, she waited for a response.

It was a minute before it came. Conor's eyes fixed on the road.

'Are you sure it was, Ed?'

'One hundred percent. You'd know if you could see the video and photos.' She again berated herself for having to get rid of her phone. 'Like I said, I can't access the accounts to show you. There's no doubt about it.'

He took a moment. 'But you said you did doubt it?'

'Well … yes … at the start … I'd be crazy not to. But as soon as I saw his hat, I knew.'

'But you didn't actually see Ed? Didn't see his face?'

'No, I didn't, but…'

He cut across her. 'So all you're going on is a walk and a hat seen through a camera screen?'

She was quiet.

'You said the man's voice was different to Ed. He was speaking in Irish. Looked thinner. Had a beard, which Ed hated. I just think,' he paused. 'I just think you need to prepare yourself. This may not be Ed at all.'

'I know it's him. The passports explain why he speaks Irish. But more than that, men are chasing me, they're hunting Ed and threatening Dad. That all tells me I'm right. Ed is alive.'

Conor took a long pause. One hand on the top of the wheel, the other resting at the bottom.

'Jay, the men are chasing you because you *said* you saw Ed. You *said* he was alive. Not because you *actually* saw him.' He emphasised the words before he glanced across and met her eye. 'That doesn't mean he's alive.'

She took a few seconds to absorb this. It hit her hard. She hadn't seen it that way at all and she couldn't find a reply.

'I just want you to be prepared. This could all be one big mistake.'

She swallowed. Felt tears coming to her eyes. Blinked them back. Eyes forward on the road.

'I know what I saw.' Her voice steely, talking through gritted teeth. 'It was Ed.'

Conor didn't reply. His hands tensed on the wheel.

She looked out of the side window. The rain was falling faster now. Grey sky across the horizon. They were passing green fields, bracken and hedgerows. And at intervals along the road, houses. Much sleeker than she'd imagined. Not quaint cottages but new buildings. Some with white fencing and long tarmac drives.

She turned back to Conor.

'The child in the passport is Ed. He's Sean O'Neill. I'm sure of it. Everything fits. From the security issues to—'

Conor interrupted her. 'That still doesn't mean you saw Ed.'

'What about George sending the men to my house?'

He took in a long breath. 'I can't make sense of that. He loves you all like family. He'd never do anything to hurt you.'

She felt lost. He had questioned everything she'd seen.

'Let's leave it for now,' she said. 'We can talk more later. I'm going to rest for a bit.'

She laid her head back and closed her eyes. She'd looked for an objective listener and she'd got one. But being met with disbelief made her feel a little less certain.

A few minutes passed.

'Jay?'

She pretended to be asleep.

'I know you're awake.'

'How do you know?'

She could almost feel his smile.

'Your breathing.'

'What's wrong with my breathing?'

'It's erratic.'

She couldn't even pretend sleep to fool him.

'If it is Ed…' Conor took a long breath in. 'He has a hell of a lot of explaining to do.'

Jamie gazed out into the distance. She didn't reply.

'Jay?'

She looked across at him. Her eyes bright. Tears close to the surface again. Conor met her gaze. Seconds later, he was signalling and pulling to the side of the road. He stopped, put the hazard lights on, and focused his eyes on her.

'I'm sorry.'

'Don't be. I know this whole thing sounds crazy.'

His eyes didn't leave her face. Searching. 'Are we OK?'

She held his look. His face tense. Eyes concerned. As though he knew he'd failed her. Been too brutal. Or too honest. She put her hand out to his. Felt the steel grip. 'Always.'

He gave her a tight smile and turned forward. Hands gripping the wheel, he glanced in the rear-view mirror and drove off.

40

They'd called an uneasy truce. She knew what Conor was doing. Initially, his doubts had affected her. But as the car ticked through the miles, her confidence bounced back. She knew what she'd seen. And she knew, deep in her gut, that her husband was alive and that every mile they travelled took her closer to him.

She looked across at Conor and decided to move to easier ground.

'You'll never believe who I saw at work last month?'

She saw his whole body relax, the tension disperse. This terrain was better for both of them.

He looked across at her. 'You giving me twenty?'

'You'll never get it.'

'Tell me then.'

'Matt Yates.'

Conor blew out a breath. 'Wow. A blast from the past.'

'Quite literally.'

They looked at each other and laughed.

'What was he doing at the DMRC?' Conor asked.

'Interviewing for a job.'

'Tell me he didn't get it.'

‘He didn’t get it.’

‘That’s a relief.’

‘His fame had preceded him.’

‘I’m not surprised. He nearly took us all out.’

‘I don’t need to check the handbook. It’s red not green.’ She mimicked the words in a cockney accent.’

Conor shook his head. ‘There’s only one thing worse than an incompetent soldier, that’s one who believes they’re smart. I’m still not sure how we even made it out of there alive.’

She took another look at Conor. At how well he looked. It was still impossible to believe. To take in. After ten years of deteriorating health, excruciating pain and dwindling independence, things were changing.

‘Is the drug trial still going well?’

‘It is.’

‘No real side effects or anything unusual?’

‘It’s all good.’

‘These last few months. You’ve improved so much more.’

He glanced at her. ‘It’s cumulative, I think.’

‘I can’t believe you’re sitting here, have been able to drive this far.’

‘I know.’

‘It’s impossible to believe. Last year, you couldn’t even sit at your table to eat. When you look back—’

‘I’m not looking back.’

His words were sharp. Cutting her off. His eyes still fixed on the road.

She was quiet. She understood. Who wants to relive their worst nightmare? But she couldn’t help but look back and remember everything.

All the things Conor had tried over the years. The barrage of medications – from opiates, to antidepressants, and anti-convulsants – too many combinations to even remember. Surgery, ablation, freezing nerve branches, spinal cord stimulation, spending thousands on dubious cures. So many charlatans ready to feed on his anguish and despair. Getting worse with each medical intervention. She'd been by his side through it all. Watched as his weakened body failed him. Living out of his bed. Lying on his side. Not even a shadow of his former self. Pain preventing him from doing even the simplest of things, like sitting up. And unable to do the things which, in his eyes, made him a man.

And then the phone calls of despair. Where she tried to say the words which would keep him alive while she travelled to him. Reminding him that she needed him. And that he needed to hold on to hope.

And finally, finally, it had happened. Originally ineligible, he'd got a late place on the Tolacaine trial eighteen months ago. And he'd never looked back.

Conor turned to her. 'Thank you.'

'What for?'

'Keeping me alive.'

He'd read her mind.

'You were right, Jay. Something good did happen.'

'I'm always right,' she laughed.

'Almost always.'

And she caught his smile.

They were quiet for a few minutes before Jamie spoke again.

'I was with someone yesterday at work and I mentioned you.'

Conor's eyes flicked back towards her.

'Not by name.'

He nodded.

She couldn't believe it was less than 24 hours since she'd kneeled in front of Timothy Dane in the gym. It felt like a lifetime ago.

'We can't get his pain under control.'

'You haven't got access to Tolacaine yet?'

'It's just been approved for limited use in our clinic. I'm hoping he'll have access to it soon. He's really struggling. And … he's at risk.'

Conor's eyes stayed fixed on the road. 'Chronic pain is its very own war zone. It can take you down piece by piece.'

She watched his profile. Saw his jaw tense.

They pulled to a stop behind a line of cars. Road work signs in front of them. A man ahead holding a stop sign.

'I'm going to need to stop soon.' She tapped the water bottle and looked at Conor. She'd been extensively rehydrating after her ferry debacle.

He raised his eyebrows. 'Pick the next services then.'

She pulled out her phone and did some route checking. 'We're fifteen minutes from Birdhill Services at Limerick. Halfway to Lough Acoose.'

'Let's go with that.'

They relaxed back into quiet, companionable silence then. She took another glance at his profile. At ease now. Strong and steady. His sleeves rolled up. The extensive tattoos taut again across his muscular arms. It was incredible to see. She was getting Conor back.

He glanced across at her.

'What ya looking at?'

'Nothing,' she said and smiled. Turning her head back around to look at the road ahead.

41

They pulled in at Birdhill Services twenty minutes later. After visiting the bathroom, changing out of her new clothes and back into black, Jamie found a secluded table by a window.

She pulled the package out from her backpack as Conor walked towards her with a tray. He put the coffees and burgers down in front of them. Sat and shook four small packages of sugar into his black coffee. He started stirring his drink while Jamie scraped off the green relish inside her veggie burger.

'Sorry, I couldn't stop her from loading it with—'

She waved her hand. 'It's fine.' She looked around her, then pushed the black package towards him. 'Here are Ed's things.'

Conor put his spoon down and reached forward. Undid the zip and pulled out the contents. He turned the disc over in his hands. Reached for the passports and opened each one, lingering over the child. Over Sean O'Neill.

'It's Ed, isn't it?'

He looked up at her and nodded his head. 'I can see the likeness. But this guy,' he pointed to the picture of the father,

Frank O'Neill. 'Take away the beard and Ed is the spit of him.' He put the passports down. 'What was the article you found on the family?'

She pulled the article up on her phone and passed it to him.

Reading it through, his face did not move.

'Have you heard of this kind of thing? Paramilitaries and drug dealers?'

He glanced up at her. 'It's well known. Goes back decades.'

'But if you look at his mother's letter.' She reached across, opened it, and waited for him to read it. Then she pointed to the crucial line.

...whatever is said, whatever story is told, you know us...

She watched his face. 'You're not convinced?'

Conor folded up the letter and passed it back to her. 'Well she's not going to say they're drug dealers.'

'You really think Ed could be involved with drugs?'

Conor shrugged his shoulders. 'If this is Ed, and we don't know that yet, we have no idea what he's involved in. Paramilitaries act on information on the ground. They don't carry out punishment killings for no reason. And if Ed is alive, he's being tracked down by men with weapons. He must know something or be involved in something. It can't be anything good or he'd have gone to the police. He wouldn't have faked his own death and disappeared.'

Jamie flinched at the last words. Hearing them spoken aloud, so matter of fact from Conor's mouth, made it all the more shocking.

'He couldn't go to the police,' she said. 'The police are involved in this. O'Malley was at my house. And there's George.'

He went to speak. She held up her hand. 'I know we

disagree about George. But Ed must have known the police were involved.'

She held Sean O'Neill's passport in her hand. 'I think the family was going to disappear. The second passports, all the documents, and what the mother says about the forces against them. And maybe Paul Arthur Tole really is connected to their deaths, like she says in the letter.'

Conor shook his head. 'I find that very hard to believe.'

'I just can't see Ed being involved in drugs,' she carried on. 'You know him. We both know him better than that.'

'We *thought* we knew him.' Conor said, taking another huge bite from his burger, chewing his way through it and looking out into the distance. 'These tell us', he wiped his mouth with a napkin and pointed back to the package and documents, 'that we didn't know him at all.'

Jamie watched Conor. His face set. Eyes narrowed. Always protective, he was thinking of her. Of what Ed had done to her. His betrayal. It fired it back up inside her. Conor was right. She hadn't known her husband at all. She felt the dark thoughts rising, pushing up to the surface, the scales tipping back from compassion to anger. She gathered the documents together and put them back into the black zipped case.

They were both quiet now. Eating. Drinking. Thinking.

Jamie looked back at Conor. 'How did I miss this?'

He looked up, his coffee midway to his mouth. 'What do you mean?'

'How did I not know, not see, this was going on inside Ed? I was his wife. I thought,' she took a breath. 'I thought I knew him.'

'We never know all of someone.'

'Of course, I know that.' She moved her hand impatiently. 'But we know the important things. The heart of them.'

'I'm not even sure about that.'

'What?'

He looked her in the eye. 'Anyone can deceive someone, if they want to, if they have the motivation, and the person trusts them enough.'

Jamie took a few seconds. 'That's very dispiriting ... And cynical.'

Conor shrugged. 'It's a fact. Ed didn't just deceive you, he deceived me, too. I had zero idea anything was wrong.'

And she saw it then. The reason for Conor's controlled but visible anger. It wasn't all about her, it was about him. This was a personal affront. Ed, the soft-hearted computer geek, had fooled him, the pragmatic, elite soldier. That rivalry she knew was there, however much they tried to hide it from her, was coming to the fore. Even with all his skills, Conor hadn't seen through Ed's façade.

'So how do you trust someone like that again?' Jamie said.

Conor shook his head. 'Hell if I have any idea on that.'

'And if it comes to it, can I ever forgive him?'

'Well…' he drew out the word. 'You know forgiveness isn't my best quality.'

Their eyes met. She knew all too well. A father who had abandoned a wife and an eight-year-old son. The son never speaking to him again, even when called to his deathbed. With no regrets. Conor knew how to play hard ball. And like he said earlier, he didn't look back.

'You just need to be prepared,' Conor focused on her. 'We could be going into all kinds of danger here.' He paused. 'And you might not like what we find out.'

'You think Ed is alive now, then?'

He took in a long breath. 'Maybe. I don't know either way.'

Jamie fought back the emotion building inside her. More waves of anger. The position she was in, that she'd pulled

Conor into. The uncertainty they were facing. She pushed the black package down into her bag with force. 'Whatever there is to find out, I need to know. I need to know the truth.'

He glanced across at her. 'Truth? If it is Ed, there's his truth and the real truth. They may be different things. How will we trust anything he says?'

Jamie felt like she was drowning. She put her head in her hands then looked up and out of the window.

Conor reached his hand out, placing it on her arm. 'You'll get through this. You're going to be OK. Whatever we find out.'

She didn't reply.

'Jay?'

He nudged her. 'You listening?'

'I am. But…' she stopped talking. Eyes focused out of the window.

'But, what?'

'I just saw a black Mercedes circle around the car park again. I'm sure it's the same one I saw when you were filling up with diesel. I only caught the end of the registration number, but it's the same.'

Conor whipped his head up to scan through the glass.

'Did you see the driver?'

'No.'

Conor was on his feet. He waved his hand. 'Come on. We need to move.'

Jamie grabbed her bag and followed him. The half-eaten food and drink left on the table.

Conor's eyes scanned around the car park. He opened the car door and popped up the bonnet. 'Check underneath the boot and the wheel arches for a tracker. I'll check the front.'

Jamie searched her way across, feeling her way and using the light from her phone. She started walking around to the front. 'I can't see or feel anything.'

'I have something.' Conor spoke under his breath.

He held out a black tracker in his hand. It's red eye blinking.

She peered down at it. Couldn't believe it. She could have led the hunters right to Ed's door.

Conor continued to scan the car park before looking back at Jamie. 'It was underneath the right front wheel arch. Here,' Conor pointed, shaking his head. 'It's just not possible. It doesn't make any sense.'

Jamie's mind started to whir. 'When I was in the loft, they mentioned Hayley. They knew her movements. They'd been tracking her. What if—'

He shook his head. 'There's no way—'

'What if,' she persisted, 'they've been tracking you?'

His eyes blazed. 'Who are these people that could manage something like that? It's not even my car. When did they put it there?'

His temper was up now. His eyes roving the car park.

'They know we're friends. Know I might turn to you. I'm coming to Ireland after all.' She wanted to calm him. 'We found it, that's the main thing. We're ahead of them.'

He didn't answer. He was silent as he moved around to the boot of the car. Stepped to the Skoda in the parking space next to them and slipped the tracker underneath its wheel arch, out of sight.

He opened the boot and leaned in. Started moving and banging things around. He yanked back the carpet on the right side and exposed a hidden compartment. 'I have extra plates. They may use number plate recognition as well.'

As he pulled out the plates, she saw a cache of weapons.

'Conor, what the hell…' She pushed the carpet back down and looked behind and around her.

'You said men were chasing you with weapons, what did you expect?'

And she thought again what a terrible mistake she'd made bringing Conor into this. He was right, what had she expected? Now she had even more to worry about. An angry Conor who wouldn't hesitate to defend her. Wouldn't hesitate to put himself in the line of fire. And wouldn't hesitate to go up against anyone to protect her. Even Ed.

42

As they travelled the rest of the way west across Ireland, Conor was silent. Jamie stole looks at him. His face was a mask, his jaw set rigid. She knew better than to engage with him in this mood.

She could feel the emotion building inside her. The vice-like sensation she'd felt on the ship was back. But it was different. Fear and excitement now intertwined. Fearing what she was going to find but desperate to lay eyes on her husband.

She turned back to her phone. She'd travelled the road around Lough Acoose, using Google Maps, until she knew each twist by heart. From the online tour, she knew the land-mark she was looking for. And with the Sat Nav on, she knew they were close.

'Slow down.' She put her hand out and pointed at the front windscreen. 'It's around this bend on the right.'

As they turned the corner, she saw what she was looking for.

'Pull in here.'

Conor checked his mirrors and pulled across the road, parking the car in a lay-by. Jamie got out of the car and looked at the stunning Lough. There was no sun today. But the hanging mist across the water, and the distant shapes of the mountains, still looked majestic and beautiful. Just yesterday evening she had seen this through the lens of David Marr's camera. Now she was here. It seemed impossible.

She cast her eyes up. Saw the long, winding road that David Marr had walked on. That Ed had walked on. She was ready to start the search. She grabbed her pack from the back seat and closed the door.

Conor was already moving towards the boot. Jamie followed him. He opened the hidden compartment and pulled out a Glock, putting it into the back of his waistband, and adding spare magazines to his open backpack.

'Conor, do you really think…'

'Jay, I don't know what to think. But I'm not moving into the unknown without some kind of protection. We could be walking into a drug den. You need to take something.'

He held out another Glock, pushing it into her hands.

She dropped it back into the compartment. 'I don't want it.' She stepped forward to close the boot.

'Jamie.'

His voice made her turn. 'This is not just about you. You pulled me into this. We might need this kind of backup.'

Conor retrieved the gun and passed it to her. She held his eyes for a long moment. Then she took the Glock from his outstretched hand and put it in her backpack, along with the spare magazines he handed her. He pulled the boot closed.

'Which way are we going?' he said.

She pointed ahead to the long winding road.

'OK. Let's get moving.'

43

They had been up and down the Lough Road, together and apart, for almost two hours, in mizzling, miserable rain.

Conor's mood had not improved.

'Are you sure we're on the right stretch?'

She hesitated. 'Ummm, yes.'

'You don't sound sure.'

Jamie looked back towards the car. Doubting everything. Desperation creeping in as she travelled each step. Could Ed have started running as soon as the camera got past him? He'd disappeared quickly. But could he have gone farther than she thought? She'd travelled well past the lay-by and around the corner and found nothing. He couldn't have got any further than that.

She turned back to Conor. 'It's definitely this stretch.'

She walked and Conor followed.

'How's your knee and back doing?'

'Not great. I'm pushing it.'

'You stay here then. I'll try again.'

A flash of relief crossed his face.

She moved away from Conor and again began the walk

away from the car. Trying to recall every detail of the tour and David Marr's words. The things he talked about and the time it took. She tried to walk as he did. Estimating the distance. The place where he zoomed and scanned in on the mountains. The curve of the road where she first saw Ed. Then the moments as her husband got closer.

When she was sure she was far enough along the road, she turned and began the walk back. Tracing what she was sure were Ed's steps. The Lough on her left, the brush, grass and trees on her right. She walked slowly. Again. Scouring the route. Going off the road onto grassy verges where she could. Pushing aside bushes and looking through trees. Looking over barbed wire fencing where she couldn't get through. Searching at every point. Searching for anything that suggested a hidden track. A way off the road.

She pushed wet hair away from her face and pulled back her hoodie. It had finally stopped raining. A hint of blue sky showed over the Lough and the sun was peeking through. She stepped forward off the road, close to a verge of bracken and trees. Scanning every inch.

And then she saw it.

A glint.

Just one flash reflected as the sun hit yellow and green foliage. And then it was gone.

She moved towards the spot, stepping over more low-level wire fencing. Walking up a small rise and pushing through bracken and foliage, ignoring the scratches to her hands.

And there it was.

A small black box.

A security camera.

So many emotions flooded through her. She couldn't begin to name them. What she could name was the relief. She hadn't been going mad. She had been right.

And she was sure, with every breath in her body, that her husband was looking into her eyes right now.

44

The piercing alarm went off at 1:15 p.m.

Ed ran to his study and checked the screens. Relief hit him in waves. It was Jamie staring into his first line of defence. One of his cameras close to the Lough Road.

'Conor!'

Her shout echoed through his speakers. He saw her waving and watched as Conor came into frame minutes later.

Seeing her. Hearing her voice. He wanted to sit here, watch her for a while, but he couldn't. The hunters wouldn't be far behind. He was surprised they weren't here already.

He reached for his phone and opened his security app. Moving out of the study, he pulled on his coat, picked up his weapons, and made for the door.

On his phone, he watched Jamie and Conor move at a decent pace. Following the main track and taking the correct path at the intersection. Conor was pointing at the ground, noting the indentations in the grass of Ed's own footprints that he'd made less than twenty-four hours earlier.

Ed received alerts from each camera they passed. Heard each trap they set off. His eyes fixed on the screen as he walked. His ear buds in to ensure his phone remained silent.

Watching Jamie, his heart rate rocketed – his mind a heightened mixture of fear and excitement. He was also watching the interactions between her and Conor. They were very different from the airport. More like their normal behaviour. Maybe the airport display had been a cover. An act. He couldn't help it, hope built inside him.

She was so close now. He needed to focus. He had to get them all to safety as quickly as possible. This was the most dangerous moment since his error two years ago behind the firewall of the computers of Tole Pharmaceuticals. The catastrophic error which had led to his disappearance.

Ed had watched them walk for fifteen minutes. And they were now in his sights. He circled around and behind them. Approaching with stealth.

Jamie and Conor were both on the ground. Binoculars up. Eyes on his cottage. Scoping the area. He wouldn't expect anything less. Especially from Conor. They were just twenty feet away from him.

Ed looked down at the ground. Took another deliberate step forward onto a large twig. The crack resounded throughout the silent forest.

He raised his hands in preparation.

Watched Conor pull his weapon from his belt, spin around, and raise his Glock. Aiming it directly at his chest.

45

Jamie heard the sound. Saw Conor pulling his weapon. Turned herself around. And there he was.

Real.

Alive.

In the flesh.

His hands up.

Eyes focused on Conor.

Her husband.

She struggled to her feet. Hand on her chest. It felt like her heart had stopped beating.

Ed was standing just feet away from her. And yet it wasn't him at all. The beard, the longer hair. A rifle over his shoulder, a Glock in his waistband, a hunting knife looped into his belt. It was like an alternate universe where they'd swapped places. He the soldier, her the civilian.

He held out his hands. Palms facing the ground.

'Ease it down Conor.' His voice was calm. 'If I wanted to hurt you, you'd already know about it. I've been tracking you since the first camera.'

Hearing his voice in person, for the first time in two years, robbed her of her breath. Conor looked across at her and lowered his weapon. He tucked it back into his waistband and got to his feet. His face echoed her own shock. Pure disbelief.

Jamie's eyes were fixed on her husband. Unable to move from her spot, she couldn't speak. It took all she had to stay upright. It was one thing believing he was alive, another to see him standing in front of her. She willed him to meet her eye, but he didn't. His face turned away from her. His eyes still on Conor, stepping towards him and holding out a long electronic device.

'I need to check for trackers. Can you raise your arms, Conor?'

She saw Conor hesitate, then follow the instruction. Jamie watched the wand wave across Conor's body. Heard the electrical sound with no extra high-pitched buzzing.

It was her turn next. Her husband moved towards her. His eyes down.

She held up her arms as he executed the search without meeting her eye. He was so close to her and yet a wall stood between them. He was like a stranger. His head bowed, unwilling to meet her eye. And something in her heart broke. She wanted to fall to the ground. It was clear. Her biggest fear realised. He wasn't hers anymore. She felt the loss at a visceral level. Fearing even more what she was going to find inside his cottage. Who she was going to find there and how she was going to face it. To live with it.

A sound echoed from the forest. She looked up. A calling bird.

Ed's eyes shot up in its direction.

She saw the fear then. The anxiety.

'We need to get back to the house. We're too exposed here.' Ed said.

He started walking. She looked at Conor. They had no choice but to follow. Still, she couldn't move. Conor came beside her and dragged her forward. As she began to stabilise and put one foot in front of the other, Conor stepped up his pace. He moved ahead of her, alongside Ed.

'Eddie, what the hell is going on here?'

'We'll talk later, when it's safe. Focus on the ground, Conor. It's uneven.'

And that was all she heard of her husband's voice.

No gentle softness. No reunion. He was brusque and distant. And as she kept pace over each uneven step, anguish lacing around her heart, she could feel something else rising to drive her forward. Raw anger building back inside her.

46

They were quiet as they walked. Ed followed by Conor, then her. Her husband kept looking back, looking around, and checking his phone. The pace was relentless, the route to the cottage more difficult than it had appeared from their visual sweep through the binoculars.

Conor was keeping pace, but his jaw was fixed. Rage coming off him like a mist. He wasn't used to being ordered around by anyone anymore. Least of all Ed.

Jamie watched her husband. His hyper-vigilance intense. Searching all directions, including the sky. It was a very different Ed in front of her. Different to the man she had lost two years ago. And different to the one she'd been married to for six years before that.

Each step she took, she was fighting to contain the emotion building inside.

After a few relentless minutes, the cottage came into view. A final steep track upwards and they would be there.

She passed a vegetable patch set out neatly, in sections, with raised beds. A fire pit with two chairs alongside it. Ahead of them, a brick-built garage covered with solar panels was attached to a quaint cottage, its wooden doors half open.

She glimpsed a Land Rover and a motorbike inside and a pile of logs sheltered in one corner. A half-made cabinet was sat up on a wooden bench. Ed was still working on his favourite hobby. Not everything had changed.

She was lagging, her focus on all she could see around her. A window into her husband's new world. Searching for clues about his life here. An ordinary life, as far as she could see. And no children's toys.

She took two steps up onto the porch.

Conor had taken off his backpack and was sitting on a bench just outside the front window, catching his breath and massaging his left leg. He looked at her as she passed by him.

'I'll stay here for a bit.' He put his hand out to hers. Gave it a squeeze.

She held it for a few seconds, then dropped it.

47

Jamie watched Ed unlock the door and step back, gesturing her inside. She walked straight into a living room and heard the door close behind her.

She stepped forward, scanning the space. Took off her backpack and placed it on a nearby chair. Her eyes moved to the coat rack in the corner.

'It's just me here.'

She turned back to her husband. Their eyes locked for the first time. It was like an electric shock to her heart. He had read her mind.

He held out his hand. She slipped off her coat. He hung it on an empty peg between two of his own coats. The symbolism was not lost on her. He turned back.

She could finally look at him. Really look at him.

His face was thinner. His jawline sharper. And his body leaner. For the first time, she met unguarded eyes. And she saw it then. Saw she had been wrong before. Very wrong.

He took a step towards her.

She took a step back.

He looked as if she'd dealt him a physical blow.

Eye to eye, they waited.

She looked away first and turned her back to him. It was easier that way.

'Have you been here the whole time?' she said.

'Yes.'

His voice so soft. Just that one word made her whole body ache.

She moved a few feet further and reached towards the chair. Picked up the beanie hat and held it in her hands. She brought it up to her face and inhaled. Stroking her fingers across the delicate embroidered icons.

'I looked for it everywhere…' Her eyes misted. She stopped herself. It seemed like a lifetime ago, that moment on the Lough Road.

'It's distinctive.' She glanced back at him. Watched his realisation. And let the hat drop.

Her eyes checked every inch of the room. There was a card she'd made, a pen sketch, the year before he'd died. Before she thought he'd died. An image from their last holiday together. Gondolas bobbing on sparkling water. The only other item from his past she could see in this entire space. It was on top of the cabinet. Framed.

She walked towards it. Felt the memory like opening a window in her mind and letting light in. The moment she'd given it to him in their hotel in Venice. Balcony doors open, light flooding onto the bed, the bustling Grand Canal below, the sound of water buses going by. The look on his face. Pure joy. He'd kept it on his desk at work. When she'd cleared it out, she had been distraught it wasn't there.

Seeing it should have comforted her. It didn't. It fed her anger. Fed her increasing heartbeat.

She looked back at him. His eyes were fixed on her. Watching her, reading her thoughts, the way he always could. Waiting for the right moment to speak.

Then she spotted something else. She moved past him.

On the coffee table were several magazines. She pushed the top one aside, recognising the edge of the image below. Her image. On the cover of *Soldier* magazine. The irony struck her. How the interviewer had wanted her to talk about the death of her husband. She'd refused. She'd taken the interview to raise the profile of injured soldiers and their rehabilitation. Her grief was not fodder for selling copies of their magazine.

Trying to hold her anger in check, she picked it up and turned to him. Held it up. 'Have you been following what I've been doing?'

He looked her in the eye. She saw the wariness. He really did know her so well. He nodded.

'You've been watching me? Tracking me?' She threw the magazine down, didn't wait for an answer. 'Did you hack me?' Her voice was rising now, however hard she tried to stop it. 'Did you turn on the cameras? Have you been watching me at home?'

'No.' His voice raised for the first time, meeting her pitch. A hint of the fire she knew he had inside him. He put his hands up. A defensive, calming gesture. 'I just needed to know how you were doing. I texted George every month to make sure that you and Dad were OK.'

She waited. Tried to hold herself together. She had so much to say about George, but this wasn't the time.

'You texted to check…' she could barely speak, 'that I was, OK? You thought I was … OK?' Her voice finally broke. Her anger burned. She started to tremble, struggling to stay on an even keel. '*You* had to know how *I* was doing? When I thought you were…'

She stopped herself. Her heart now pounding in her chest. She looked down. Afraid of what she might say next. The missile she might launch at him.

She'd been searching for 24 hours to get to this moment.

Crossed the Irish Sea, travelled through two countries, running from men who were hunting her. All the time looking for answers. And now she was in front of him, she couldn't trust herself to speak. Couldn't get answers to any of her questions.

Two years of separation. Of loss. When he was here, in this space, alive and alone the whole time. Thinking of her. Missing her. While she was at home. In grief. Aching for him. All that pointless pain. Pain caused by his choices.

He stepped towards her. 'I know that…'

Jamie held up her hand. Stopped him in his tracks. She couldn't talk anymore, listen anymore, or look at her husband anymore.

She stepped across to the door and walked back outside. Strode past Conor and down to the fire pit. Waved Conor off when he walked towards her. She watched him turn and bang the door open into the cottage.

She tried to steady her breathing. Leant forward. Her heart pounding so hard her ears were ringing.

Pulling back up, she saw the views surrounding her. The woodland and forest encircling the house, distant mountains, gentle hills, gorse and bracken. Beauty everywhere. Peace. At complete odds with the physical and emotional pain she was drowning in.

She'd seen the love in his eyes. The longing in every line of his face. In every part of his being. The anguish.

Of course he'd followed her. Of course he'd watched what she was doing. If the situations had been reversed, she would have done the same.

But none of it helped her. She'd had to walk away. Everything she saw fuelled her anger. She wanted to rail and shout, but she couldn't hurt him like that. He looked as broken as she felt.

Of all the things she thought she might find here, prepared

herself to find here, it wasn't this. His heart was an open wound. Matching hers.

Even seeing that, knowing it at her core, the rage still burned inside her. Her mind fixed on his betrayal. The deception. Lies. Abandonment. Lack of trust in her. Like a record stuck in a groove, a train in its track, the thoughts played on a loop.

Minutes passed before she heard a sound. She turned to see Conor walking towards her. His limp more pronounced.

He sat down and looked at her.

'Talk to me, Jay.'

'I can't.'

'Try.'

'It's too complicated, there's so much swimming in my head.'

'Is it that complicated?'

She looked at him as though he were mad.

'Every day for two years, what would you have given to have him back?'

'It's not that simple.'

'Isn't it?'

She looked away from his stare.

'Jay,' his voice forced her to look back at him. 'That man is dying in there.'

She didn't answer.

'You had everyone. Work, Tom, friends. He's been here alone. With no one. Every single day for two years.'

Her temper flared.

'How is that my fault? His choice, not mine.'

She held Conor's gaze. Saw disappointment in his eyes. Something she'd never seen before when he'd looked at her.

He stood. Started to walk away. Then turned back.

'And there was me thinking, Jamie, that you really did know what love was.'

Conor's parting shot stabbed her like a knife in the heart. Like a punch to the stomach, landing and bending her double.

And in that instant, like a mighty wall crashing to the ground, the rage fell away. Her mind at rest. Quieted. Her heart back in control. Driving her.

And it *was* clear. And it *was* simple.

She ran inside to her husband.

48

She was back. Standing in front of him. Just feet away from him. A step. A chasm. Her eyes changed. The anger gone, replaced by anguish.

'Why didn't you tell me? Whatever it was, it wouldn't have mattered. I could have come with you. I would have come with you. All this time,' her voice cracked. 'All this time we could have been here, still together.'

Ed looked into those blue eyes. A window to a soul he thought he'd never see again.

He shook his head. 'Captain Jamie Shaw, decorated for outstanding service in Afghanistan. Stories and articles across the internet. In magazines.' He pointed back to the table. 'How could you disappear? There was nowhere you could go. I'd have forced you into a cage, buried alive here. You think that would have worked?' His voice ached with sadness. 'I couldn't do that to you.'

She was silent for a moment.

'That wasn't your choice to make.'

He didn't know how to answer that.

'You thought I'd rather live without you, lost, alone and broken, than disappear with you?'

He tried to find the words. To explain. But she kept going.

'And what happened to, "Us against the world?"'

Like stones thrown, her words wounded him. Still he stepped towards her. This time, she didn't move away. He took her hands. She didn't flinch.

'It wouldn't have worked. I wanted you to be safe. And…' he faltered, less sure of himself now, 'I didn't want you to lose everything, too. It was my fight, not yours.'

The tears were now rolling down her cheeks. Her eyes held pain he'd never seen before. Pain he knew he'd put there.

The silence was long. Then she spoke.

'But I did lose everything. Everything that mattered to me.'

Her quiet voice shattered him. He was helpless in the face of these words. In this moment, he questioned everything. Turned his mind in the circles he'd been plaguing himself with for two years. He knew whatever he'd done, he couldn't have won. If he'd told her, he knew she would have come with him. Her life would have been so small. A prisoner here. He couldn't watch that. Be responsible for that. He did what he thought was best. Best for her. That's what enabled him to survive. He wanted her to be safe. To still have a life, even if it was without him. Do her work. Maybe find happiness with someone else. Even though it killed him. That's how much he loved her.

Seeing her in front of him now, he realised he'd made a terrible mistake. In his desire to choose what was best for them both, he'd almost destroyed them both.

He put a hand up to her cheek to touch the falling tears. Stroking them from her face.

'Jamie…'

He stopped. Saying her name nearly brought him to his knees.

'Forgive me.'

His words a whisper. His eyes imploring. Acknowledging everything. Accepting he'd been wrong. Surrendering to her.

It felt like the longest time before she spoke.

'Don't leave me again.'

He saw soft, vulnerable eyes, but heard an edge of steel in her voice. A warning.

'I won't,' he said. Tears in his eyes. Close to falling.

He knew it wouldn't be this easy. But he couldn't wait any longer. Couldn't hold back anymore. He moved forward and pulled her into his arms.

He inhaled her scent from the base of his lungs. It felt like the breath of life. He held her close. Felt her arms tighten around him. Then the tears fell down his cheeks. He didn't hold them back. Couldn't hold them back. Their force was too powerful.

After two desperate, desolate years without her, he could finally breathe again.

49

Jamie breathed in the scent of her husband. It took her straight to the place of memory. Heady. Floating. The longing. Night after night. Finally, in his arms again. Living arms. Not just ones from her dreams, when she woke in horror and despair, tears soaking her face. This was real. Her body against his. Melting and bonding to him.

His heart was beating against her chest. His arms holding her as though his life depended on it. Heat radiated from him. One hand, stroking her hair. Gentle strokes. Threading fingers through the fine brown strands.

He tilted her head back. She looked into those brown eyes which had captivated her from the first moment she'd looked into them. Eyes she'd always thought she could read. Tears running from them now.

There was a fragility between them. Bridges needed to be built. To be crossed. That would take time. But before any of that, she knew one thing. Clear and stark. Whatever he was involved in, it didn't matter to her. She would have run with him two years ago, and she would run with him now. It shocked her, this realisation. The power of her love. What she was willing to sacrifice of her own self. Her own morality.

But looking at him now, feeling his arms around her, she wasn't letting him go. She wasn't losing him again. And the answers to all her questions could come later. For now, she wanted to be lost in him.

Her heart was pounding as she ran trembling fingertips, damp with his tears, over his face. How her mind and body had ached for him. Through days, through long anguished nights. She could barely believe he was real. She touched the soft hair on his cheeks. Brown with flecks of grey. Moved to his lips. Her thumb stroking across the top. Across the bottom. His eyes full of a fire that she knew so well. He was fighting for control. She could see that. Feel that. But he was waiting. Waiting for her.

She moved forward. Her lips touched his. Gently. Their eyes open. Watching each other. Searching. It felt like the first time. That vulnerability. Uncertainty. Her hands moved, curled around his neck. She pulled his face towards her, arched her body and deepened the kiss. The fire exploded. All restraint gone. His arms, his hands, were on her body. Crushing her against him. His lips taking hers.

She felt herself sink into oblivion. There was only sensation. Falling deeper. And deeper. Until she heard a voice. Distant shouting.

Conor's voice.

Jamie jarred away from her husband. Dazed. Both turned in unison to the window.

Conor was running towards the house as fast as his body would allow. His hands waving them back. His words hard to comprehend.

She thought she understood.

'Go! Go!'

She looked at her husband. Neither retreated, both moved forwards. Towards Conor.

The hinges almost gave way as Conor barrelled into the door, calling at the top of his voice.

'Drone! Drone!'

Ed was closest to Conor. Tried to catch him as he stumbled, overbalanced and hit the ground. All the weight on his damaged left side. They heaved him up, one on each side. Ed guiding them towards a door at the back of the living room.

Jamie saw the camera. The keypad. And watched Ed scan his eyes and hit a sequence of digits before the door opened. He started pulling Conor inside. Her eyes turned back to the room. She couldn't go without them. The letter and documents from his parents and the footage of their father under threat.

'Wait!'

She propped Conor on the door jamb. Ducked down. Darted back into the room. Picked up her backpack and threw it on her shoulder. Put her arm back under Conor's and was pushing him inside the room within seconds.

The door closed behind them with a deep thud.

It was pitch black until lights flooded the space. A small, windowless room. Ed's office. And she was sure, by the sound of the door, a safe room. She saw another similar door of steel on the opposite wall.

Ed moved to a desk with several computers laid out. Her eyes followed him. The screens were full of images. Forest, grass, hills, bracken, tracks and roads.

Jamie felt herself almost overbalance. She was holding the full weight of Conor as he leaned on her, struggling to stand. Not able to catch his breath.

She looked around, pulled him towards a chair and sat him down. He was trying to get enough air to speak. Jamie knew the memories he was revisiting. The men in his team killed by a drone attack in Kandahar. Him on a distant hill, the sniper with his rifle drawn, everything visible through his scope. Running towards his team afterwards, against orders, knowing it was hopeless.

Jamie knelt down. Held his hands.

'Breathe, Conor. Breathe.'

Jamie looked up at Ed. She went to speak, when ear-piercing alarms shattered the room. One after the other. A cacophony of agonising screeching. She put her hands over Conor's ears. Looked across at her husband, his eyes fixed on the computers. Hitting keys with force. Red alerts were flashing across several images. Figures moving across multiple screens.

Jamie scanned the computers. Understood immediately. 'How far out are they?' she shouted.

'Two miles.'

Two miles was long enough for them to get away. It was difficult terrain. All the figures were on foot. They'd take time to get here. She'd seen a car and a motorbike in the garage. She knew her husband, he'd have a route out of here. An escape plan.

She felt a pull on her hand. Conor's hand was gripping hers, hurting her. 'The drone…' his words came between gasps, 'it's … armed.'

And as Jamie heard his words, and looked across at Ed in horror, an explosion rocked the entire house.

50

It was pitch black. An eerie silence. The lights had gone out with the bomb.

Jamie was sure she was unhurt, but she knew soldiers who'd experienced explosions had not even known their own limbs were missing.

She ran hands over her body. She was intact. Still standing, but disorientated.

'Jamie.' Ed's voice came into the darkness. His phone lit up the space in front of her.

She reached out her arms and he moved towards her. Conor was still on the chair beside her. She put a shaking hand on his shoulder.

'Are you OK?'

He nodded. His hand reached up to grip hers.

A whirring noise sounded and the lights came back on. The computer screens started to flash.

'Back-up generator,' Ed said. Stepping towards the screens.

Jamie looked at him, needing the chair to keep her balance. 'What did they hit?'

‘Check the garage.’ Conor said quietly.

She could see him steadying himself. His hands tense around the sides of the chair, trying to look in command. But she saw the look in his eyes. The shock. But there was more than that. She saw rage.

She turned back towards the desk. The computers were all now online and red alerts were still flashing. Ed pointed to an image. The garage, the entire right side of the house and part of the living room was demolished. The car and motorbike were underneath the rubble. Conor was right. And the explosion was aimed at one thing, to remove their means of escape.

Another explosion rocked the building. Jamie gripped the chair. On the screens, more flames shot up from the garage.

‘Petrol from the tanks,’ Ed said.

‘We need to move from here asap,’ Conor said.

Jamie could see black smoke billowing. Sparks flying out into the air. The fire would move into the living room next to them in minutes.

‘How is this room not damaged?’ Jamie said.

‘It’s reinforced steel and concrete.’

She watched her husband. He was the calmest of them all. Focused. In spite of the attack. But she felt jumpy, like a tiger caught in a trap, panic washing over her. Ed turned to speak and saw it. He came forward. Put a hand on each arm. His eyes direct to hers.

‘We’re OK. We have another way out. There’s a mine shaft outside.’

Ed turned away, back to the screens, punching more keys at speed. She tried to breathe more evenly.

She looked at Conor. His eyes were fixed on something behind her. She turned and saw a wall full of images, text, photocopies of newspaper cuttings, and handwritten notes. It was like a police incident board. Red crosses covered photos of many smiling faces. Names were written beneath each of them.

She recognised the pictures from the passports. Prudence, Frank and Sean O'Neill. A red cross struck through the parents in the happy family portrait. Her eyes swept across the wall. There was a cross over a beautiful woman. A family with young children. And there were many more. All of the lines from these crosses of death pointed to the centre of the board. To a photo of Paul Arthur Tole. She took in a breath. It was clear, Ed believed Tole was connected to his parents' murders. Was at the heart of his story. At the heart of Sean O'Neill's story.

Her eyes turned back to Conor. He pointed to Ed's parents. He mimed the words, 'The papers?'

She touched her backpack.

'We can't take anything trackable with us.' Ed's voice made her spin around.

She handed him her burner phone. Pulled out the black zipped package from her pack and gave him the extra phone and SIM cards.

His eyes held hers. 'You were in the loft space.'

Before she could answer, he turned away and began to factory reset the phones, his own tablets and laptops, and snap the physical SIM cards.

She looked over at Conor. He was mirroring Ed's actions with his own phone. His eyes casting around the room. Fixing on the other door.

'Where's the mine shaft, Eddie? What's the plan?'

'It's 150 yards away. In that direction.' Ed, still looking at his screens, pointed to the other steel door. 'We need to handle the drone, then get out of here.' He tapped the keyboard, opening new windows, zooming in on images. 'Somehow it evaded the radar. But I see it now. High up. Hovering away from the cottage.'

He turned around to Conor. 'Can you shoot it down?'

Conor inhaled. 'Not with this,' he said, putting his hand on the Glock in his waistband. 'What have you got?'

Ed opened a steel cabinet bolted to the wall.

Conor whistled. 'Now you're talking.'

Jamie looked from the cabinet to her husband. The man who hated guns had an arsenal in front of her. He'd changed. It was inevitable. Out here alone. Afraid for his life. What mark would this leave on his psyche if they ever got out of this nightmare alive?

As if reading her thoughts, Ed reached out his hand to find hers.

'We need to move now.' His voice soft. His eyes softer. Still her Ed.

Conor got to his feet. Winced and staggered but managed to stabilise himself. Standing in front of the cabinet, he reached in and held a long-range rifle in his hands. Put it back and picked up a pump action shotgun instead. Pulled forward a box of cartridges and a waist pouch and left them sitting on the shelf.

Jamie's eyes fixed on Conor. 'Did you see how many missiles the drone was carrying?'

Conor paused. Looked directly at her. 'Two.'

'You can't go out there. It's too risky.'

'You have an alternative?' Conor's eyes were locked on hers.

She turned away, looked at Ed, searching for support, then at the screens. At the figures moving towards them and the drone holding them in place. They were helpless. Someone had to go outside to break this standoff.

'If they wanted us dead, they'd have fired again already.' Conor said.

He was right. He was always right in these situations.

Conor moved across the room. Scanned the computer screens.

'Where is it?'

Ed maximised one of the windows. The image was blurry. Smoke across the camera lens. 'There,' he pointed. 'I think it's a quadcopter?'

'A small one.' Conor said. 'But it's been adapted. It's military spec by its size, with missiles on board, and able to evade radar. I haven't seen one quite like it before but they're experimenting all the time.'

'What about the missile, if you shoot it down?'

'Should be alright. It only fires on launch.'

'Should be…'

Ed's words hung in the air. Conor shrugged.

'You need it closer, to have a chance at bringing it down.' Ed said.

He nodded. 'Right now, it's too high up and visibility isn't good.' He pointed to the other steel door. 'Is this the back of the house?'

Ed nodded.

'Show me outside.'

He brought up several images side by side showing a small, covered area over the back of the cottage, a shed about ten feet away, and a derelict structure with no roof on another screen.

Conor pointed to the derelict building. 'How far is this?'

'Straight ahead. A little to the left. About 50 yards.'

Conor looked between her and Ed. 'You ready to go if I get this thing down?'

Jamie watched her husband hit keys on his computer keyboard, then open the drawers of his filing cabinet, and turn around to Conor.

'I'm ready.'

Conor looked at her. ‘Are you ready?’

She hesitated. ‘No. This is a bad plan.’

Conor zeroed in on her. ‘You have a better one?’

She paused. Looked across at the screens and at the two men.

‘I do.’

51

Both sets of eyes were now on Jamie.

'I'll be a decoy, run out to the derelict ruin and bring the drone lower. Conor, you slip out to the shed here.' She pointed to the screen. 'You stay hidden and then shoot it down. Divide and conquer. You'll maybe have three or four shots before it goes too high and back out of range.'

Both men were shaking their heads.

Conor spoke first. 'Too dangerous.'

Ed followed. 'No. No way.'

She looked directly at Conor. 'If they wanted us dead, they'd have fired again already.'

He didn't reply. His eyes narrowing.

Her eyes stayed on Conor. 'We both know the drone is too high up and visibility is poor. The minute you go out there and it sees your weapon, it'll either shoot at you or move even further away. You don't have a chance at getting it down. You need a decoy. Look.' She pointed to the screens. The men in camouflage were moving towards them from multiple directions. The fire was creeping into the room next to them. 'It's the only way we have a chance of all getting out of here.'

Her eyes did not move from his. She had a look of her own which he knew very well. And she was using it.

Conor ran his hand around his neck. Exhaled. She saw it in his face. She'd won.

'Jamie's right,' said Conor. 'If she … plays decoy, I have a better chance at shooting it down.'

'Don't…' Ed said, looking at her. 'They want me. I can lead them away.'

'No,' Jamie said. 'We get the drone down. We go together. And we stay together.'

Both men looked at each other, the time ticking down. She tried to think of the words to push them forward. She couldn't find any.

She chose action.

She went to the gun cabinet and loaded the shotgun with five cartridges. Poured ammunition into the pouch, turned towards Conor and held out the weapon.

She knew these would need to be the shots of his life. She'd seen how difficult it was to shoot down a drone in Afghanistan. Almost impossible with a rifle. More chance of success with a shotgun with its spray of lead at every release.

Conor looked at Ed. Back at Jamie.

Then he put out his hand. And he took the shotgun.

52

Jamie strapped on her backpack over the jacket she'd taken from the weapons cupboard. A damp scarf protected her nose and mouth. Her hoodie was up. She was ready.

She avoided looking at Ed or Conor. Didn't want to see their doubt, fear, or concern. They had agreed on their plan. She just wanted to put it into action.

Jamie felt Ed watching her as she stood at the door. She didn't look up.

'Ready?' His voice was tight with tension.

She put her thumb up.

He clicked the locks, hit numbers on the digital keypad, and opened the back door.

The heat hit her first, like a blast from a boiling hot hairdryer. Her eyes stung with the smoke. Then she heard crackling flames.

She held her breath and started running. Weaving across the ground. Seconds later, she heard the buzz of the drone intensify. It was lowering, getting closer to her. Her chest was tight, her breathing heavy, and her heart was pounding. It was one thing to be told the drone wouldn't fire on her, another to be exposed and out in the open.

She was close to the derelict building now. The buzz loud and insistent. She circled around it, then began heading back towards the cottage. The flames from the garage were licking into the air. The entire roof of the cottage was now on fire. She was within 30 yards of the back door when she heard the first distinctive crack. There was a pause. Then a second. She looked to the sky. The drone was already moving back up, spinning itself around, changing direction. She glanced back down, saw the barrel of a shotgun pointing out from the shed, and heard the third crack. A different sound. The drone tilted in the air. Conor's fourth shot was fatal. The drone spun out of control, crashing to the ground.

Conor was already limping to reach the drone and smashing the camera with the butt of the shotgun when she saw Ed leaving the cottage, running towards her.

They both reached her a few seconds apart.

'We need to move fast.' Ed said. 'They'll send another one.'

She put her arm in Conor's, Ed took the other side.

The terrain was rocky with no level ground. Treacherous for Conor at speed. But they got into a rhythm. Passed the ruined shack and kept moving.

'Almost there.' Ed shouted. 'The trees ahead.'

There was a small copse in front of them. Ed pulled them into the centre. Conor leaned against a tree and Jamie looked up. Evergreen trees created a thick canopy above them. Hiding them from aerial monitoring but not from a drone's heat sensor.

Ed lifted up a long steel rod hidden in the grass, pulled away an edge of turf and began to lever something forward. It took all his strength. Then Jamie saw why.

Layers of thick foliage and grass covered a wooden platform attached to a steel manhole cover. He propped the cover open.

'You go first, Jamie.' He reached into his pack. Put a torch on her head and switched it on. 'There are thirty-eight rungs. Go slow. Go steady. We'll be close behind. Rap the ladder when you're down. It won't take two people.'

She took a step down into the unknown. Into the darkness. The rungs of the ladder were slim and damp. It was precarious. Her feet slipped several times as she counted, but finally she was down, smelling damp earth. She tapped the steel rung with her Glock.

'I'm down!' she called. Not sure if Ed could hear her.

She scanned around the small circular space. Her head torch bounced light around the walls. Just one tunnel led off from the centre.

She heard sounds on the ladder, echoing off the walls. Then Conor was beside her. Meeting her eye. Pain etched on his face. Breathing heavily. He leant against the wall as she tapped the rung of the ladder again.

'We're both down!' Jamie shouted.

She looked up. Waiting for a sound on the ladder. Waiting for Ed. She glanced at Conor.

'Where is he?'

Still trying to catch his breath, Conor shook his head.

She looked back up the silent mine shaft.

Ed wasn't following them.

53

Ed heard the second rap ringing on the steel ladder and heard Jamie shout. They were both safely down. He pulled the only phone he'd brought from the house out of his pack.

He'd already erased the data across all his computers. But he needed them to be obliterated. The fire was taking hold, but he had to make sure the papers from all his work over the last two years were also gone. He had to set off the explosives he'd laid in the safe room.

His finger lingered on the keys. The cottage had been a prison, but sometimes even a prison can feel safe. It surprised him, how hard it was to key in these numbers. To destroy it all.

He heard the ladder clanging. Jamie's voice echoing up to him.

'Ed! Ed! Where are you? I'm coming back up.'

He tapped the ladder. Bellowed down. 'No! Don't! I'm coming!'

It was enough to push him forward.

He keyed in the first code and heard the deep rumble. The inside of his safe room would be fried. Everything charred or burnt to ashes.

He was ready with the next code. Charges set all the way around the rest of his house. This would reduce everything to rubble and keep Keller's men busy. It would be hours before anyone could search inside the house.

He took a breath. Keyed in the numbers and hit the final button.

Ed watched his house explode. He felt the vibration under his feet, reaching up through his body. The sound bounced around the mountains, echoing through the landscape. The trees in the copse shook and pieces of debris flew around him. He jumped down into the mine, knocked out the prop and let the cover drop above him. He sealed the lid from inside and set the tamper-proof charge. If anyone found the entrance or broke the seal, the mine would collapse. Entry and exit from this point would then be impossible. He hurtled down the ladder as though the walls would crumble around him.

He was forty feet underground and next to Jamie in twenty seconds. She pulled him close.

'What the hell was that?' Conor said, looking at him.

He pulled away from Jamie. 'Just tidying the place up.'

Conor blew out a breath. 'No stone left unturned.'

'The only way,' Ed said, looking between them. 'Are we ready to move? The underground bunker is fifteen minutes' walk. It's cramped, though. Hard going.' He looked at Conor with concern. 'We'll stop there to eat and sleep and move again at dawn.'

'Won't they search the mine and the tunnels?' Jamie said.

'They don't exist. I wiped them from the land registry and every paper and online history that I could find.'

'What about local knowledge?' Conor said.

'A few locals know of the mine, but they don't know any of the entrance points. I doubt the men will have time to canvas the neighbourhood.'

Ed checked the time on his watch. 3:50 p.m. He wouldn't feel settled until they were in the bunker.

'Let's get moving,' he said.

54

Ed took a slow pace. He couldn't afford anyone to have another injury. A twist of the foot, or worse, could spell disaster.

The tunnel was cramped, difficult underfoot. Only room for one person at its width. And the ceiling was clearly hewn by a smaller man. Jamie had enough headroom to stand, he was slightly stooped. But it was Conor, with his six feet plus, who would struggle the most.

He looked back. Jamie was about fifteen feet behind him. Conor was further back, moving steadily, using the tunnel wall to stabilise himself and the shotgun on his other side. Ed put a thumbs up. They both responded.

The space was airless. A musty atmosphere you could almost touch. He had a ventilation system running, powered from the bunker, but it didn't work well. It was difficult to breathe and his chest felt tight. It was hot and sweat was soaking through his clothes.

He'd travelled this route many times. This escape. But he'd never practised the retreat with three people, one carrying an injury. All the plans he had in place would need to be changed.

It had been the beginnings of a small zinc mine more than a century ago. An unfinished speculation by the landowner. It had taken him a while to clear areas of fallen rocks, but he'd found the mine in remarkably good condition. He'd pored over the plans and decided on the best route out. The hunters would not find them down here, even if they found out the tunnels existed.

He turned around. Jamie had slipped further back. Conor was now a long way behind her. He could barely see him. He stopped at a crossroads between three tunnels. Checked his watch. They'd been walking for ten minutes. It felt like much longer. His lungs hurt and his body felt heavy. It was like being on a high mountain at altitude. The lack of oxygen debilitating.

Jamie reached him. Thirty seconds later, Conor was beside them, his face pale and drawn.

'How are you both doing?' His eyes stayed on Conor.

Conor nodded. Grimaced and looked away from him. Jamie took the water bottle he handed her and took some gulps. Her hair was soaked, sweat dripping from the ends.

'How much further?' she said.

'Only five minutes. We'll rest here for a bit.'

Conor took a few mouthfuls and passed the bottle back to Ed. He took deep swigs, finished the bottle, and threw it on the ground.

Conor's eyes were fixed on him. Things were no easier between them.

Earlier, after Jamie had left him standing inside his cottage, Conor had come storming in. His eyes on fire. Spoiling for a fight. Conor had gone to lash out, but Ed had stopped him. Defended himself and almost knocked Conor to the ground. He'd seen the shock on Conor's face. No longer just a computer geek, he was strong. He'd learned how to fight. And Ed had used that strength to force Conor to listen. His words finally getting through.

'I disappeared for Jamie. To keep her safe. I left her behind to give her a chance at a life. It killed me.'

He'd seen the fire ebb in Conor's eyes as he talked to him. And he'd calmed. Up to a point.

Now, in the darkness of this fetid tunnel, he put a hand on Conor's shoulder. Trying to bridge the gap that remained between them.

'Are you ready to go?'

Conor nodded. Ed saw the pain etched across his face, with no word of complaint.

He looked at Jamie, reached out and touched her hand. She smiled at him. He let her hand drop and started walking ahead.

The footsteps on the ground behind told him they were following.

55

They had made it to the bunker. A space around ten feet by twelve, with a low ceiling, propped with thick wooden beams.

Jamie scanned the cramped space. A lamp offered low light on a table with a laptop and a folding wooden chair. A single gas ring burner with crockery and other items sat to the side. There was also a steel cabinet, batteries connected to a wire running up the wall, bottles of mineral water, an air filtration unit, and a put-up bed.

Conor collapsed down onto the bed. Pulled his coat off. His arm went across his forehead as Jamie stepped towards him.

'How's the pain?'

'Not good.'

'Let me help?'

He nodded.

She knelt down and massaged his thigh and calf. His face contorted. The muscles were knotted. Trigger points within each band of tight muscles. She massaged the soft tissue around his left hip and he winced. She touched his knee and he gasped.

This was serious. After the suicide bombing, multiple reconstructive surgeries had left his hip and knee severely weakened. The exertion over the last few hours had affected him badly.

'What about your back?'

He shook his head.

Jamie knew the constant pain he was in from the shrapnel embedded near his spine. He needed to rest. Put minimal weight on his back, hip and legs for a few days. His knee was an urgent issue. It was swelling.

She touched the swollen knee. 'We need to ice and strap it.'

Conor's eyes moved around the space. 'Good luck with that.'

Jamie glanced around the bunker. Ed was clicking computer keys, focused on his task. Oblivious to them.

In a small recess in the wall she found a first aid box and a thick bandage inside. With no ice available she reached for a bottle of water and soaked it, kneeling back beside Conor.

Conor pulled a flick knife from his trouser pocket. The silver casing had his engraved initials visible on the side. He clicked the button to open it and sliced the blade down the front of his jeans to allow access to the knee.

Jamie held the wet cloth onto his inflamed knee. She soaked it a few times and wrapped it around the swollen joint. It would do very little – the surrounding flesh was red and burning hot.

The memories of Afghanistan and Conor's rehab time at the DMRC flooded back to her. His weeks in bed when she'd devoted herself more to him than any other patient. Caring for him during the intensive rehabilitation that followed. Keeping him going physically. Keeping him going mentally when the nerve damage at his spine nearly broke him. They had been tough months. Even tougher years.

She soaked the bandage again, wiped his face, resting her hand on his forehead.

'You're on fire.'

'I know.' He put his hand out to reach hers, touched it and smiled. His hand dropped down, exhausted. 'I need my meds.'

'Where are they?'

'Blown to smithereens on the porch.'

That wasn't good.

'When are you due the next dose?'

He checked his watch. 'In a few hours.'

They had to figure out how to get hold of the drugs he'd need. There was one downside to Tolacaine. And it was a big one. Withdrawal began within hours of the last dose.

She strapped his knee. Searched through the first aid kit and found some anti-inflammatories. He swigged them back.

'You need to rest now.'

Conor nodded. Unusually compliant.

She looked across at Ed. He was watching them. He turned away quickly. Eyes back on his screen.

She stood and moved towards her husband. 'Shall I make coffee?'

He gave a weary smile. 'That would be great.'

As she was about to light the gas burner, a picture came on screen. What was once the cottage was now a pile of burning, smoking rubble.

'That was … comprehensive,' she smiled.

He looked up at her but there was no smile across his face. It was more than weariness. She put her hand on his arm.

'What's wrong?'

He beckoned her closer to him. 'I don't know how to get us out of here.'

'What do you mean?' She whispered.

'I had a plan.' He looked across at Conor lying prone on the bed then back at her. 'But it's not going to work for us now.'

He looked as though the weight of the world was crushing him.

She touched his shoulder. 'We just … need a new plan.' Her eyes met his then she looked away.

She knew this was her fault. She had brought dangerous men to his door.

'We were so careful.' She hesitated. 'We avoided the three men at the port.' She raised her voice, looking across at Conor. 'But we found a bug on Conor's car, they must have been tracking him. We got rid of it and changed plates. I guess—'

'Three men at the port?' Ed cut across her. 'There were four men.'

She felt Conor bolt upright.

'There were three.' Conor's voice could have cut steel. He propped himself up onto his side, elbow supporting him, eyes trained on Ed.

Ed took the laptop over to Conor and played the footage.

The screen showed a man in jeans and a black hoodie jumping out of a black Subaru on the road into Dublin port. Then three men in suits emerging from the car after it parked up.

Jamie had rarely seen Conor's face change so rapidly.

He put his hand up to his head. Banged the cave wall with his fist. Wincing at the pain. 'That's who put the tracker on the car. I missed it. 'I'm … sorry, Eddie.' He ground out the words. They pained him.

Ed closed the laptop. 'It was inevitable. From the moment Jamie saw me they were always coming. It was only a matter of time.'

She glanced at Conor. Could see he was struggling to

contain his anger at being bested by the hunters. And even worse, being found wanting in front of Ed.

'We're here. We're safe.' Ed said. 'That's all that matters.'

Conor met these words with silence and lay back down. Arm bent over his eyes, unwilling to meet anyone's gaze.

56

Jamie watched the saucepan boil then turned off the gas.

There were only two mugs on the table and no more on the open shelves. She spooned coffee into each. Emptied little UHT milk cartons into Ed's and one teaspoon of sugar. Left Conor's black, adding three heaped spoons of sugar.

She pulled forward a bottle of water for herself. Took a quick swig of Ed's milky, sugary coffee. It tasted vile to her, but it was wet and warm. Somehow the normality of it was soothing.

She handed Ed his drink. He took a sip and pulled a face.

'What's wrong with it?'

'I don't take sugar anymore.'

'Really?'

He shrugged. 'A health kick.'

She had to smile. How many more unlikely changes was she going to see in her husband. Two years really was a long time.

Jamie reached out to take back the drink, but Ed grabbed her hand, held it, and smiled back.

'It'll be good.'

Jamie picked up Conor's mug and went to his makeshift

bed. He opened his eyes, sitting forward as she propped pillows behind him. He sipped the steaming drink with his cast-iron lips.

Jamie sat down beside him.

'I can't believe I missed that.' Conor said.

'Forget about it. It's not important now.'

Her words were pointless, she knew how important it was to him.

'What were you whispering about?' he said.

She didn't answer.

'Something else is wrong. Tell me?'

Jamie glanced across at Ed. He took four steps and sat on the floor next to her.

'We have a…' Ed paused. 'A logistical problem.'

Conor's eyes were fixed on Ed. Not saying a word. Waiting. His signature move.

The silence went on.

Jamie plunged in. 'Our escape plan is…' she searched for the right words, 'in need of revision.'

'You mean we're…' Conor drew a finger across his throat.

'That's exactly what I mean.' Jamie said.

Conor looked at Ed. 'What was the escape plan?'

'I have a motorbike stowed at the end of the tunnel. The plan was either to ride or hike over the mountains. Then rent a cottage and lie low until things died down.'

Conor paused. 'I don't see a problem. We split up. You and Jamie take the motorbike or hike. I can hole up here, then find another way to get to you.'

'No.' Jamie shook her head.

Conor ignored her. 'Eddie, you know it's the right thing to do.'

'We're not splitting up.' Jamie said.

But Conor was not done.

'I'm not risking both of you. I want you safe.' His eyes rested on Jamie, then went back to Ed. 'I'll figure things out my side.'

Jamie shook her head again. 'By tomorrow, you'll barely be standing on that leg. And what about your drugs? You'll be in withdrawal. You won't make it out of here alone.'

'Is there any way,' Ed hesitated. 'Could you manage to get on the back of the bike, Conor? Jamie could drive. I could hike and we—'

'No,' Jamie spoke even louder, stopping him mid-sentence, before Conor had a chance to answer. 'He'd never manage it. And we're not separating.'

There was no reply from either of them.

'I'm not losing you again,' she said, her eyes locked on Ed. Tears threatening. 'We stay together. OK?'

The men both paused. Then nodded. But she saw the look between them. For once, it felt like she was on the outside. That they were already deciding on an unspoken plan and she was not part of it.

Jamie moved back to the small gas burner. Reached up and pulled down two bowls and three tins of beans and spaghetti from the open shelves. She poured them into the saucepan and started stirring. A glance behind her showed Ed and Conor in deep, whispered conversation.

She blinked away glistening tears. It was more than she could do, to leave Ed now she had him back.

As the food warmed, she opened the steel cupboard, searching for another bowl. This time she wasn't surprised by what she found. Another weapons cache. Along with phones, laptops, clothes and more. She shut the doors and turned around.

Ed was stirring the beans and spaghetti. Then pouring it into the two bowls. He took one to Conor with a spoon, handing him a bottle of water and a paper towel. Then he pointed to Jamie to sit on the floor next to him. Handed her a spoon and the other bowl. Kept the pan and fork for himself.

The three of them ate in silence.

Jamie struggled to push down any of the sickly sauce and springy strands of spaghetti. Her stomach in knots of tension. She looked up as Conor's bowl clicked onto the floor. He held her gaze. She sensed the moment before his words entered the space.

'I think it's time, Eddie.' Conor paused. 'Time you told us everything. What the hell are we mixed up in?'

At last. The question she was desperate for an answer to, that she'd travelled across two countries for, had been spoken aloud by Conor.

57

Ed could feel both sets of eyes piercing into him.

He knew they had his black case from the loft. Had seen the whiteboard in his office. He just didn't know how much they'd pieced together. And what they believed.

He turned to his right, towards Jamie, sitting beside him on the floor.

'The package from the loft. You opened it? You saw the DVD and the passports? You read the letter?'

She nodded.

'My name, my birth name is…' He couldn't say the words. Had been banned from saying them for so long that he couldn't get them past his lips.

'Sean O'Neill,' Jamie said. Her voice soft, hands reaching out for his.

'It's so long ago and yet…' he looked away. Drifting. He pulled himself back. Back to Jamie. He gripped her hands. 'I know I've put you in danger. Lied to you. Betrayed you in the most terrible way. There's no reason for you to trust me now. To believe in me. But I'm going to tell you everything.'

He took in a breath.

'Nineteen years ago, my birth parents were murdered.'

Jamie hesitated. 'I read … did a search online…'

It was her turn to struggle for words now. He could imagine what she was thinking. He knew every word of every article she might have found and read online.

'Vicious lies.' He tried to contain his anger. 'My parents weren't involved in any kind of criminal network.'

'The police reports said they were murdered by paramilitaries. Punishment killings for drug dealing.' Conor's voice was sharp.

Ed's eyes flared. 'You don't think it's easy to copy their methods?'

Ed could feel his heart rate increasing. He needed to stay calm. Lay it out piece by piece. He looked at Jamie. She was the one who mattered most.

'They were murdered because of what they knew. They were whistleblowers.' He took a steadying breath. 'My parents…' He hesitated, struggling to say the words. He tried again.

'Paul Arthur Tole had my parents killed.'

The words he'd never spoken aloud to anyone were finally out of his mouth.

He could see the doubt in Jamie's eyes. But not surprise. Not shock.

'The head of Tole Pharmaceuticals?' Conor said. 'That's impossible. I can't believe it.'

Ed watched Conor but ignored his words.

'And there have been many more deaths. More murders ordered by Tole.'

Conor held his eye for a long moment. 'Were they the red crosses on your board?'

He met Conor's challenging stare and nodded.

'Do you have any proof of this?'

'I do. And proof of my own death sentence.'

Ed stood and moved to his computer. Brought over the laptop and sat back down. He searched and tapped on a folder of audio files.

'I'll play the shortened version.' He glanced between Jamie and Conor as he hit play.

Mr Tole.

Yes, Keller.

Regarding Sean O'Neill. Our suspicions were correct. He is still alive. What do you want me to do, Mr Tole?

Find and kill Sean O'Neill.

The words reverberated around the room. Bounced off the walls like bullets ricocheting. Two different voices. Both men revealed.

He looked at Jamie first. She was shell-shocked. Hearing the proof. The voice from news interviews. The hero of the moment. The acclaimed. The fêted. Paul Arthur Tole.

If it was possible, Conor looked even more shocked than Jamie. His face tense, body rigid, focusing on every word. Words Ed himself had only heard yesterday, courtesy of his continued hacking and tracking of Tole's network.

'Who is Keller?' Conor said.

'Michael Keller.' Ed clicked and turned the computer towards him, showing a face on screen. 'He's Tole's fixer. He deals with all the dirty work. He controls a large part of Dublin's underworld. He's ruthless … It was his men at the port.'

Conor paled and Ed saw his jaw clench. Realising what a close call they'd had in Dublin and how costly his mistake could have been.

Ed turned back to Jamie. He could see she was reeling. But the worst was still to come. He pointed to the date on the audio file.

7:46 p.m. Friday 5th April 2024.

Yesterday.

Her eyes met his. And all he could do was watch as she pieced it together.

58

Jamie stared at the screen. Felt the shock come in waves. She registered the time and the date in slow motion. Her brain barely willing to acknowledge it.

'That was … after I called George … telling him I'd seen you. He must have called someone. To tell them.' She turned to Conor. 'I told you George was involved in this.'

'No.' Ed grasped her hands. 'George would never betray us.'

'But—'

'No.' Ed cut across her. 'George has been helping me.'

'Then how did—'

'Chief Inspector Denis O'Malley was sent over to work with George. He was there to keep an eye on both of you.'

'How do you know about O'Malley?' Jamie said.

'George went to our house in Reed Close and saw him there.'

'You're sure George didn't send the men?'

'I'm sure.'

She breathed in. She had been wrong. Conor right. It was a relief. One less betrayal.

'He saw Dad too…' Ed carried on. 'Keller's men have him.'

Jamie felt her stomach cramp, pain cutting into her chest. She saw the anguish in her husband's eyes. 'I know. I … I saw them take him … I couldn't stop them.' Her mind flashed to their father, weak and vulnerable, rough hands on him. And that crushing feeling of guilt swept over her. She pushed away the memories. 'I think they were hacking my phone because—'

'They would have been.' Ed said. 'You couldn't have known.' His hands continued to exert gentle pressure on hers.

His words and touch didn't help. Overwhelmed by guilt and regret, she bowed her head.

'I knew I shouldn't have come. I knew it was selfish. Now they've found you. And it's all because of—'

'No.' He put his hand under her chin and lifted her head up. Looking into her eyes.

'Yes,' she said. Defiant. Shaking off his hands. 'I brought them here. It's my fault. You're in danger because I—'

'No!' Ed's angry voice hit the walls of the bunker. 'None of this is because of you. It's all because of him. Because of Tole.'

Jamie could feel her heart beating faster. She glanced across at Conor. His face was as tense as she'd ever seen. She heard those terrible words echoing inside her head. *Find. Kill.* It didn't matter what Ed said, this was down to her. She had brought these men to his door. Men who wanted to kill him.

'Why is this all happening?' she said. 'Why did Tole have your parents killed? And why does he want to kill you?'

She waited as Ed got himself back under control.

'You saw the DVD in the black package?'

She nodded.

'It has all my mother's notes and research on it. And a folder of digital files taken by my father from behind the firewall at Tole Pharmaceuticals. He retrieved them two weeks before my parents were murdered. There's information on a cover-up which my parents were investigating.'

She paused, taking this in. 'What—'

But Ed didn't wait for her question. 'I know who Paul Arthur Tole really is, Jamie. The man behind his carefully constructed façade. I know the people he controls and the influence he has. He killed my parents for what they found out and that's why he can't allow me to live. He thinks I may know some of his secrets.'

'What secrets?' Conor's voice was swift and sharp.

She watched Ed take in a deep breath. And she knew this was the moment. The moment she had been waiting for. She was finally going to hear why her husband had betrayed her.

59

Jamie waited.

'Back in 2005,' Ed finally began, 'there was a woman called Zoe Bridges who worked at Tole Pharmaceuticals. She was the company's archivist. She found a document she should never have seen. Zoe was digitising all the old research and clinical trials when she came across a file in an archive box, misplaced, tucked inside other papers. It had printed words in red stamped across it. "Top Secret. To Be Destroyed."

'What was in the document?' Conor said.

'It had details of secret drug trials undertaken by Tole Pharmaceuticals. They took place in Africa, across several locations in Nigeria. The participants were poor people. Powerless people. And there were no official records of the trials. My parents uncovered some of what happened. I've spent years trying to uncover the rest.'

Ed paused before carrying on. 'The doctor who co-ordinated the secret trials in Africa is dead, along with his family. The trial participants I've been able to trace and identify have all died in suspicious circumstances. Zoe, the archivist who found the file and shared the information with my parents, died in a hit-and-run accident which was never solved. The secretary, who dealt with the correspondence, is missing. And my parents who investigated it all … well …' He tailed off. 'And that's just the beginning.'

Jamie felt nausea rising in her stomach. This was worse than anything she'd imagined.

'These secret drug trials,' she said. 'What did they find out?'

'I don't know. The digital files my father retrieved are in one of the folders on the DVD. And that folder is encrypted.'

'Can't you decrypt them?' Conor said.

Ed looked across at him. 'I've tried, but it's above my skill set. I've contacted experts across the dark web – white and black hackers – but Tole had military grade encryption even back then. The files will self-delete if anyone attempts to hack them. No one will touch them. It's too much of a risk.'

Ed's eyes came back to hers. 'That's what I was doing two years ago. Before I had to…' He took in another breath. 'Before I had to leave … disappear. I'd made it behind the firewall at Tole Pharmaceuticals several times before, but I hadn't found the encryption key to unlock the files my father downloaded. I knew time was running out and I pushed too hard. Something went wrong on that day. I got out from behind the firewall fast, but not fast enough. Somehow,' he shook his head, 'part of my IP address was exposed. I knew they could trace me, I just didn't know how long it would take them. I thought it would be hours, days at the most. It turns out I had longer. It took them a few months to even spot the breach.'

He was talking fast now. His breaths uneven. The emotion overwhelming him. She felt his hands reach for hers. A tremble in them.

'I had to leave. To protect you. To keep you safe. It was

the only thing I could do … The worst thing I've ever had to do.' His voice cracked. His head bent down unable to meet her eyes.

She stroked his hands. Calming him. It was instinctive. As she did with her patients. But her own mind was racing. Trying to make sense of his words and the story they told.

'What do you mean, time was running out?' Conor said. 'What do you think is in those files?'

Ed pulled himself up. 'The file Zoe found had a name stamped across it. The same name as the files my father downloaded from Tole Pharmaceuticals. It's one of the company's drugs. Something is wrong with it and Tole doesn't want anyone to know about it.'

Jamie felt a chill creeping down her spine. Inch by cold inch. She pressed on her husband's hands. His eyes came back to her.

'What's the name of the drug?' Jamie's voice was just above a whisper.

'That's why it was so urgent. I'd been monitoring it for over a decade. I knew the last phase of the trials was being resumed after the pandemic. The drug was going to thousands of—'

'What's the name of the drug, Ed?' Jamie cut him off, pressing harder on his hands, her voice louder.

'It's the one all over the news. Tolacaine.'

60

Ed had expected shock, but Jamie's face turned ashen. He looked at Conor. Saw his usual steel-like mask had slipped. Shock clear across his face.

And then it was obvious. Conor's improvements during the last two years. The timescale of the latest round of double-blind trials. He looked between them both. 'No.' Ed said. Shaking his head. 'Don't tell me … don't tell me you're on Tolacaine?'

He didn't need an answer.

Ed bent over his computer and clicked up his parents' research file. Pushed the computer towards Jamie. 'Here's one of the documents from the DVD, written by my mother. It's all the information they gathered. I've added some of my own research notes.'

Jamie started to read.

'There's so much here,' she said. Scrolling down. Scanning through the document. I need to read it properly.' She looked back up at him. 'When did these secret trials on Tolacaine happen?'

'Between 1998 and 2004. Over a period of six years.'

She paused. 'And when did Tole Pharmaceuticals say they started work on Tolacaine?'

'From 2005, when my mother was working on the drug discovery team.'

Jamie sank her head back into the computer.

'You said you think there's something wrong with Tolacaine.' Conor said.

Ed turned towards him. 'There has to be.'

'What do you think it is?'

'That's the problem, I don't know.'

'So you haven't found any actual evidence?' Conor said.

'Not yet.'

Conor paused. 'I've been taking it for eighteen months and I've had very few side effects. If there was something wrong with it, I'd know by now.'

'Not necessarily.' Ed focused on Conor. 'It could be something that only shows up with long term use. It could show up in the next generation – think of thalidomide. It could even be something to do with the fact that Tolacaine is now the most addictive painkiller we have.'

Conor was silent.

'I remember reading early on,' Jamie said, 'that there were concerns about how addictive it was.'

He nodded. 'They had to pause the trials because of legal challenges. The fear of another highly addictive drug, like fentanyl, entering the marketplace. The side-effects of prolonged opiate use – even at prescribed levels – are stark.' Ed looked at Conor. 'Physical dependency, breathing and cognitive issues. Now we have Tolacaine, an even more addictive drug. What effects will it have long term? We don't know yet. What we do know is that withdrawal occurs within hours of the last dose.'

He saw Jamie look at Conor.

'If Tolacaine is more potent than opiates,' Ed continued,

'how will it affect the neural pathways of the brain? The respiratory system? And what cognitive effects will it have longterm? What about its effect on an aging brain?'

'What are you thinking?' Jamie said. 'Some kind of dementia? Mental illness?'

Ed shrugged. 'I don't know. That's the problem. We don't know. What we do know are the positives. The trial data shows Tolacaine has real, measurable benefits.'

'The best drug in a generation for chronic pain.' Jamie added quietly.

'That's the strapline.' Ed said. 'And it's true.'

'But if there was so much concern about it, and there were legal challenges, why did the trials go ahead?' Conor said.

'Because the *actual* benefits of Tolacaine outweighed any *possible* issues. And Tole pressed hard. After a while, many of those concerned parties went quiet. Tole is an influential man. This was business for him. He was unrelenting. Ruthless. Not out of compassion for those in pain and suffering, but because Tolacaine is going to make him billions. This drug was always coming to market. Even if something was wrong with it.'

Ed finally took a breath in. His chest tight. He couldn't hide the vitriol in every word he spoke.

He swallowed, his throat dry, watching Jamie and Conor as they absorbed his words in silence. He could see their minds working. And he waited for them to catch up.

It was Jamie who challenged him first.

61

'But…,' Jamie shook her head. 'If Tole knows something is wrong with Tolacaine, he also knows it will be uncovered in time. Why would he push forward—'

'That's what I thought at first,' Ed interrupted. 'But just think about it. Look at the tobacco industry. As early as the 1940s and 50s, companies already knew the link between smoking and lung cancer. They kept it secret. Kept producing tobacco. And kept denying there were any issues with it. By then, people were addicted to it. Even later, when the evidence mounted that it could kill them, people were hooked. Some quit, others didn't want to stop, some couldn't stop. In spite of the warnings, many are willing to gamble with their future. They'd prefer to enjoy life now rather than look ahead. It's part of the human condition: a willingness to sacrifice the future for present pleasures. Tole is playing into that human weakness.'

He looked across at Conor. 'The improvement you've had from Tolacaine, it's … remarkable. Much more than I knew was possible, than any of the data has shown. Is all your progress down to it?'

Conor nodded.

'That's incredible … But here's my question to you. If *you* found out something was wrong with Tolacaine, would you give it up now you've had the benefits?'

'Nothing would stop me taking it.' Conor's reply was instant, looking Ed straight in the eye.

Ed glanced at Jamie. Her eyes were fixed on Conor.

'Not even if something is wrong with it?' she said.

'You know where I was, Jay. For me, it was a living death. No. Worse. A living hell. Nothing anyone says would make me choose to go back to that. If I get a few better years, whatever's coming later doesn't matter to me.'

Jamie turned away from Conor's gaze, looking back at Ed.

'You think Paul Arthur Tole, knowing something is wrong with Tolacaine, is planning to get people reliant on it, have them see and feel the benefits, make his money, and worry about the backlash later?' she said.

'I do. And I don't even think Tole will worry about any backlash. As long as there's no evidence he knew anything was wrong. That's the crucial thing. Without any proof that he knew there was a problem with Tolacaine, he'll shake off any challenges. And he'll tie up the courts for years. That's why he's hunted me for so long. His fear over what I might know and be able to reveal.'

'But don't—'

'Think of the litigation history with tobacco.' Ed kept going, drowning out Jamie's words. 'The denials. The delays. Cases drowning in legal battles. It took decades just to get warnings on cigarette packaging in the UK. And while Tolacaine is physically addictive, it will reduce debilitating, life-limiting pain and give people some of their life back. And don't forget, millions of people across the world live with some kind of long-term pain. From minor to severe and disabling. Think of the positive effects on healthcare, welfare and the economy. Tolacaine will help get people off benefits and back into work. It'll save the economies of the world hundreds of billions every year. If people actually experience those benefits, no one's going to want to stop taking it…'

Conor was nodding in agreement.

'…and there would be uproar if doctors stop prescribing it. People will deny it's even a problem rather than have to stop it. And governments won't want those people back on welfare.' Ed finished.

'But there's nothing in the data showing any problems.' Jamie said. 'I've read all the reports.'

'I know, so have I. And you're right, there aren't any issues reported.'

'Could they be falsifying the trials? Hiding what's wrong?' Conor said.

'It's been done before. The data can be manipulated. But I haven't found any evidence of that from the initial trials right through to the blind trials. The data looks sound. The one thing I do know is that no one participating in these current Tolacaine trials has been on the drug for longer than three years.'

Another silence hit the bunker.

Ed looked between them. 'And remember, Tole Pharmaceuticals completed six years of trials on Tolacaine in Africa. And kept them secret. What did they find out? Was there an issue with longer term use? What else could it be? Why would everyone who knew about the trials be dead or missing? Why would the research scientists, like my mother, who thought they were working on a new drug, not know there had been years of unmonitored trials on it? Why would a Pharma company conduct trials on poor, powerless people, and then dispose of them? There has to be something wrong with Tolacaine. It's the only explanation.'

Ed looked at Conor. He'd never seen him this shaken. He

turned to Jamie. She was deep in thought. Then her eyes came up to his.

'Is anyone else still alive who knows about these secret trials?'

'There's us.' And he felt the weight again. People in danger because of him. 'There's Tole. Keller must know. And there is one other person I know of. I've searched for him for years. He's been impossible to trace. But I finally had a breakthrough and found him a few months ago.'

'Who is he?' Conor said.

'He's mentioned only as 'the Professor' in the document Zoe found and elsewhere. I believe he's been in control of the Tolacaine trials from the very beginning. He must be a powerful man. Tole's most important ally. Tole has gone to great lengths to cover up their connection. His name is Professor Jeremy Wyndham. If anyone has answers, it has to be him.'

'Where is he?' Conor said.

'He lives ten minutes from Tole. Overlooking Killiney Bay in Dublin.'

'Playground of the rich and famous.'

He nodded.

'We need to go there.' Conor's eyes were intense. Still focused on him. 'We need to make him talk. Tell us what's going on. There are thousands of people on the trials who are already taking Tolacaine. And it's about to go public.'

'I know. That's why it's so urgent. I've been making indirect approaches for months to the Professor. Tried several different routes, under different guises, but it's been impossible to make contact without giving myself away. But now Tole knows I'm alive, I don't need to hide. I can go direct to the Professor. Meet him face to face.'

'We all need to go,' Conor said.

Ed hesitated. He wasn't at all sure that was a good idea.

And he wondered how it was even possible in Conor's current condition. But as he took in Conor's face, he couldn't refuse. Ed had never seen him this agitated. After all, he was already dependent on Tolacaine. He had a right to know what was going on and what he might be facing. His eyes met Jamie's. He wasn't letting her out of his sight. It was an easy decision. Somehow, they'd all go together.

Ed checked his watch. It was gone seven in the evening. It felt much later. He suddenly felt exhausted. His brain a whirlpool, his body aching and tired. But he dragged himself onto his feet. There was still work to do.

He moved across to the steel cabinet, grabbed phones and another laptop and powered them up. He went to sit back down, this time between Conor and Jamie.

He looked at Conor. 'We just have to get out of here, and get in front of the Professor, without Keller and his men tracking us.'

'Let's start planning.' Conor said, reaching out his hand.

Ed handed him the laptop. And he saw the nod of Conor's head. It was intangible and yet he could feel it. Things had changed between them. He saw something in Conor's eyes. Something he'd never seen before.

Respect.

62

Jamie sat on the floor, the laptop on her knees. The notes from Ed's parents on the screen. Her mind reeling.

Of all the emotions competing inside her mind and heart, the most selfish trumped them all. Relief. Relief that her husband wasn't a drug dealer mixed up with a cartel. Relief that he was the good man she loved.

But next to that, and gaining ground every second, was stone cold terror. The danger her husband was in. The danger she had brought right to his door.

She heard Paul Arthur Tole's chilling words again. *Find and kill Sean O'Neill.* Spoken with ice-cold calmness. Almost matter of fact. As though it was nothing to order the death of someone. His voice so at ease with the order.

Her eyes moved to the time on the laptop. 7:17 p.m. Just twenty-four hours since she'd seen the man walking on the Lough Road. Since she'd known her husband was alive.

She looked to her right. Ed and Conor were talking, exchanging ideas, working together. It was something she'd never seen before. Them as allies.

There's his truth and the real truth. How will we trust anything he says?

Conor's words. Spoken just a few hours ago at the service station. Words which were now history. It was clear, Conor believed every word Ed had said. And so had she. His truth was the real truth. It was written in every beat of his heart, every traumatic word he'd spoken, and every desperate look in his eyes. It was visible, the weight he carried of all he knew. All he'd done and uncovered these two years, and all the ones before. All done alone.

She thought of Tolacaine. If there was something wrong with it and people knew, but kept it hidden, this would be the biggest medical scandal in decades. But she also realised that, if they found out what was wrong with Tolacaine and revealed this to the world, it would have to be taken off the market. All the people it was helping would be back where they started, their hope extinguished, having had a taste of a better life. It was cruelty in the extreme to take that from someone. To take it from Conor. She shuddered at the thought of it. But they couldn't stay quiet. Couldn't be complicit in the coverup. They couldn't watch people walk unknowing into catastrophe.

She bowed her head to the screen. Looked at Ed's mother's typed notes. As she scanned, she saw that they were written in diary form. Ed had inserted extra comments and links throughout the document.

She scrolled to the end and found a long list of names. At the top were Frank & Prudence O'Neill. She clicked on another name. Dr Musa Ibrahim. This opened a message full of notes, photos and newspaper photocopies. She scanned. *Brutal death of respected local doctor and his family during civil unrest in Tocotan.* A photo caught her eye. The doctor with his wife and three smiling young children. The photo she'd seen on the whiteboard.

She scrolled further down the long list. Clicked on Zoe

Bridges. A beautiful, young face appeared alongside newspaper headlines. *Hit and run on the Falls Road.*

She moved to another name. Clara Meath. Clicked to view the newspaper reports. *Missing woman.* Her eyes flashed across the article. *Wife and mother.* Clara's husband was convinced she had come to harm. *She would never leave her family willingly.*

Her head pounded. The words blurring. Her mind went back to Conor. What damage was Tolacaine doing to him? How soon would that damage show itself?

'Jamie?'

The voice cut into her spinning thoughts. She looked up. Ed held out a phone to her.

'We've each got a clean phone. I've put our numbers in just in case we get separated. They're charged but turned off. We won't use them until we're clear of Keller's men.'

She pocketed the phone. Looked between the two of them. 'You have a plan?'

'We have a couple of options,' Conor said.

She closed the laptop.

'OK. Let me hear them.'

63

Paul Arthur Tole sat at the dining table, impatient for the latest report. His wife sat opposite, her afternoon tea barely touched, her red lipstick pristine.

He checked his watch again. 4:05 p.m.

Tole rarely wanted a running commentary on a clean-up, he just needed to know the job was done. But this was different. His life depended on resolving this crisis. Of finding, of killing, Sean O'Neill.

He glanced at the Financial Times to the side of the table. *Share prices skyrocket at Tole Pharmaceuticals.* Tolacaine was doing all that he planned and more. A global success which would continue to soar. His patent on the drug was indefinite. There would be no generics further down the line, as usually happened. No cheaper drugs, with less money for him. He'd made sure that couldn't happen. Tolacaine would make him billions. In a couple of years, he'd have the most successful Pharma company in Europe.

He should be feeling satisfied. The culmination of over two decades of work and strategy. Instead, he felt uneasy. Deep in his gut. Something he'd not experienced since childhood.

The phone rang.

Keller.

He picked up.

'It's not good news, Mr Tole.'

He waited.

'As my men were closing in on the house, it exploded.'

Tole stood from the dining table without glancing at his wife and moved to the hallway.

'Deliberate?'

'Yes. I'm sure. Heat signatures from the initial drone located three people inside the cottage. We presume O'Neill is with Daly and Shaw. But we haven't had eyes on the target yet. It'll be hours before we can search the rubble, but we can't stay here. The emergency services are already on the way. The fire was called in by a local. We're on borrowed time in this location.'

'So you've lost them?' Tole held on to his burning rage, kept his voice even, his hand clenched at his side. Keller was the one person he couldn't afford to alienate.

'We have another drone up but the smoke is affecting visibility and any heat signatures. The surrounding area is woodland and forest. It's good camouflage territory. For the moment,' Keller paused, 'we don't have a precise location on them.'

Tole kept his voice steady and ignored the double speak. He could feel his usual quiet heart begin to pound. 'Any phone activity? Are we getting any information through?'

'Nothing. It's a dead zone. No signals.'

Tole felt another twist in his gut. 'Send in everything you have.'

'That's already underway. There's only so far they can get. I'm confident we'll have them within the next few hours.' Keller paused. 'There is one thing. I think we need to reevaluate the kill order on O'Neill.'

'What?' Tole's voice was sharp.

'After today's events, I think we've underestimated him. I believe we're dealing with someone who is capable of far more than we realised.'

Tole noted the emphasis on 'we' and he waited.

'A kill order alone is insufficient. He'll have an end game in place if something happens to him.'

'How could you know that?'

'This man is a planner. He'd protected his surroundings in a way only an expert could. If he'd wanted to, he could have killed all my men as they got closer to his cottage. We're not just dealing with a man in hiding, someone good at hacking your system on a computer, and gathering information. He's now much more than that. And much more dangerous.'

Tole considered the words. His accelerated heartbeat told him that Keller was right.

'Your assessment?'

'We need to bring him in first. And the others. Ensure we have everything he knows. Everything the others with him know. And any other plans he has put in place. Once we have the information we need, we can finish them all.'

Tole could go along with that. He'd get what he wanted. An image of Sean O'Neill dead on the ground. Maybe he'd even see it happen. It would just be delayed.

'Agreed.' Tole said.

'We're widening our search area. But I need to know, could they be heading anywhere specific?'

Tole took in a breath. There was only one place worth going. One person worth seeing. The only man left alive who knew everything. Who could reveal all of his secrets.

He thought O'Neill had found him. Someone had been reaching out to the Professor over the last few months. He'd had his suspicions, but now he was sure. It had been O'Neill.

'There's one place. One person.' Tole said.

Keller waited.

Tole paused, his razor-sharp mind thinking it through, a smile crossing his features. 'If they go there, we could bring this all to a close.'

For the next few minutes, he filled Keller in on a masterful Plan B and the unique opportunity it afforded to wrap this all up once and for all. To remove the only other living link to the true history of Tolacaine. If successful, Keller would receive a handsome reward. He'd shown himself worthy of Tole's trust.

Tole allowed himself a moment to imagine this victory. Then he issued a final order to Michael Keller.

'End this. Do whatever it takes.'

With those words, he hung up the phone.

64

Jamie walked in silence. Ed up front. Conor next. Her bringing up the rear. The tunnel continued to narrow with its slow incline upwards.

They'd all been quiet this morning. Unease between them. They knew Keller would continue to scan the area for mobile signals. The plan, to walk two miles to a nearby bed and breakfast to use their landline phone and get transport out of here, was not supported by Ed or Conor. The arguments last night had been intense. But Jamie wasn't budging, no matter the persuasive words. She wasn't leaving Conor behind. She wasn't going anywhere without Ed. They were not splitting up.

On waking this morning, Ed had fashioned a brace from the steel framework of the camp-bed. They'd strapped Conor's leg to it and also created a crutch of sorts.

Now, as Jamie walked, she could see Conor's slow progress ahead of her. Hear the muttering discontent and angry words, his body letting him down. His staunch disagreement with the plan of action they'd decided on was having visible and audible repercussions.

Conor's words this morning, 'I'm losing more sensation,'

gave Jamie extra cause for concern about the shrapnel lodged near his spine. She was also worried about his withdrawal from Tolacaine. She knew the dangers. Other than a vile temper, she'd seen no signs yet of fever, shaking, or confusion. But they'd be coming soon and she didn't know where to get the drug from. She pulled her mind back. One step at a time. Getting out of this mine and forest, and to the next location, were problems enough.

Up ahead, Ed held out his hand. They caught up to him and came to a stop beside a motorbike.

His laptop open, Ed checked the area outside the mine. Jamie watched the screen. It was still dark, but the infra-red cameras showed no activity.

Ed glanced up at Conor. 'All quiet.'

With a nod from Conor, Ed unlocked and pulled a steel door towards him. Thick foliage hung down like blankets across the entrance. Ed pushed aside the greenery and created a gap. Conor struggled across the uneven threshold and followed Ed outside. Their head torches lit up the surrounding space.

Jamie stepped through the open doorway and saw a dark mass of forest ahead. A small rocky area with boulders was within feet of the exit and Conor had moved towards it, propping himself up. The relief on his face was visible.

Jamie glanced around. A hint of light was breaking through ahead of the dawn. And the moon, visible like an orb of white brilliance, offered them some extra light.

She turned to see Ed pushing back the door, locking it, and ensuring the hanging branches covered the entrance.

Conor beckoned them both towards him. 'You need to rethink this plan.'

Jamie went to speak but he held up his hand.

'Eddie. Take the motorbike and go with Jamie. Get safe ... I have the route to the house … I'll take my time. I can make it .... if I get in trouble ... I'll come back here to the mine.' His words inspired no confidence. His voice breathless from his battle through the tunnel.

Jamie had never seen Conor plead. But she saw it now. Before Ed could answer, she took Conor's hands. 'I'm not leaving you.'

His pleading eyes changed. Conor shook her hands off him. 'I'm not talking to you, Jamie. I'm talking to Ed.' He looked away from her. 'Do what's right, Eddie. You know I'm right.'

Jamie turned to her husband. He'd have to physically drag her away to stop her from staying with Conor. She could see he knew that.

'I think Jamie's right.' Ed said. 'We need to stick together. If you stumble, fall ... it's difficult terrain until we get to the road.'

'You're making a big mistake...' Conor fixed her with a harsh glare, pausing for another deep breath. 'You're both risking everything for me. And I don't want it.'

She swallowed. She had never seen Conor this angry with her.

Silence lay between them. A clash of wills. Both staring each other down.

Ed's voice cut through their silent standoff.

'We need to get moving.' He stepped forward. Went to Conor's left side and held out his arm. But Conor ignored him. He pushed up from the rocks and began his slow movement forward into the heart of the dark forest. In silence.

65

Ed had seen nothing like this before. Jamie and Conor at odds. More like daggers drawn. He knew Conor was right, but he wouldn't side with him against Jamie. He knew there was no point. She wouldn't change her mind. He wouldn't win that argument.

His eyes continued to scan around and ahead of them. There was safety in the depths of the forest. Good cover. But the ground was treacherous.

Conor had begun under his own steam. Limping badly, using his crutch, his braced leg holding. But he was now leaning heavily on him. With each step, Ed was bearing more of Conor's weight.

He glanced to his right. To Jamie. Her eyes were fixed ahead. Her look unyielding.

A few minutes on, and little progress had been made. Conor was panting. Now Ed believed Jamie had been right. Conor would never have made this route on his own.

Every minute that passed, the trees of the forest became more visible, and their surroundings came to life. Birdsong echoed between the trees. Flitting creatures crossed their path. So many delicate, beautiful sounds emerged around them.

Then Ed heard another sound. Unfamiliar noises echoing. Alien to the forest.

He stopped. Turned to Conor. And saw the recognition.

Dogs.

Barking in the distance.

He spun around to locate the sound.

'Which direction?' he said to Conor.

Conor pointed. It was as he thought. The sounds were coming from the east. There was time. They were moving west.

'How far off are they?' he looked again at Conor.

'Impossible to tell in this terrain … sound carries.' Conor took a breath. 'Could be one mile, could be three.'

Ed needed to think fast. With Conor's injury, their pace was slow. They could go back to the tunnel. He could get the bike and leave with Jamie. Leave Conor behind in the mine. But the dogs would catch their scent now. Keller may have something of his from the cottage. Maybe even have things belonging to Jamie. Conor would be a sitting duck in the tunnel. Captured. Like his own father. Someone else Tole could use against him. Someone else to threaten him with.

'Now will you go?' Conor was gripping his arm. Turning him around. Eyes desperate. 'Take her Eddie. Go back … Get the bike. Leave me.' He paused to get his breath. 'They don't want me.'

Ed turned around in the space. Felt a spinning in his head. As though all the trees in the forest were voices competing inside his mind.

He gripped Conor under the arm. Waved to Jamie to take the other side.

'We need to move faster.'

66

Ed felt more urgency in their movements now as they pressed forward. One of them on each side of Conor. The strain for all three intense. The distant barking pushing them on. Piercing noises from excited animals moving faster than they could.

'We're here.' Ed saw the road coming into view. 'It'll be easier now.'

His words were met with stony silence.

They stepped onto the single tarmac road, the dawning light making the path ahead clearer.

They travelled along the left side of the road, trying to gain a rhythm and some momentum. Conor stumbled, almost taking them both down. A muffled cry of pain seared through him. They righted themselves and kept moving forwards.

The minutes felt long. The black, even tarmac not helping in the way Ed had hoped. Conor was tiring more with each agonising step. Sweat pouring down his forehead, guttural sounds he could not hide each time his feet hit the road.

'We're … too … exposed.' Conor's voice came through heaving breaths.

Ed knew that. Knew Conor was right. His eyes went to the sky. If the dogs were out, the drones would follow.

He looked at Jamie. She still had not spoken. Her body tense with effort. Helping this six-foot man stay on his feet.

Conor suddenly stopped in his tracks. Ed almost fell forwards.

Then he heard it. A car engine.

Jamie pointed to the side of the road, to a low-lying dry-stone wall. She was already changing angle, pulling them towards it, dragging them with her across the sodden grass verge. As she reached the wall, Jamie jumped behind it, hands out to help Conor. But Conor wasn't moving. Ed didn't see how he could possibly mount the wall, but Jamie was tugging at him. Conor stayed firm, shook off her hand and leaned on the wall. His eyes fixed on Ed.

'Come on,' Jamie's voice was urgent.

He scanned Conor's eyes and understood immediately. It was a risk. But a calculated risk. Conor couldn't make another mile and a half in his state. This was the better of the options on the table. Ed started to move back towards the road.

'Ed. Ed, what are you doing?' Jamie called in a hushed voice.

He turned. 'We need that car, Jamie.'

'Ed, get back here.'

But he kept walking. He would not be torn between them anymore. He'd do what he thought was best for them all.

The noise of the car was closer now and Ed moved into the centre of the road. As the car rounded the long bend, he held up his hands to flag it down.

The headlights were still on in the half-light. The car pulled to a cautious stop. Then the lights changed. The full beam blinding him. His arm went up towards his eyes. Through the gap, he saw two car doors opening. He felt the beat in his chest increase.

Caught in the full beam of bright headlights, he raised both of his arms above his head.

67

Jamie saw two men step out from the car. Both in combat gear. Both with guns drawn. And she watched as Ed raised his arms in the air.

Her heart pounded. Hiding behind the wall, with Conor as a shield, she could see it all. But she already knew what she'd see as the car pulled to a stop. How could Ed be this reckless and put himself in the firing line? After all they'd done to get here. It was always going to be Keller's men in that car. And he'd sided with Conor against her. She'd seen that unspoken decision crossing between them. Her hands shook with anger. With fear.

Her eyes darted around from her hiding place. Blinding headlights lit the scene. The two men moving forward. One weapon trained on Ed. One now turned towards Conor who also had his arms raised.

She ducked back down. The gunmen were splitting off from each other. Each moving towards their prey. Twenty feet out.

'Where's Shaw?' One man shouted.

Jamie didn't hear a reply. She had already started moving

to the right. Crawling on hands and knees. The wall as her cover.

Twenty feet on, she stopped. Peered over the wall.

One gunman was now twelve feet from Ed. Almost within touching distance. The other was fifteen feet from Conor.

After all her husband's fight and struggle. Years of sacrifice and anguish. Had it really come to this? Killed on a back country road. Lost to her again. All because of her. Because she'd led the men here. And she'd insisted they all stay together. This was her fault.

Find and kill Sean O'Neill.

Jamie heard the words pounding in her head. She would not let that happen. Could not let it happen. She pulled out her Glock. Steadied her shaking arm and raised herself up above the wall.

'I'm here,' she called out. Both men looked up. The man with Conor in his sights moved his gun first. Towards her. He wasn't fast enough. She fired. Twice. The sound enormous in the silence. Two shots to the chest. He dropped onto his back.

In her peripheral vision, she saw the man closer to Ed, his face now turning towards her. She had her weapon raised, knew Conor's hand would be moving to his belt, but Ed was already stepping forwards, the distraction all he needed. In one explosive movement he kicked the man's legs from under him. As the man landed heavily on his back, Ed dealt him a savage blow to the side of his head, and the man lay still.

Ed opened his backpack, grabbed ties and bound the unconscious man's hands and legs. As he was searching the man's pockets, Jamie jumped the wall and ran to the man she had felled and kicked away the gun. Keller's man was clutching his chest. Gasping for air. Winded and in pain.

She looked up and Ed was beside her. He bent over the

helpless man on the ground. Searched him. Pulled a phone and walkie talkie from his pocket. Using more ties, he bound the man's wrists and ankles.

He glanced back up at Jamie.

'How did you know he was wearing body armour?'

Jamie looked down at the man. The man sent to kill her husband. She looked back up at Ed.

'I didn't.'

As Ed's eyes held hers, the walkie talkie crackled into life.

'Team three. Status. We have a report of two gunshots. Repeat two gunshots. Over.'

Jamie pulled the walkie talkie from Ed's hands. Knelt down. Held it to the man's lips. Put the gun to his temple. 'Tell them it's all quiet. False alarm.' The man didn't respond. She pushed the gun harder against his head. 'Tell them.'

'This is Team three. All quiet. False alarm. Travelling west on Miller Road. Over.'

'Stay vigilant. Out.'

Jamie turned around. A limping Conor was struggling to come towards them. She stepped back to help him.

'We need to take them with us.' Conor gave his assessment as he viewed the scene. One man down on the tarmac. The other on the grass verge. Both men disabled. Both now a problem.

Jamie and Ed dragged the men to the boot and heaved them inside. It took all their strength. The conscious man struggled but knew it was futile. His eyes empty. Believing he knew his fate, as the boot slammed closed.

Jamie and Ed both moved to get into the car. Conor was already in the driving seat. The car revving. Ed jumped in the passenger seat, Jamie jumped in behind him.

Conor began to turn the car around. Jamie could see he'd

loosened the brace, allowing his knee to bend the small amount it could. She heard a gasp as his foot released the clutch and the car accelerated forward.

68

Jamie didn't know how Conor was driving. The agony of his leg as it bent, pushing onto the pedals, and the sounds of pain he could not disguise.

'I'm taking you back to the forest path. When I get there, you get out and go back to the mine for the motorbike.'

Conor was shouting instructions as Ed sat tense in the passenger seat, looking behind at her.

'The drones must be coming. You need to run fast.'

More directions from Conor. He'd taken charge. Taken over. And this time, with him behind the wheel, neither she nor Ed could stop him.

The car screeched to a stop. Ed was out of the car and running as Jamie pulled open her door and jumped out. She moved around the car, to lean into the driver's window to speak to Conor, but the car revved, and he was gone. Streaking off into the distance.

She felt something inside her break. Detach itself as she watched him drive away. Injured. Alone. Angry with her. But doing what he'd wanted to do all along. Saving her. And saving Ed.

She felt Ed pulling on her arm. She snapped into action.

Moved fast, keeping his pace. Twigs cracking beneath their feet as they ran through the forest. The barking dogs getting nearer and louder. The sounds pushing them to run harder.

It took less than two minutes at speed and Ed was at the mine entrance, dragging back the branches across the door and pulling leathers from the pegs on the wall.

She looked behind her. The dogs sounded much closer.

Ed passed her the leather jacket and a helmet. He pulled on trousers and a second helmet. Wheeled the motorbike out, put it on its stand, then helped Jamie cover the entrance to the mine.

Ed took the bike off its stand, jumped on and turned the key which was already sitting in the ignition. The engine came to life. He reached out to her and she climbed on behind him.

Clinging onto his waist, her head leaning on his back, face to the side, he revved. And then they were riding. Jolting on the uneven terrain.

Moving away from the dogs.

Away from the men hunting them.

Away from Conor.

69

Ed felt Jamie's soft, even breaths rippling onto his bare chest. His eyes were wide open, tracing every line on the ceiling in the run-down bed and breakfast.

The journey across Ireland had felt interminable. They'd stopped only for fuel and rest breaks – avoiding watching cameras. Five hours later, their bodies aching, sore and frozen to the bone, they'd arrived in the valley of Glencullen, North of the Wicklow mountains. Twenty minutes away from their final destination. Twenty minutes away from the Professor.

Ed stretched his stiff back. Jamie stirred beside him but did not wake.

He thought of Conor and his latest message. *I'm safe. Holed up in a hotel.* He'd seen the look in Jamie's eyes when he'd told her. The relief. Then sadness. Conor had not called her. Ed had caused a breach in that relationship, along with everything else he'd done to her. It made him think of George, his most loyal friend. He hoped he was safe with his family. He wanted to contact him. Talk to him. But right now, it was too much of a risk.

He closed his eyes. Longing for sleep. But sleep was

impossible. His mind fixed on the Professor. Things were moving fast. Too fast. It's when mistakes were made.

This visit was riskier than anything he had previously planned. It was a dangerous move. If the Professor was as powerful as Ed believed him to be, he would be well protected. He may not even get close to him. But he knew he had to try. He could only run so far, and for so long, exposed and out in the open. And it was harder to run now he wasn't alone.

He listened to Jamie's breathing. Breathed in step with her. It calmed him. He touched the fine strands of brown hair lying across his chest. The lamplight highlighting the auburn undertones. It was as though they'd never been apart. Those two years had vanished the moment he'd held her in his arms yesterday. But he felt an ache deep in his chest. Then fear in his stomach. Fear of this new plan. Fear that he would not make it back to her.

He had everything in place if something should happen to him. Things he had set in motion long ago. But there was more he needed to do. Things he needed to say.

Jamie stirred. This time, she pulled her head back. Stretched. He slid down the bed and turned towards her. Pushing the strands of hair from her face. Tucking them behind her ear. Face to face, he watched her.

She rubbed her eyes. Put a hand to his cheek. 'Did you get any sleep?'

'Not much.'

His fingers grazed across her lips. He kissed her gently. Amidst all the madness, it was a perfect moment. He should stay in it. Let his thoughts be. His conscience rest. Deal with it all later. He'd already filled in so much about his past in quiet tones as they lay in the bunker together. And since arriving in this room over eight hours ago. But that was all factual, practical information. He hadn't said the things he desperately wanted to say. The things he needed Jamie to know. And now he couldn't stop himself. There may be no later. He had to speak these words aloud.

'I'm sorry,' he whispered. Stroking his fingers across her cheek. 'So sorry. For all of this.'

Her fingers came to his lips. To shush his words. Touching his now bare cheeks, the beard already a distant memory.

He took the hand away. Kissed her fingers. The words were burning inside him. Had been building for years. He couldn't wait any longer.

'I need you to know some things…'

She looked wary. 'We don't need to talk about anything right now.'

'I need to. I need to talk about it.'

She paused. 'OK.'

'After we met, I want you to know that I stopped the research. Put away the files for four years. I couldn't believe I could be so lucky. To have someone. To have you. It was more than I ever expected. I fought so hard. Fought so hard to put it all behind me and do what my mother said. To be happy with you. But it was like…' He stopped and searched for the words, looking away from her. 'Like I was … betraying my parents. Giving up on them. Making their lives, their deaths, meaningless. It felt like I had no choice. Something was driving me from the inside. I sacrificed us because of it. And that day, Jamie. That day…'

He looked back into her eyes. She went to speak, but he stopped her.

'Please … let me…' He faltered again.

His eyes locked with hers.

'Once I made the error behind the firewall, I thought they'd find the breach within hours, days at the most. I knew I had to leave fast. Leave you.'

‘You could have told me. Why didn’t you just come to me? Tell me. Be honest. All those years. You didn’t trust me.’

‘It was never about that. Never about not trusting you. I know you think I should have told you, but I couldn’t risk anything happening to you. Everything I did, I did to protect you.’

‘And to protect yourself.’

The words cut him. Halted him. But she was right. And he saw something change in her eyes.

‘You knew that morning, didn’t you?’ she said and paused. ‘I remember it so vividly. Have lived that day a thousand times. I got up early, to do some work, and you came to me in the office.’

He held her eyes. He remembered every second just as vividly. The last moments he would ever see her, hold her, again. How it had taken everything he had not to tell her the truth. Taken every piece of love in his heart to leave her behind, knowing she would be safer. He’d gone to retrieve the package from the loft, but Jamie was sitting at the desk. He’d had no choice, he had to leave it behind.

‘You knew you weren’t coming back,’ she carried on. ‘You had it all planned out with George and Sheena, when you kissed me goodbye.’

A statement. Not a question.

Ed tried to hold her eyes but couldn’t. He looked away. He shouldn’t have begun this conversation. Finally, he looked back at her. To face it. To face her. Those deep blue eyes looking back at him. Still soft, but there was something else there he couldn’t place.

‘Yes,’ he spoke quietly. ‘I had it all planned out when I said goodbye.’

He watched her take in the words.

‘I…,’ she paused. ‘I always thought I could read you … that I knew you.’

'You do know me.'

He grasped her hand. Crushing the fingers.

'I didn't know about any of it. For all those years. I had no idea what you went through. What you were going through. And no idea what you were doing.' She took a breath in. 'Did Dad know?'

'No.' He shook his head vigorously. 'No. No. Of course not. He didn't know anything. Neither did Mum. They didn't know who I was.' He watched her take in the words. They seemed to help her. He waited for her to speak.

'The problem is … I didn't see it. Any of it. Your … deception … How can I ever trust my judgement again?'

'I'm so sorry. So sorry. I was wrong. I know that now. The choices I made. If I could go back…' He spoke fast and bowed his head, unable to meet her gaze.

Silence sat between them.

He felt her hand still touching his and looked back at her, trying to find the right words. 'Do you think … Can you believe in me again? In us?'

She hesitated. 'You mean take a leap of faith?'

'It's how we began, isn't it?'

Her blue eyes held his. She nodded slowly. 'But it's different now. You've shown me what you're capable of.'

A puncture wound to his heart. But she was right. Her words were fair and not unjustified. And the fear spread. Not just in his stomach but permeating his body. After all this, was he going to lose her all over again?

'Do you think you can ever forgive—'

She waved her hand. 'It's not about forgiveness. I've already forgiven you. It's not about love. I love you.' Her hand reached up to his face. 'And I understand all of it. In my mind.' She tapped her head. 'I know why you had to search, to find out what happened to your parents. I get all of that. I would have done the same. I couldn't have let it rest. But that doesn't change what you did. All without me knowing. Looking into my eyes every day and lying to me. I didn't have a clue. So how can I ever believe in you again? Believe you're being true to me? Believe that what we have is real? How can I trust you? I wonder…' She paused. Struggling to get the words out. 'I wonder if … however powerful our love is, if it's enough.'

There was no anger in her voice. No malice. It was worse. Aching sadness.

'I know I've broken things between us. We've lost something and that's all on me,' he said.

She didn't reply.

'I know we can't go back to how it was. And there's nothing I can do to erase it. To make it right. I know that. I can only say that I'll never lie to you again. And never let anything, or anyone, come between us again.'

He waited. Eyes locked with hers. She looked away. His heart dropped. Then she turned back to him.

'There's no way back if I find out you're lying to me again, Ed.'

'I know,' he said quietly. 'I won't.'

She was silent.

He had to fill the space.

'I know it'll take time. I'll spend the rest of my life proving you can trust me again.'

She shook her head. 'I don't want that. I don't want you living to prove your love to me. And anyway, you can't prove it because I'll still never know. I didn't see it before when I trusted you. This is about me. I have to believe it. Believe in you. I have to decide to trust you again. I have to take that risk.'

'Can you?' He held his breath. Eyes flickering across her face.

She put her hand up and ran her fingers over his cheek.

He could see that beautiful mind working. But for once, he wasn't at all sure what was going on inside it.

The pause was long.

She still hadn't answered when the alert sounded on both of their phones at 8:30 p.m.

70

Jamie checked her watch. It was 8:58 p.m. and already dark as Ed pulled the bike to a stop on the Knock-Na-Cree Road, behind Conor's black BMW. It was a tranquil residential area, half a mile from the Professor's house. Within touching distance of Tole's partner in crime.

Conor was out of his car before Ed turned off the engine. He was limping forward. Crutches in both hands. Limping into Jamie's outstretched arms. They didn't speak of earlier. No words were needed. All that had gone before was forgotten. Jamie pulled back, looking into his eyes.

'How's your back and knee? How's the pain? Did you manage to—'

'I did, finally,' he grimaced. 'I contacted a friend who's in Dublin. He's on the trial. He gave me a few tablets to tide me over. They're starting to kick in. I'll sort out a new prescription in the week.'

Relief flooded through her. Seeing his face no longer drawn with pain. And more than that, the look in his eyes as they settled on her. What was always there between them was back.

'And I got an automatic car,' he looked back towards the BMW.

She followed his gaze. 'What happened to the men in the boot?'

He paused. 'They won't be a problem. They'll be found in a day or two.'

She looked back at him. 'Alive?'

His eyes narrowed. 'Of course, alive. What did you think I was going to do? It wasn't me who shot one of them.'

She was about to reply when she felt Ed's arm on her back.

'Good to see you, Conor.' Ed stepped forward and put a hand on his shoulder. 'How long have you been here? Have you seen anything?'

'I've been checking the area for two hours. Parked up in different places. No sign of anything out of place.'

Jamie saw Ed exhale. Felt some of his tension release.

'What about the Professor's house?' Ed asked.

'No security gates. Just cameras on the house itself. You can walk straight up the drive.'

'Still no security gates? I thought Google Maps may be outdated.'

'No. It's pretty much as is. But he'll have other security. Less obtrusive. Panic alarms. And CCTV. That's a bigger concern. It's risky. He may even have guards, although I couldn't see any.'

Ed shook his head. 'The CCTV isn't a problem. I can handle that. We'll check for guards. Is he even there? Is he alone?'

Conor shook his head. 'I didn't see anyone, but the lights are all on. We'll have to go in blind.'

Jamie watched the two men glance around. Vigilant. Looking for any hint of danger. She did the same but saw nothing suspicious. No one lurking. But she felt something. The vice was back around her chest. The warning.

She turned a circle. Killiney Bay was now on her right, twinkling lights on the dark water. The distant, lit-up chimney stacks she'd seen on her way into port were shining like beacons. Traffic whizzed by them. So close on this narrow road. She looked to her left to the steep slopes and large houses. Lights were on in many windows. No curtains drawn. She turned again towards the bay. Felt uneasy. An icy chill sitting in her stomach.

Ed touched her arm. She jumped. Put a hand to her chest, the beat inside building.

'We're going now.' He looked closer at her. 'Are you OK?'

She nodded and gave him a forced smile.

As they got on the bike, Conor pulled off and they followed.

Up ahead, Conor signalled left. They did the same and took a sharp turn onto Torca Road. It was claustrophobic. High trees and hedges loomed in the darkness. Grand houses towering. Many set back from the road, on sloped ground, to get the best view of the bay.

Jamie watched the houses pass them by, on either side of the road. Watched as the surroundings altered to trees on a narrowing road. The wooded area now all around them. The darkness only lit by headlights.

Conor slowed. Ed matched him. Jamie recognised the high yellow hedges of the neighbour's house come into view. She knew the Professor's house was next. It was set well back, with a large open frontage. A low wall met the narrow pavement.

They went past the house and parked up. Then walked back to the edge of the property. Tucked behind high hedges,

Ed pulled out his laptop and went to work on the Professor's security system.

'No sign of any guards,' Ed said, looking at Conor. And I've disabled the CCTV.' He paused, clicking a final button on his laptop. 'Are you ready to go?' He glanced between Conor and her.

Both of them nodded in sync.

Then the three of them stepped forward. Walked along the pavement, through the open driveway, and onto grey block-paving. Lights lit the entire area. They bowed their heads. It was blinding. Like being pinned on an airport runway.

Ahead, up a steep incline, was the large two-storey detached house. It had double bay windows and a distinctive wooden railing on the upper floor with a wraparound veranda. Designed for the stunning views over Killiney and Dalkey Bay.

As she took each step, she felt the tension in Ed's body increase. His hand gripping hers so tightly it hurt. As they approached the door, Conor moved out of sight and Ed hit the bell.

The impending opening bars to Beethoven's fifth symphony rang out. The bell sounded hollow inside the tiled hallway. A man walked towards the glass door, visible in the brightly lit corridor.

Jamie had to do a double take, she barely recognised the stooped figure from the photo Ed had shown them. It was impossible to believe he was only sixty-four. She'd have guessed he was in his eighties. He walked slowly. His skin looked sallow, his body thin and haggard.

Lit up by the porch lights, the Professor looked between her and Ed through the thick glass door which separated them and protected him. He pressed a button on the intercom.

'Can I…'

The Professor stopped mid-sentence. His mouth stayed

open and he let go of the button. He moved closer to the glass, peering out. Then he turned the lock, clicked off the safety catch on his door, and pulled it towards him. Stepping forward, he looked directly at Ed and paled.

His hand gripped the door jamb.

'Frank … Frank O'Neill?'

His voice shook as he struggled to push the name out. His bony right hand moving up towards his mouth.

Ed shook his head but didn't speak. Jamie's eyes moved between her husband and the fragile-looking man. The two men were stuck in time, looking at each other. Finally, Ed put out his hand.

'It's Sean, Professor Wyndham … Sean O'Neill.'

The Professor's knees buckled. Ed stepped forward just in time to stop him from falling to the ground.

71

Jamie helped Ed walk the Professor inside. Conor followed them.

They settled him into a large easy chair inside a tastefully furnished living room of yellow and gold. A walnut-coloured baby grand piano sat in the bay window.

The Professor trembled. Unable to catch his breath.

'I need to get you some water. Where…'

The Professor pointed Jamie towards the door. She rushed across the hallway into a cottage-style kitchen. Seconds later, she was kneeling beside the shaking man.

She took his hand. 'I'm a nurse.' She felt for his pulse. It was racing. Shock taking hold. 'Just breathe slowly.'

The Professor took some deep breaths in. Steadying himself. Then took small sips of his drink. He began to calm. Jamie checked his pulse again. It was slower.

'How?' The Professor finally managed to get some words out. Looking up at Ed. Looking at Sean O'Neill. 'Where have you been all these years?'

'It's a long story.'

'I have time.' His voice was soft and raspy.

Ed stood in front of him, looking down. 'I'm not sure that we do. Tole knows I'm alive.'

The Professor took in a breath.

'He's hunting me. Hunting us all.'

If it was possible, the Professor paled even more. His hands began to shake so violently, Jamie took the glass from him.

'He'll … know … you're here.' The Professor struggled to get the words out.

Ed shook his head.

'He will,' the Professor said in a shaky voice. 'His people monitor the CCTV.'

'It's OK.' Ed offered a calming gesture to the petrified man. 'The CCTV won't show anything. I've dealt with it. No-one will see we've arrived. But we can't stay long. It's dangerous for us all. I just need your help. I've come for answers.'

Jamie stepped forward to intervene and slow Ed down, but it was too late. He was blind to the fragility of the man in front of him, so intent on his task.

'What do you know about my parents' death?'

The Professor's head snapped back up. 'I had nothing to do with it. I…' his words faltered. 'I would never be involved in anything like that.'

'But you knew it wasn't true, the story in the newspapers?'

He nodded.

'Then tell me. Why were they murdered?'

He shook his head. 'I can't.' His words were laced with fear. No. Terror.

'What about Zoe? Did you know…'

The Professor started to rock in his chair.

Jamie moved forward. Pressed Ed back. Knelt in front of

the Professor and placed her hands on his thin, trembling ones.

'Professor?'

He didn't raise his head.

'Professor Wyndham?' She said again.

Her soft voice made him look at her. She was horrified. Tears were rolling down his cheeks. The man looked broken. Not at all the powerful ally of Paul Arthur Tole they had expected to see.

'Are you in danger?' Jamie asked gently.

The crumbling man bowed his head again.

Jamie waited.

'My family have been in danger ever since…' he tailed off.

'Ever since what?' Jamie said.

He shook his head.

'Maybe we can help?'

The Professor shook his head again. 'He's too powerful.'

'You mean Tole?'

The man jerked as though hit by a taser.

'Ed…' She quickly corrected herself. 'Sean … has evidence. Documents. He can prove things. But we need you.'

The Professor raised his eyes to hers.

'We need you to tell us what happened. What Tole is hiding.'

The man had calmed a little as Jamie's hands stroked his. Her calmness seeping into him.

'I don't know if I can.'

'Do you want to?' she said.

He didn't reply.

'I know you're afraid, but we have to do something. Our lives depend on it. We need you to help us.'

She saw the battle in him. His eyes glancing up to Ed and back to her.

After what seemed like an eternity, his agonising stopped. With a look of weary defeat, he nodded.

72

'It was Zoe. She found … then it was … Well, she said to Prue … then Frank…'

The Professor was barely coherent. Jamie could feel Ed beside her. Struggling to be patient, to stay quiet. Desperate for answers.

'Professor,' Jamie pressed his fragile hands. 'Take a breath.' She breathed in and out with him. 'Go back to the beginning.'

He breathed in again. Trying to focus.

'Zoe, our archivist, found a file that should have been destroyed with the others… She told Prue. Your mother.' He glanced up at Ed and took more steadying breaths. 'Prue was such a smart woman. We never met face to face. All our correspondence was via email or on the phone. I admired…' His eyes filled with tears again and he looked back down into his lap.

He tried again.

'The file was about secret trials on a drug called,' he hesitated, 'a drug called Tolacaine. Zoe found the file and told your mother about it. Zoe wanted to understand what had happened and why the trials had not been registered. She started making phone calls. Investigating. She didn't realise she was being monitored. Watched. In Belfast, they … they ran her over. Left her dead on the ground … in the pouring rain.'

He was shaking again.

Jamie kept stroking the man's hands.

He swallowed and carried on. His eyes on Sean O'Neill.

'Zoe must have told your parents what she was investigating before she died, because a few months later there was an IT security breach. Your father's login was identified. There was no other reason he would go looking behind the Infinity Firewall. He shouldn't have even known it existed.'

The Professor shook his head.

'When I saw the newspaper report … what he'd done.'

'Who? Tole?' Ed said.

The Professor nodded. 'How did you get away, Sean? I've thought of you. Thought you were dead. Buried in a ditch somewhere. You've haunted me.' His voice broke. 'How did you manage out there alone?'

Now Ed came beside Jamie and knelt down in front of the fragile man.

'I had help. I was loved. And I managed because I never gave up fighting for them. To get to the truth. I need to put it right. Get answers. Get justice for them. And lay them to rest. Will you help me?'

The Professor shook his head. The intensity of Ed's words seemed to remind him of the stakes. The terror was back again. 'You'll never do it. He's untouchable. The people he knows, the power he wields … It's beyond what you can imagine.'

'What power does he hold over you, Professor?' He turned to Jamie's soft voice. 'We can help you.'

She watched the emotions pass across his thin, lined face.

'You can't help me. No-one can.'

'How do you know?'

He didn't answer.

'Let us try,' she said.

Jamie could see in his eyes. He wanted to share the burden he was carrying. The burden that was weighing him down. She pressed his hands again and looked in his eyes. 'Let us try to help you.'

She watched. Then she saw it. A decision.

Professor Wyndham pulled his hands away from hers and pushed himself up onto unsteady feet.

'Let's go to my office. It's safer there.'

73

Ed walked silently beside Conor along the hallway. He needed to adjust his thinking. Swiftly. The Professor was not what he expected at all. He was not a powerful man. But a desperate man. Weak and terrified of Paul Arthur Tole.

Up ahead, Jamie and the Professor pulled to a stop. Rifling in his pocket, the Professor pulled out a key. Then he unlocked and opened the mahogany door.

Ed stepped into the large, square room. The office was warm and welcoming with deep, golden yellow walls. On his left, were books from floor to ceiling. On his right, a large mahogany desk close to a wall covered in family pictures. Comfortable chairs were dotted around the room. Straight opposite were French doors. A small table, next to the floor-length gold velvet curtains, held a game of chess laid out. Mid-game.

As the Professor moved towards his desk, he already looked stronger. His decision to help seemed to give him some momentum and make him stand a little taller. As Ed was looking around, Jamie crossed the space and closed the curtains over the French doors then moved back into the centre of the room.

The Professor sat down. He held out his hand to offer Ed the seat across the desk from him. Ed moved forwards. As he settled into the chair, he glanced across at Jamie standing a few feet to his right. He looked behind at Conor, standing close to the door, his eyes scanning the room. On alert.

As he turned back to look at the Professor, Ed could feel the tension rising in his body. He was so close now. So close to hearing the truth he'd been searching two decades for.

'Is it you who's been reaching out to me over the last few months?' The Professor said.

'Yes. I've been desperate to talk to you.'

'I wondered what was happening. I wasn't allowed to…' the Professor stopped. 'Anyway, that doesn't matter now. You're here. What do you already know?' His eyes lifted up to look at Ed.

'I know about the cover-up. The secret trials in Africa. The deaths in Nigeria and elsewhere. And the people who have gone missing.' Ed leaned forward. 'And I know you were testing Tolacaine in secret for years before you reported its discovery.'

Across from him, the Professor did not move.

Ed kept his eyes fixed on the man. 'When my father breached the firewall the first time, he wasn't detected, and he downloaded a folder of files called *Tolacaine 1998-2004*. I presume it's the data from those early, secret trials?'

The Professor looked surprised. 'It will be.'

'My father wasn't able to access them, and neither can I. They're heavily encrypted. He was trying to get behind the firewall again, to get the encryption key, on the day…' Ed looked down as he felt his voice give way. 'On the day he and my mother were murdered.' He looked back up. Straight at the Professor. 'What was in that trial data, Professor? What is wrong with Tolacaine?'

The Professor's face changed. He looked puzzled.

‘What was wrong with it? What do you mean?’

‘There’s something wrong with it. There must be. Why else would you cover up all those years of trials? Keep that data secret. Test the drug on poor people and then get rid of them. What is it about long-term use that the trials discovered? Dementia? Genetic problems? Physical problems? What is it that you’re covering up?’

Ed could feel his voice rising with each word he spoke, but he couldn’t stop himself.

The Professor stayed silent. He leaned forward. Pulled a handkerchief from his trouser pocket with trembling hands. Wiped the skin above his lips, the sweat beading.

‘I’ll tell you everything, Sean. But … I need to explain first. I need you to understand.’

74

Ed's eyes were locked on Professor Wyndham.

'I was nineteen when I first met … Paul,' he began. 'We were at Cambridge together. I was studying Pharmacology, and he'd received a Classics Scholarship. Only a handful of those were around in the 1980s. He must have really impressed the Admissions Board. We were not alike at all. My parents were wealthy. His were dirt poor. But we gravitated towards each other. "The two Paddys" they used to call us. Can you imagine back then, in the early 80s? The Irish were always the butt of jokes. And there was ongoing hostility because of the IRA. Elite scholars? They were worse than children. And Paul, well, he was a fish out of water. Mercilessly mocked and humiliated by the other students, those entitled snobs, born with silver spoons in their mouths.'

The Professor paused, shaking his head.

'Paul had come from a terrible place. Sometimes I heard his nightmares. His father was a violent drunk, his mother doped up on tranquillisers to cope. I saw his body once. His back and chest were covered in scars from whippings and beatings. He was angry I'd seen them. Shouted that he didn't want pity. But by the time our final year came around, you wouldn't have recognised him. He talked differently. Acted differently. Like a sponge, he'd learned everything he needed to know. From etiquette to business to the stock market. He'd talk to those rich kids for hours about their father's financial investment strategies. "Taking an interest," he called it.' The Professor gave a thin smile. 'By the time Paul left Cambridge, he knew more about finance and investments than most of the business lecturers.'

Ed knew all about Tole's stock market successes. It was all across his Wikipedia profile. How the gifted student had started to make his fortune while studying the Classics at Cambridge. But he hadn't known the rest. He tried to summon sympathy for the young, brutalised boy. In this moment, he couldn't.

'I thought we were friends,' the Professor carried on. Looking off into the distance. His mind in another place and time. 'That we both wanted to change the world. All those late-night debates. Telling him what I was working on. I thought we could make a real impact. I decided to specialise in pain medications because of my mother. She was crippled with Rheumatoid Arthritis. All the money we had back then made little difference.'

The Professor looked almost wistful. Then his eyes changed.

'But I was just a vehicle for Paul's ambition. None of it was real. He was just using me because … well … not to put too fine a point on it … I was a genius. At least that's what the university said.'

Ed heard no pride in the Professor's voice. Just emptiness.

'After we finished at Cambridge, we both came back to Dublin. Paul started his company, Tole Pharmaceuticals. I took up a position at Élan Pharma. We kept in touch. He always showed such a keen interest in my research.' The Professor shook his head. 'I was so naive … Blind … A few years later he headhunted me. He offered to set me up with my own lab researching pain medications. No-one knew we were working together. It was an incredible opportunity. Independence. Everything a young research Pharmacologist could ever wish for. I said yes, of course. I had the most cutting-edge technology and facilities and a small team around me. I worked relentlessly. We discovered several important drugs during those years.' He paused, taking in a deep breath. 'But there was one drug I worked on alone. After ten years in the lab, night and day, I went to Paul with what I'd found. Triumphant. He insisted we do the trials in Africa and keep them secret. I didn't understand why, but he wasn't someone you disagreed with. When the results came in on Tolacaine, they were unbelievable.'

Ed felt his arms tense on the chair. He looked across at Jamie, she was riveted to the Professor's every word.

'But then,' the Professor started shaking his head, 'he said the company wouldn't be releasing Tolacaine. I was stunned. I argued of course. For weeks. But Paul refused to listen. That's when I realised, he had his own agenda. And I'd made a catastrophic error in judgement. I'd trusted the wrong person. Made a deal with the Devil. He owned me. And he owned everything I discovered. That was in the fine print of the contract I'd signed right at the beginning.'

The Professor sank back in his chair.

Ed had followed every word, but the story didn't make sense. Tolacaine *was* being released into the world. Right now.

Ed was about to speak when the Professor looked directly at him. 'Paul changed then. He disbanded my team and started to cover things up. He shredded all the physical trial results from Africa. He must have missed that one document Zoe found.' He stopped again, struggling to go on. 'Clara, his secretary went missing. Then there was Zoe and your parents.' He glanced up at Ed. 'Later I found out that he'd traced some of the trial participants in Nigeria and … had them killed… even Doctor Ibrahim who coordinated the trials. And his family.' The Professor's voice shook. He looked down at his hands, picking at his pale fingers. His distress clear to see.

Everything Ed had discovered was true. The Professor was confirming it.

'But why,' Ed said. 'Why did Tole cover up those trials in Africa? And why did he have my parents, and all those people killed?' Ed leaned forward. 'You have to tell me everything. Because you know Tole *has* released Tolacaine. And you know it's about to go public. You have to tell me what's wrong with it.'

The Professor now looked directly at Ed. Shaking his head. 'You don't understand, Sean. That was the problem. There was nothing wrong with Tolacaine. Nothing wrong with it at all. Quite the reverse.'

Ed waved his hand impatiently. 'But that doesn't make any sense. Why else would everyone connected with those trials be dead or missing?'

The Professor leaned forward. Hands clasped on the desk. The fear back in his eyes. 'You don't know what you're asking of me.' His words were whispered. His eyes darting around the room. 'If I'd had the courage I would have revealed this long ago. I just didn't, don't, have that kind of courage.'

He bowed his head. His eyes glistening. 'When I told Paul,' the Professor paused. 'When I told him that I'd speak out, reveal what I'd found, I got a phone call from him. Her little voice. I can still hear every word now, over twenty years later. *Hello Papa, I'm with Uncle Paul. I'm on a high wall. It's amazing. It's so, so high, and I'm looking all the way down at the ocean.*'

He stopped talking, trying to gather himself together. His hands shaking. 'I'll never forget that moment. I knew what he was capable of. I knew he'd do it. My little daughter Maisie. And after I'd just lost my wife, her mother…' The Professor broke down. 'I just couldn't lose her too. And now it's not just Maisie, it's my grandchildren.' Tears were now falling from his eyes. 'I have to keep them all safe. Please understand. I need you to understand.'

The Professor looked at Ed. His eyes desperate and pleading. 'But I know you've lost so much. Suffered so much. And you need answers. I … I want to give you that much.'

The Professor took in a deep breath and drew himself upright. 'Sean … your parents died because Paul covered up anyone or anything connected to what I worked on. They died because when I discovered Tolacaine, I discovered the Grail.'

Ed paused. He turned towards Jamie. Her eyes were still fixed on the Professor. Ed looked back across the desk. 'The Grail? What do you mean?'

The Professor reached for a glass of water on his desk. Took a sip with those bony, shaking hands and put it back down.

'I discovered The Holy Grail of pain management.'

75

Jamie heard the words. Understood the words. But couldn't believe them.

She glanced across at Ed and behind at Conor. Their faces were puzzled.

'What exactly do you mean?' Ed said again, looking at the Professor.

'I'd spent years on my research. I collected and studied every article, every paper, every medical trial. Everything I could get hold of on the subject of pain and pain management. It was my life's work. My big breakthrough came when endomorphins, the body's own painkillers, were first isolated. I immediately recognised their significance and channelled all my research efforts into them. My research was years ahead of its time. Researchers still haven't put all the pieces together. Many are wasting time on somatic discoveries, neuroscience, and psychological therapies. I've tried to help … as much as I dare. But with Paul monitoring my every move, it's been impossible.·I've written papers under pseudonyms, tried to point them in the right direction, but the researchers haven't followed my clues.'

The Professor's eyes had changed. He was gesturing with

his hands. His whole body alive for the first time since they'd walked into the house.

'Professor,' Ed said. 'I'm still not sure what—'

'I'm sorry. Sorry.' The Professor interrupted, holding up his hand in apology. 'I've run ahead. I forget myself sometimes. In layman's terms,' he paused and looked around the room. 'I found the cure for chronic pain.'

Jamie gasped. 'That's impossible,' she said.

The Professor looked across at her. His eyes bright now with a mystical zeal. 'I can assure you it was and is completely possible. If you're a nurse, you have some understanding of these things. My drug was a new type of endomorphin. A stable endomorphin analogue which targeted pain effectively. And, this was the vital finding, it wasn't addictive and didn't have any damaging side-effects that we could find. It worked on all kinds of pain. On arthritis, migraines, fibromyalgia, endometriosis, cancer and more. And on all kinds of peripheral neuropathy or nerve pain, like trigeminal neuralgia. Mild or severely disabling, it eradicated it all. It was a miracle. All the trials in Africa proved it beyond doubt. That's why Paul covered everything up and…' his voice faltered, eyes fearful again.

Jamie could barely take in what the Professor's words meant. If this was true, it was incredible. And appalling. Her mind went straight to Conor. Standing behind her. Because when he realised what the Professor—

'Hold on.' Conor's voice cut through her thoughts. She turned towards him. It was the first time he'd spoken since they'd all entered this house. And he had caught up. His hands were clenched by his side. His mouth open in disbelief.

Conor limped forward, using just one of his crutches. He pointed at the Professor with his free arm. 'Are you actually telling us that you've had the cure for chronic pain for over two decades and kept it secret?'

Conor took another step towards the Professor. He was all but shaking with rage.

The Professor reacted to Conor's words as though he'd been struck. He looked around the room, but he didn't fight back. Didn't justify. They'd already heard why. Protecting his daughter Maisie, and the rest of his family. Instead, he crumpled. Head in his hands. 'You'll never know what this has done to me. Every day knowing…' his voice broke. 'I chose my family. Every day I live with what I've done. Knowing the endless suffering I could have prevented. And knowing so many have died to keep this secret.'

Conor's face showed no sympathy for the pitiable man. Disgust and rage etched across his features.

Jamie looked at Ed. He'd been stunned into silence.

'No one will ever know what this has done to me,' the Professor carried on.

But Jamie could see exactly what it had done to the broken man in front of her.

'The guilt. The guilt is…' the Professor shook his head, his pleading eyes moving between the three of them. 'Please, please forgive me.'

'Never,' she heard the brutal word from Conor. Shouted with venom. 'I've lived through ten years of hell for nothing. Dosed up on cocktails of opiates, antidepressants and anti-convulsants. Living – existing – like a zombie. Experimented on with barbaric surgeries and treatments. I lost everything. And there are millions like me around the world.' He took another step closer to the Professor. 'What you've done is unforgivable. All that suffering. All that despair. For two decades. All that pain. You could have stopped it all.'

She put out her hand and touched Conor's arm. She'd never seen him this close to losing control. He shook off her hand without looking at her.

'You're worse than Tole is,' Conor spat out. He took

another step forward. The Professor looked terrified as Conor was getting closer with each step. Now almost within touching distance of the desk.

Jamie moved forward. She brushed past Conor. Stepped between him and the Professor. Conor's eyes finally met hers. She held his gaze. Put her hands on his arms and shook her head. As the seconds passed, his breathing began to calm. His eyes lost some of their fire and he nodded at her. She moved to his side and pulled Conor back from the desk to stand beside her.

Jamie's heart was pounding. She'd pulled Conor back from the brink, but she could hear his breathing as he stood next to her. He was fighting to get himself under control.

'I don't believe you.'

She turned towards Ed. He was up on his feet and standing at the edge of the Professor's desk.

The Professor looked bewildered.

'Tolacaine *is* about to be released to the public,' Ed carried on. 'You know this. It's a good drug, but it's *not* a cure for chronic pain. If you—'

The Professor butted in. 'You're right. But you don't understand, Sean…' he waved his hand.

'…The Tolacaine on the market isn't the same drug we tested in Africa. It has the same name. But it isn't the same drug.'

Jamie's brain spun.

76

'What?' Ed's mind was racing. Trying to catch up. 'What do you mean, it isn't the same drug?'

The Professor sat forward. 'The drug they're now releasing as Tolacaine,' he repeated patiently, 'isn't the same drug we tested in Africa. Originally, I'd called my miracle drug Valocaine, in honour of my mother, Valerie. But Paul's ego put an immediate stop to that. It had to be named after him. It had to be called Tolacaine.' He paused. 'But when Paul made the decision not to release it, he came up with a new plan. He forced me to modify it. To change the formula. Keep some of the benefits but change how it affected the brain. To make it more addictive than opiates and to increase dependency. He knew it would still be the best drug for a generation for pain. But he was determined to call it after himself, so he kept the name. Because he knew Tolacaine – even the modified version – would make him famous.'

The room went silent. Ed turned to look at Jamie. But she was still watching Conor.

'You're saying…' Conor's eyes were wide. Horrified. 'You deliberately made the Tolacaine we now have on the market less effective and more addictive for people suffering and in pain. You deliberately did that?'

The Professor stayed silent.

'Why? Why would you do that? Why would you cover up your discovery, then release a less effective drug?' Conor was shouting. Ed had never seen him this close to the edge. Jamie still had her hand on his arm, holding him back, stopping him from moving nearer to the Professor.

'Paul's whole empire is built on pain management drugs,' the Professor finally replied. His voice quiet. 'If he'd released my drug, three quarters or more of his medications would be obsolete. Imagine how much money he'd lose overnight. Even a miracle drug wouldn't replace that revenue.' The Professor raised his hands, helplessly. 'I realise I was a fool. I see that now. I hadn't even considered the implications on the market of a drug which eradicated chronic pain. I just—'

'So this all comes down to money?' Conor cut across him.

The Professor paused, looking at each of their faces. 'Yes … I'm afraid it all comes down to money. Paul was, and still is, protecting his business empire.'

Ed turned back to Conor. He looked like a volcano ready to explode. His chest heaving. With a look of hatred and contempt, he shook off Jamie's arm and limped back towards the door. Banging his crutch down at each step.

Ed sank back down into his chair. In shock. Everything he'd believed for years was completely wrong. He felt sick to his stomach. He thought he knew Tole. Knew the depths he would sink to, but this was at a whole new level.

Ed looked at the Professor. 'Why has Tole allowed you to live when you know all of this? When so many others have died?'

'Because I have all the research. It's all encrypted, but I have the encryption key. They've ransacked this house, but they'll never find it. I have copies of all the trials, all the data and every report. I have the drug formula, manufacturing methods, everything. And Paul still needs me. He wants a supply of the drug for himself. I make it for him. He couldn't possibly trust anyone else with the formula. All of this is my insurance. It's keeping me and my family alive. I have all the proof that my creation is everything I ever hoped for.' His voice cracked. 'And it's more than I could ever have dreamed of.'

The Professor slumped back in the chair. Exhausted. The defeated man looked like a dry and empty husk.

Finally, Ed knew what his parents' sacrifice was for. It was far worse than he had imagined. One man's greed, and his quest for money and power, had stopped millions of people from living pain-free lives. It was too appalling to take in.

He looked at Jamie. She was watching him.

He glanced back at Conor. Leaning on the wall next to the door. Fighting to get himself back under control.

He looked across the desk at the Professor. At a broken man. He seemed small. Insignificant. It was hard to visualise the brain of a genius sitting in this withered excuse for a man. Yet he held the world hostage.

The Professor had made the choice to protect his family. Ed understood that. But he compared the Professor's actions with his own and those of his family. What his parents had been willing to risk – their lives – and what he himself had given up – his happiness. It affected how he saw everything.

He knew the side he came down on. However hard. However desolate. He came down on the side of sacrifice. It was embedded in him.

He took a long breath in.

He now had the answers to all his questions.

And he knew what he had to do next.

Whatever the cost.

77

'What are you willing to do now, Professor?' Ed watched his words land on the Professor.

'What do you mean?' Panic now in his voice. In his eyes.

'I understand why you've done what you've done, but…' Ed paused. 'I can't stay silent about this. Not now I know. Paul Arthur Tole had my parents murdered, he cost me my happiness, separated me from my wife, he's denied a world full of people relief from pain, and his men have taken my adoptive father hostage. I have a lot of evidence. It won't be enough to finish him, but it'll be enough to cast doubt, to put him in a mire of allegations and investigations.'

'You want to go up against Paul? It's a death sentence.' The Professor now looked terrified.

Ed shrugged. 'I'm dead already, even if I don't try. Soon there won't be anywhere left for me to hide. For us to hide.' He glanced across at Jamie.

The Professor shook his head. 'You can't do that, you'll—'

'Yes. I will have to reveal what you've told me.'

The Professor had his head in his hands. 'He'll know it's come from me. It can only have come from me.'

‘I know he will. That’s why I want you to consider something.’ Ed paused. Thinking fast. Running through multiple scenarios. Figuring out the best move. ‘I want you to consider giving me all the information you have, Professor. Trust me. Trust that I can end this.’

The Professor’s eyes moved back to fear. ‘What are you planning to do?’

‘I already have evidence and documents on Tole and his dealings. If you give me what you have, I can expose him for who he really is…’

The Professor shook his head even more vigorously.

‘…and try to keep us all safe.’ Ed finished his sentence. He didn’t want to promise more than he could deliver.

‘You’ll never do it,’ the Professor’s voice rose in pitch. ‘He’ll kill us all! I can’t risk my family. I can’t do it. I can’t give you what I have.’ His voice was desperate. And determined.

Ed bowed his head. He’d taken the wrong route. He should have realised, he couldn’t trump the Professor’s love for his family. He needed to offer more.

He turned behind to look at Conor. Now standing like a statue near the doorway. Immovable. Unyielding. The mask was back. His rage contained.

He looked across to his right towards Jamie. Her eyes were still on the Professor. And she was stepping towards him.

78

Jamie had to pull this back. Had to reach the Professor.

She stepped forward and rested her hands on the edge of the desk.

'How have you survived knowing you created this miracle and couldn't share it with the world? she asked. Her voice soft and gentle.

He was silent.

'What do you think your family will feel when they find out what you've done?'

The Professor looked at Jamie. A flash of spirit in his eye. 'They'll be grateful that I kept them alive.'

Jamie paused, then shook her head slowly. 'Are you sure about that? How do you think they'll feel when they find out they're the reason for one of the worst injustices that's ever been known. I think they'll be horrified.'

The Professor didn't reply but his eyes held hers.

'You've been alone in this for so long that you've…' Jamie needed to weigh her words. 'You've lost perspective … They would never want you to be a hostage like this. To have sacrificed your life's work. To have denied the world ease from despair and pain. I promise you, they wouldn't want it.

And Ed … Sean … if he says he can get us all out of this, keep us safe, then I believe him.' Her eyes moved across to her husband.

She turned back to the Professor. He was watching her, but he still didn't speak.

'You'll never get this chance again. If you wait, we'll be gone. Dead. Then you'll have no hope left of seeing what you created find its way into the world. Of easing global suffering. Of going down in history. Of making your family proud that you stood up for what is right. Isn't that the lesson you want to pass on to your grandchildren? Sometimes…' her throat cramped. 'Sometimes you have to take a risk. To sacrifice things you love to do what's right.' She glanced again at Ed. His eyes holding hers.

Jamie didn't know if any of her words were having any impact. The Professor had now dropped his head and would not meet her gaze.

'I told you, I'm a coward.'

'It's not too late.'

Silence from the Professor.

'It's never too late to do the right thing.'

Jamie waited. Holding her breath.

Finally, the Professor pulled his head up and looked at her. 'You believe that? You believe it's never too late?'

'I do,' she said.

His eyes were fixed on hers. She saw a flicker, but it quickly vanished. 'No.' He waved his hands. 'No. No. I can't risk my family.'

'We can keep your family safe.' Ed said.

Jamie turned towards her husband. She didn't expect this. Wasn't sure how it was possible. But it was the only move left he could make.

'How?' The Professor said. Looking at Ed.

'We'll put them all under close protection until this is

over. It should only be a few days.' Ed looked behind at Conor. 'We can do that?'

After the briefest hesitation, Conor nodded. 'We can. I have the contacts. They'll be hidden. They'll be safe.'

The Professor looked at each of them. Jamie could almost see his mind whirring.

'You're … sure. You can keep my family safe?'

'I know we can,' Ed said. 'And we will.'

The room was silent.

After a long pause, the Professor raised his head. Pushed himself to his feet and walked slowly across the room to the wall of books. He reached to his full height, took down a large hardback volume and moved back to his desk. He took scissors from his desk drawer and slit down the edge of the book. Jamie could see a micro-SD card stuck to the inside of the spine. The Professor pulled it free, reached back into his drawer and pulled out a black USB flash drive with numbered buttons on it. Then he took a piece of paper from his desk and proceeded to write a long sequence of numbers from memory. After he finished writing, he sat up, gathered the things together on his desk and looked up at Ed.

'You promise you can keep them safe?' The Professor said, hands on the vital data.

'I promise.' Ed said.

'This is the only copy of all the files. You must use this code when you insert the SD card. You won't be able to open it if you don't and the files will be lost.'

Ed stood and stepped towards the desk.

In one small, silent movement, the Professor pushed the life-changing items across the desk. The man looked both relieved and terrified.

Ed picked up the SD card, the flash drive, and the piece of handwritten paper.

Jamie watched the emotions cross her husband's face. All

he'd fought for, all he'd sacrificed, had come down to this moment. The answers to all his questions and the knowledge now in his hands. To finally expose the truth and get justice for his parents.

Ed pulled his phone from his pocket. Captured the handwritten code on his camera then looked across at Jamie. Tears were in his eyes. They mirrored her own. She took two steps towards him. As her hand reached out to touch his, she caught a flash of movement in her peripheral vision.

She turned.

And she froze in place.

Her heart began to pound.

And her world stopped turning.

Conor had raised his gun.

And it was pointed directly at Ed.

79

'Conor. What are you doing?'

Ed spun around. Jamie moved to step towards Conor, but Ed pulled her back.

Conor held up his other hand. He looked directly at Ed. 'I just need the SD card, the flash drive and the code from the Professor,' he pointed to Ed's hand. 'And I need access to all your research, Eddie. And the DVD.' He glanced across at her. 'It's OK, Jay. You're both going to be OK.'

Jamie's legs swayed beneath her. She could feel herself falling apart. Their years of friendship like wreckage. Carnage on the ground. Like that explosion in Afghanistan. This time, pieces of her heart shattering.

She looked at her husband. His eyes were locked on Conor. Hands clutching the Professor's precious information.

'In what world do you think we're going to be OK, Conor?' Ed's words held no anger. His voice was quiet and steady.

'What have you done?' Jamie said.

Conor's eyes moved towards her.

He didn't answer.

She took one step nearer to him. Shaking off Ed's restraining hand.

'Tell me what's happened.'

He shook his head.

'Tell me.'

'A while back,' he said, 'someone asked me to help them.'

'Who?'

'I now know it was Michael Keller.'

Her heart broke a little more.

'What did he ask you to do?'

'To … watch you. See if you found anything Ed had left behind. Something hidden. Documents. Research. And to see if Ed might actually…' he broke off.

'Might what?'

He paused. 'Might … still be alive.'

Her hand went to her stomach. Deep, searing pain. It felt like a gut shot. How it must feel to be irreparably wounded.

'When? When did he contact you?'

'Eighteen months ago.'

'And what did he give you…' her voice trembled. She couldn't get the words out. Couldn't believe she was saying them. 'What did he give you to betray me?'

'It wasn't like that, Jay. Keller said Ed had documents given to him from his parents. That years back they'd stolen critical research on a drug which would change the lives of people with chronic pain. I was helping to get it all back.'

'And you believed that?'

He didn't answer.

'You really believed Ed would do something that horrific?'

'Well he disappeared without a trace and faked his own death. I had no idea what he was capable of.' There was a flash of anger in Conor's voice.

'You wanted to believe it. You've never liked…' she broke off. 'What did he give you that was worth destroying us for?'

Conor's eyes had not moved from hers.

'What did he give you?' she shouted, her eyes on fire.

'He gave me back my life,' he shouted back.

She took a breath in. It's what she thought. And it all started to make sense now.

'It was him,' she said. 'Keller. He got you on the Tolacaine trial even though you were ineligible.'

Conor nodded.

She was barely able to stand.

'This was about protecting you too, Jay. From Ed. From what he'd done. What … what I thought he'd done.' Conor's voice faltered for the first time. His eyes glancing away from her.

'Protecting me?'

She took another step towards him. They were now eight feet apart.

'This wasn't about protecting me. This was about getting something you wanted and sacrificing us.' Tears were threatening. She pushed them down. 'I know how bad things were—'

'You know, Jay? You know? You don't know anything. You haven't got the faintest idea how bad it was. You had the edited highlights. And even they were curated. You nurse people. You care about them. I know that. But you don't have a clue what it actually feels like. Every single day. A life not worth living. Losing yourself piece by piece. The pain searing paths through every part of you. Weeping like a baby. Wanting to die. Desperate to live. Praying for respite. And that doesn't include the shame. The disbelief from everyone. From doctors to friends. The embarrassment. That I could be so weak. That I couldn't even sit up at a table. Couldn't even,' his voice faltered. 'It's crushing. I hid all that. Because you needed me to keep going. Keep going for you.'

She had to lean on a chair.

'But I thought—'

'You thought what I wanted you to think. Saw what I wanted you to see.'

She couldn't find any words. How had she failed him this badly?

'When Keller told me what Ed had done. What the Tolacaine trial could do for me. What I had to do in return. How it would help so many people. It was easy. I was the good guy here.'

'The good guy … easy to—'

'Not everything's about you,' he cut across her. 'You don't think I've given up enough for you?'

His words, like knives, were slicing through her heart.

'I wasn't betraying you,' he raised his voice even more. 'I was told—'

'I heard you. You were watching me, spying on me, lying to me, and reporting back to them. What would you call that?'

'I was trying to help people. And … I was desperate. I'll admit that. You don't know what someone will do to escape hell … what I was willing to do.'

And now the tears began to trickle from her eyes. Because even in her despair, in her loss of everything she thought she knew, she could understand. And she was beginning to see what this had cost him. It made it impossible to hate him. Her tears were now rivers.

He pointed at her. 'Don't, Jay. Don't do that. I know what I've done here. I know what I've lost. But I didn't know the truth then. Now I do. And I'm going to make this right.'

'There's no making this right,' she said, taking another step towards him. The gun now fully on her, shielding Ed.

'What happened six months ago?'

His eyes shifted.

'Tell me!' She shouted the words. Swiping at the tears on her face.

'Keller came to see me again. Said they were now sure Ed was alive. He didn't go into details. But I was tired of the deception. Reporting back. Watching you. The guilt. I…' his head bowed. Then he looked back up at her. 'I didn't want to do it anymore. But he said I'd be taken off the trial. And he convinced me that I just had to make sure I was there for you … in case—'

'And to sweeten that deal?' Her eyes pierced into his.

He didn't reply.

'What did Keller give you?'

'He said he could give me a stronger dose of Tolacaine.'

'But it wasn't that, was it?'

Silence from Conor.

'You know what it was now. Don't you? I thought it was strange that you had no withdrawal symptoms. You've figured it out, haven't you? As the Professor was talking. You know what happened.'

His eyes were locked on hers.

'It wasn't just a stronger dose, was it? Keller gave you the original Tolacaine. He gave you Valocaine.'

Conor looked her dead in the eye. He didn't speak.

It all made sense now. She'd been piecing it together as she stood. Why Conor had improved so much in these last six months. Why it was far beyond any of the studies she'd read about and any other patient she knew of. How he was unrecognisable. It had been like a miracle because it was a miracle. Keller had given Conor something he couldn't resist. Something which would keep him baited on a hook, unable to stop.

'And now you want the files. To give them back to Keller.

Back to Tole. You want to deny this miracle to the world. Like he did.' She pointed towards the Professor. 'Look what it's done to him. Are you going to watch as they make us red crosses on the whiteboard? You won't be far behind us.'

He shook his head. 'No. I'm not doing that. As soon as I realised, when I saw the wall in the safe room and listened to Ed in the bunker, I've been putting it together. And I've been working on a plan. I'm going to hold the power now. You and Ed will be free. I'll force Tole to…'

She started laughing. A hollow laugh. 'You're delusional. Haven't you heard anything? Learnt anything. You think we'll be safe? Be free?'

'I've kept you both alive this far.'

'What are you talking about?'

Conor put his hand to his forehead. Exasperated. 'You think they couldn't have found Ed before we did? They hacked your life, Jay. It took them a few hours, but they found the tour footage.'

Her mind was racing. Trying to catch up.

'Ed figured that out. He was expecting an army way before we showed up.'

She turned around to Ed. Saw Conor was right.

'I've done everything I could to make sure you were safe. To control things. To stop you both being hurt.'

'Control things? Like the drone strike? It could have taken you out along with the house. You had no clue about that.' She watched Conor's head drop. She knew she'd hit a nerve. She kept going. 'You haven't been in control of anything. You've just been their pawn. They've used you to make it easier. Easier to deliver us on a plate.'

Conor hesitated. 'I can—'

She cut across him. 'You really think you stand a chance? That you can go up against Tole. Against all of them. With everything you've heard. Everything you've seen. And everything they've done.'

He was silent.

Then she saw the chink. The recognition. The realisation of truth.

'We're walking out of here, Conor. And you're not stopping us. And you're not having those files.'

His grip on the gun tightened. 'You won't get away. They'll kill you. They're surrounding the house. Dublin is locked down. There's nowhere you can go. They're just waiting for my call.'

She took two more steps towards him. The gun now pressed against her chest. 'You're going to have to shoot me to stop me leaving. Can you do that?'

She held his eyes. Worlds passing between the two of them.

'How could you do this, Conor? How could you do this … to us?'

Her voice breaking. Her despair naked. Her mind. Her heart. Shattered.

'They said they wouldn't hurt you, Jay … I didn't know the truth then … I would never … Could never…'

His voice broke.

'They lied, Conor. They lied about all of it. They used you. None of us are getting out of this alive if they get anywhere near those files. And you don't begin to have the skills to deal with this. To deal with Tole. You know that. In your heart, you must know that.'

She saw him take in the words.

Watched as his hand wavered.

Watched as he lowered his weapon.

And watched as he slumped down, broken, to a nearby chair.

80

Jamie couldn't move.

It was Ed who rushed past her. Leant over Conor, hauling him back up and onto his feet.

'Conor.'

Ed shook him.

'What are they expecting you to do?'

Conor's eyes stayed locked on hers. She turned away, looking at Ed.

'Conor. Talk to me.' Ed said. Shaking him again.

'When I have all the data from the Professor, have confirmed it's the only copy, and have access to all your files, I call Keller. And they come in.'

Jamie didn't recognise Conor's expressionless voice.

'I need you to get it together, Conor.' Ed's voice was even more urgent. 'Help me figure out a way we can get out of here.'

Jamie moved away, towards the Professor. He was shaking. Slumped in his chair.

'Professor.' She knelt down beside him. 'How many ways out of here are there?'

He looked up. Eyes glazed. 'The front. The back. The garage.'

'What about these?' She pointed to the French doors.

'Too big a drop … into the garden.'

'How big?'

'Twenty-foot … too dangerous.'

'There's nothing else?'

The man was half-crazed. Searching his mind. He shook his head.

She glanced back around towards Ed. His hand on Conor's shoulder. Talking to him in low tones. And as she watched them, she couldn't help but see it. The two men she loved as much as life itself had both betrayed her. Deceived her. What was it about her? Was it what Conor had said? Out of his own mouth. Warning her. *Anyone can deceive someone, if they want to, if they have the motivation, and the person trusts them enough.* Was she too trusting? Naive. Believed too much. Wanted a family too much. To plug the holes inside her own heart. Or maybe they were just more broken than her? More capable of deception than her.

'Jamie.'

Ed beckoned her over. She struggled to her feet. Moved past the Professor. Her legs shaky.

'Conor's going to call it in. Say we've overpowered him. Then we're heading out the garage and the front entrance. The Professor is coming with us.'

It took her a few seconds to take in the words and realise what they meant. Whatever he'd done, she wouldn't abandon Conor. Couldn't abandon him. Once someone carved their name in her heart, they were there for good.

She looked back at Conor. He was leaning for support against the wall. He had none of his normal confident and proud stature. His eyes were fixed on hers and they were emptier than she'd ever seen them. A dead man barely standing.

'We all need to go,' she said.

'It's not possible.' Conor said. 'It has to be this way. I need to do this, Jay…'

'No.'

'Ed knows what we have to do. He can…' Conor broke off. Looked helplessly at Ed.

Ed put his hands on Jamie's shoulders. 'It's not just about us anymore. This is bigger than any of us. This drug will change the world. Too many people have lost too much for this. We have to do the right thing, whatever it costs us.' He gripped her arms. 'Whatever it costs us.'

She knew as he spoke. Voice pleading. Each word ripping and tearing her apart. She knew he was right.

Conor pulled himself to his full height. 'You need to make it look good, Eddie. They have to believe…'

But before he could finish his sentence, Ed had turned and launched a blow to Conor's face. She heard the crack of bone. Saw blood pouring from his nose. Then Ed landed a vicious kick to Conor's damaged knee which made him cry out in agony and crumple to the ground.

Jamie moved to go to him, but Conor looked her in the eye and shook his head.

'More, Eddie.' Conor pushed out the words as he held out his gun towards him.

Ed hesitated. Just for a few seconds. Then he took the gun. And he fired.

Then Ed was turning her around. Pulling her away like a rag doll. Away from Conor. Towards the Professor. Unlocking and opening the French doors as they passed. Chess pieces scattering onto the floor.

'Code Red,' she heard Conor say. His voice breathless. Panicked. 'Code Red. I'm down. Everyone to the back.

They're running. They're armed. They have the package. Everyone move. Now!'

'We should stay at the front—'

'Everyone move to the back!' Conor roared into the phone.

And as Ed pushed Jamie into the corridor, she looked back. She saw tears in Conor's eyes as he looked at her. And then he slumped forward, his head hitting the ground. And something in her soul died.

81

Ed's mind was racing. His body barely functioning.

He looked at the road. Looked in his mirrors. Surely someone would have heard the car. But there was no one behind them. He glanced across at Jamie. Her face white with shock. Trembling from head to foot. Eyes staring in front of her. He needed to bring her back to him.

'Jamie.'

She didn't move.

'Jamie.' He touched her arm.

Still, she didn't register his presence.

'We don't have long. We need another car. Somewhere to go.'

He knew he was talking to himself. He tried again.

'Conor said,' he saw her body shake even more. But she still didn't speak or turn. She couldn't help him. She wasn't even the walking wounded.

He looked behind him. The Professor sat cowering. Terrified. Muttering, 'My family, my family … what have I done.' His eyes flicking back and forth between the side and rear window.

Ed knew that every camera in the city would be searching

for him. And when Keller and his team realised how they'd got away, they would track the Professor's car. It was only a matter of time.

There was only one place he could go. He had his number and knew where he lived. He'd wanted to reach out so many times, but it was too dangerous before. Now he had nothing and yet everything to lose. He was almost sure the man would never change sides. But in the circles he moved in, people were fickle. And after what he'd just seen – a betrayal of Jamie so huge that he still couldn't believe it, even though he'd witnessed it with his own eyes – it was a massive risk. But he had nowhere else to go. No other viable choice.

He signalled left. He didn't know where he was, but the road looked quiet. He turned to Jamie again.

'We have to get another car.'

She looked at him this time. 'Change plates.' Her words came out as a whisper, and it seemed to take all she had. She'd understood. Responded. That was something. And it was a better idea than his.

He checked his watch. It was close to midnight, dark clouds covered the moon, it was pitch black out, except for streetlights. He drove down the narrow road until he saw a house with a car outside on the driveway with low lighting. He parked further down the road, underneath an overhanging tree.

'Wait here.'

Jamie looked through him. Her eyes still in another place.

He pulled up his collar. Head down, he ran to the house, circled around to avoid triggering the security lights, and knelt at the back of the car. He pulled open his backpack. Unscrewed the plates without touching the body of the car. Did the same at the front. Running back, he got to the Professor's car. As he was unscrewing the second plate, he heard an engine. He darted around the car onto the pavement, hidden from view of the road. He could feel his heart thumping against his ribcage. The car slowed. Endless seconds passed before it revved and drove on. Back on his knees, he finished changing the plates then jumped back inside, sitting behind the steering wheel of the car.

His hands shaking, and his heart pounding, he looked around the car at his two helpless passengers. He paused, then turned on the car engine and made the gamble of his life.

He entered the address in his Sat Nav.

And he drove.

82

Fifteen minutes later, Ed was conducting a drive-by of a three-story detached house, partially hidden behind high hedges, in Foxrock. The only thing setting it apart from its wealthy neighbours in The Birches were two men posted at large, black, iron gates. One man on each side. Backs to the house, eyes to the road. Eyes on him as he drove by.

Lights were on downstairs, in the front of the house. Curtains drawn back. Someone was home. Was up. Even at this late hour. It didn't surprise him.

He took out his phone and dialled. He cloaked his caller ID. Even a retired crime boss could be bugged.

The phone picked up.

'Who is this?'

Ed felt it in his chest. The physical sensation of home. He'd have recognised the voice anywhere. It sounded no different twenty years on. Gruff. Impatient. And fierce when it needed to be. Like now.

'I said who is this?'

'Uncle Perry?'

He heard the intake of breath. The noise in the background stopped. The line went silent apart from heavy breathing.

'I still have it.'

Silence.

'Heads or tails?'

And as a stream of profanity and blasphemy came down the line, punctuated by unalloyed joy, Ed let out a long breath. And the heart beating out of his chest began to calm.

Turning the car around, he made his way back to the house and drove through the now open gates and up the gravel driveway. He stepped out of his car as the front door opened. A man rushed forward to meet him. Still sprightly, but bigger than he'd been before. His hair thinner and grey. His body cloaked in an incongruous silk kimono. His face radiant in the house search lights.

And before Ed could put out a hand or speak, Uncle Perry had pulled him into his arms and crushed his body so hard he thought his bones would break.

83

'You're really here,' Uncle Perry said.

'I am.'

Ed smiled. It seemed wrong to feel this happy. But he couldn't help it. He'd never thought this day would come. As he sat at the large oak bench, he watched the face across from him. On closer inspection, he saw aging. The skin wrinkled around the eyes, the mouth, and frown lines on the forehead. But for sixty-five years of age, Uncle Perry looked good.

'I knew they were looking for you. There's been chatter for eighteen months and over the last six months things escalated. But the alerts went crazy across the network on Friday night. I didn't believe any of it. Thought they were chasing ghosts. Tole's continued obsession with you. But it was real. *You* are real.'

Ed smiled again. His hand reaching across the table to his uncle's arm.

'You know Keller has an army out searching for you?'

Ed nodded. He knew it.

He looked across the large open dining and kitchen space. Aunt Kathleen was pouring tea and talking to Jamie and the Professor at the table. It felt so normal. Like he'd never been away. He didn't think he'd ever seen joy like it when his aunt laid eyes on him. Held him. And he'd had to stop himself from falling to the ground when he saw the resemblance to his mother in her smile.

'What do you need my boy?'

Ed looked back at Uncle Perry.

'Can you protect the Professor and his family for a few days?'

'For as long as you need. What else can I do?'

'I need a safe place. Just for a few hours, maybe a bit longer … I have work to do. I have to figure some things out and then…'

Uncle Perry's face took on a solemn expression. 'Then?'

'I'm going to Tole.'

'Seany…' His uncle gripped his arms across the table. 'You'll never get out of there.'

'I think I know how to.'

His uncle paused. Sat back in the chair.

'I always knew you were smart, Seany. Remember what I used to say? But this…' He shook his head. 'At least let me give you some men, to go in with you, for protection.'

'We'll see.' Ed gave Uncle Perry a tight smile.

Ed took a breath in. Remembering the sacrifices that had gone before. That had brought him to this point. Zoe. His parents. And all the others. He thought of the Professor, his family relying on him. Of Jamie and his desperation to keep her safe. He needed to get to work. He pulled the laptop out of his backpack and Uncle Perry reached across and plugged in the charging cable.

Ed knew he had just one chance. One chance to see if he could make all that had been lost count for something. To see if it really was possible to change the world.

And live to see it.

84

Jamie tried to focus on the woman talking. But her mind was in shock.

Conor betraying her. Conor on the ground. It's all she could see. All she could feel.

She'd heard Ed's words distantly talking about where they were going. And she remembered who his aunt and uncle were. He'd told her about them as he filled in his story at the bed and breakfast in Glencullen. As he told her how he'd got away from Ireland and who had saved him and helped him escape.

She'd seen the love and joy on his aunt and uncle's face as they held Ed closer than she'd ever believed possible. And she thought of the twenty years Ed had been separated from his family. All that pain and loss. For all of them.

Sitting at the table now, with Aunt Kathleen and the Professor, she knew she needed to rally. Aunt Kathleen was talking again.

'More cake, Jamie.'

'No, thank you.'

She felt a hand touch her arm and turned. Ed was standing beside her.

'Professor, we need details of your family's whereabouts, to get them to safety. And I need your help with the files.'

The Professor's still-trembling hands put down his cup and he pushed himself to his feet.

Ed looked at her next. Put his hand on her shoulder. Tentatively.

'Conor … he's going to be alright ... I was careful, the bullet…' He broke off. Must have seen her face as she looked up at him.

'He didn't look alright,' she said.

'I know ... I know he didn't.'

And she saw pure and utter devastation in her husband's eyes. And a question.

He reached his hand down for hers. Jamie tried to forget that this hand had wielded the weapon which had taken Conor down. She raised her hand up to meet his and held it.

'I'm going to start work on the files with the Professor now.'

She squeezed his hand. 'Let me know if you need me.'

He let her hand drop with a final squeeze of pressure.

As the two men walked away, Jamie watched them. Then she turned back around. Ed's aunt was looking at her intently.

'He really loves you,' she said.

'I know.'

'And you really love him.'

'I do.'

Jamie looked down. Away from her intense gaze.

'Has he told you … about … before…' The older woman hesitated.

Jame raised her eyes.

'He's told me everything now.'

Kathleen started shaking her head.

'Terrible. So terrible … what happened. It nearly killed

Perry, sending him away. I can't believe he's here. That he's back.'

'It must have been dangerous for you all.' Jamie said.

Aunt Kathleen nodded. 'It was. Perry had decoys out. Used misinformation. Different cars and houses. It was the only way he got Sean out. He went grey overnight.'

The woman had tears in her eyes. As Jamie looked at her, she saw a clear resemblance to the photo of Ed's mother on the passport.

'Ed … Sean,' Jamie altered, 'explained about you and his mother.'

She looked puzzled.

'That you were sisters.'

She was shocked. 'He wasn't meant to know about that. Just that we were old family friends.'

Jamie gave a half smile. 'He said that. But you know him.' She turned around and looked at Ed. Buried in his laptop, the Professor pointing at the screen. Uncle Perry on the phone, writing notes on a piece of paper.

Kathleen smiled. 'Yes. I do know him.'

'What was he like?' Jamie said. 'When he was a child.'

'Such a sweet boy. Tender. Kind. But serious. Always so serious. Thirteen going on thirty his mother used to joke.' Her tears were back.

She wiped her eyes with a tissue from her pocket and reached across the table to a large purse. Opened it and pulled out a photo and passed it to Jamie.

The small boy must have been about six.

'You can see it even there. Serious. Watchful. Nothing got past him, even as a child.'

Jamie looked at the photo. It was the strangest thing, to hold a piece of Ed's history. To be sitting opposite someone who knew him all through those lost years that he had never spoken of.

Aunt Kathleen took out another photo.

'Sean's mother and me. My half-sister.'

Jamie took the photo. The resemblance was even more stark in this picture. 'Sean said you didn't know each other until Prue came to live in Dublin?'

'She found me after overhearing her father talking. She looked for me, searched for me, the illegitimate daughter from one of her father's … dalliances.'

'Did your mother ever—'

'No. No. I never told her about Prue. She wouldn't have understood.'

'So you kept your relationship a secret because you didn't want to cause your mother more pain?'

'Yes. Partly. To protect our families. But also…' she paused. Sadness crossing her eyes. 'Because of Perry's … connections.'

She wanted to ask more, but Kathleen stood. A forced smile back on her face.

'More tea?'

Jamie smiled. 'Thank you.'

When they were opposite each other again, Kathleen looked across at Ed. 'We've missed so much. Do you think…' She paused. 'Will this ever end?'

Jamie took in a breath. It was the question she also wanted an answer to. 'I don't know. I hope so.'

Kathleen looked at her and Jamie could read her mind. The curiosity, just as she'd had. Longing for information from the missing years of her beloved nephew's life.

'Was Sean happy with his new parents?' Kathleen asked. 'Did they treat him well?'

'They loved him beyond measure. Were devoted to him.'

Kathleen's face relaxed a little at this news.

'His mother died just a few years ago. His father,' her own voice choked. 'Tole's men are holding him.'

One hand flew to Kathleen's mouth, the other reached for Jamie's hand. Her eyes drifting across to her beloved Sean.

And Jamie could still see the questions in her sad eyes. So she began to tell Aunt Kathleen what she wanted to know. All the stories of Ed's life and the history that she had missed.

Kathleen sat riveted. Her eyes not leaving Jamie's face. Taking everything in. Living it. Gasping at the mention of Ed's death. At all Jamie hadn't known. Reaching her hand out again to hers.

After she'd finished, the woman looked emotionally wrung out.

'That was…' Kathleen shook her head. 'To pretend he'd died. That was really terrible to do that to you. Really terrible. Can you … do you think you can forgive him?'

'I can forgive him. But trusting him…' Jamie broke off. 'Trusting him is more difficult.'

Kathleen paused.

'I know it's very different, what you've been through. But Perry. Well … I knew who he was when I married him. At least I thought I knew. I really didn't know at all.' She gave a weak smile. 'As time went on, I turned a blind eye. If I saw, how could I still love him?' She glanced across to the table where the men worked. 'I never thought, when I was young, that I'd be in this position. Married to a…' She didn't say the words. 'My two sons … carrying on the family business.' She looked across with loving eyes at the table where her husband sat. 'It's not in any CV, is it?' Her glance back at Jamie was hard to pinpoint. 'And … it's cost me. In many ways. But I still wouldn't change any of it.'

Jamie was quiet. She had no idea what response was appropriate to this confession.

'What Sean did…' Kathleen stopped then began again. 'It's very different. I'm not belittling the deception. Not at all. But it was for a good reason.'

Jamie had already talked herself around this circle. 'It doesn't make any difference. He should have trusted me.'

'I think he was trying to protect you.'

'That's not what I wanted. I wanted truth in our marriage. Honesty. He knew that about me. I don't know how to live without it.'

Kathleen took in a breath. She was struggling to justify the unjustifiable. Defend the indefensible.

'Maybe he made a wrong choice for the right reason. I don't know, Jamie. All I know is that love makes us do things we wouldn't have thought possible. Forgive things we never thought we could. And keep trusting someone who has betrayed our very soul.'

Jamie glanced over her shoulder, watching Ed poring over his laptop. And she remembered her own moment of truth.

Whatever he was involved in, it didn't matter to her. She would have run with him two years ago, and she would run with him now.

And she realised her choice had already been made in that moment. How she would live with that choice was a different matter.

She turned back to look into Kathleen's face. Her eyes. The dark stories held inside. Her hand again rested on Jamie's. Tapping gently.

'My dear. Life is … complex.'

And with those simple, loaded words, Aunt Kathleen stood. Turned her back on Jamie and began preparing food on the expensive, green granite worktop.

85

It had taken hours, but Ed had done it. Afterwards, he'd collapsed with exhaustion into one of the many guest bedrooms, Jamie lying by his side. Now he was ready to leave. To finish this. To face Paul Arthur Tole.

At the front door, he shook hands with the Professor before grasping Aunt Kathleen. He felt a near-desperate tightness in her embrace. Reminding him of his mother on that last day. He watched his aunt's forced smile as she held Jamie and patted her on the shoulders, not able to speak. That would have pushed Aunt Kathleen's resolve past breaking point. He saw her close the door to the house before they drove off, unable to bear another moment of pretence.

It was clear to him.

She didn't think he was coming back.

They were all quiet on the drive to Killiney Bay. Uncle Perry and his driver were up front, Jamie and himself in the back.

As the car turned into Marino Avenue West, it pulled up to solid, white gates. A security guard stood to attention in front of each pillar.

The internal light switched on in the car and Uncle

Perry's window slid down. The guard on the left came forward and Ed saw the shock on his face as he approached the vehicle.

'Mr O'Keefe … Sir—'

'We're here to see Mr Tole.' Uncle Perry cut across him.

'Sir, I haven't been told you have an appointment. I'm sorry … I … I can't open the gates for you.'

Uncle Perry put out a hand to calm the nervous man. 'Tell Tole…' he hesitated. 'Tell him Sean O'Neill is here.'

'Yes, sir.' The guard moved backwards and touched a walkie talkie on his shoulder.

Seconds later, the electric gates opened.

Uncle Perry turned around. 'Sean, at least let me come in with you, let me…'

Ed shook his head. His hand reaching for the man's arm and holding it. Seeing a rare thing in his uncle's eyes. Fear.

'Then I'll wait here for you. I'll wait for you to come out.'

Ed grasped his uncle's arm one last time before looking at his watch. 8:35 p.m. It was time to go. He turned to Jamie.

'Are you ready?'

She nodded. He could feel her calm strength. He needed it. He knew how difficult this was going to be.

Ed opened the car door and Jamie did the same. He came round the back of the car to stand beside her.

He looked into her eyes one last time. Then he took her hand. And side by side they walked. Unaccompanied. In the cool of a spring night. Walking on the black, tarmac drive. Walking towards the fortress of Paul Arthur Tole.

86

The checks were as stringent as Ed knew they would be and took as long as he expected. Multiple electronic scanners took the place of physical, intrusive searches. He was unconcerned. He knew they'd pass this test. There were no bombs, bugs, phones or recording devices on either of them.

As they moved into the house, the level of security intensified. Three bulky, armed men were waiting. One moved to the front, the others formed a barrier around them as they walked along the corridor.

He had expected to feel fear. But what he felt was terror. An ice-cold, jagged rock sat in his stomach and his rapidly beating heart pounded on the walls of his chest. Voluntarily walking into this lion's den was a dangerous strategy. He knew that. But it was the only way to end this.

As they moved forward, his hand reached across Jamie's back. She turned towards him. He could feel the tension in her body. He shouldn't have let her come. But she'd given him no choice. Anyway, he was no longer doing things on his own. He was proving that to her now.

As they continued to follow the guard in front, Ed glanced around one of the most coveted houses in Killiney Bay. A house as stunning as the pictures he'd seen. But the opulence, the décor, the beauty, were all tainted. Gained by pure evil. He knew every inch of the house from his research, the initial building plans, and an article courtesy of *Hello* Magazine – Tole's beautiful wife shining from each colourful page. He knew all the entrance points and exits, but he didn't plan on using any of them. He aimed to walk straight back out the front door. At this moment, that felt like an impossibility.

The man up front stopped. Knocked on what Ed knew was Tole's study, then stood aside. Ed already knew what to expect. A large, grey room with few personal possessions and floor to ceiling glass doors on one side.

The heavy door opened. Michael Keller stood in the gap, filling the doorway, broad and imposing. The prominent holster on the side of his chest was visible over his black shirt. His Glock proud and ready for use.

Ed followed Keller inside, it was exactly like the pictures. Two television screens were on the wall next to the door, behind him, with analogue clocks to the side showing different time zones. Opposite, at the far side of the room was Tole's oak desk sitting in front of a fireplace. To the left, the grey wall held one picture. A portrait of Paul Arthur Tole. To the right, he could see lights flickering across the dark water of Killiney Bay through the wall of glass.

As he moved forward, it was all he could do not to react when he saw Conor standing near the glass doors. Crutches beside him. His leg fully braced, and a thick bandage on his right arm which was held in a sling. He had been desperate, wondering how Jamie would ever forgive him if the worst had happened to Conor – if that bullet had done more than he intended. He met Conor's eyes. They did not flicker. He glanced at Jamie beside him. Her eyes were locked on Conor.

Tole was standing in front of his portrait. Keller positioned himself on Tole's right-hand side. Two other men stood in the room, without jackets, their gun holsters visible. One near the door and one the other side of Tole. Another younger man sat close to the desk, laptop open, nervously looking around.

The man closest to Conor flipped a switch on the wall and the glass doors and windows turned opaque. A simple action designed to send Ed a message. He received it. Loud and clear.

Ed turned and fixed his eyes on Paul Arthur Tole.

'You're a hard man to find, Mr O'Neill.'

Tole's commanding voice filled the space.

Ed held his penetrating gaze. He could not calm his pounding heart. Fear and anger coalescing inside him. After almost two decades, he was face to face with the man who had ordered his parents' murder. Who had issued his own death sentence. Stolen so much of his life. And so much of his peace and happiness.

In the flesh, Tole looked surprisingly ordinary. A large man. His features unremarkable. Only his highly tailored clothes hinted at grandeur. But in his presence, Ed felt more than fear. More than intimidation. Because he knew what Tole was capable of.

Michael Keller made a different impression. A commanding figure who exuded strength. His uncle had told him more chilling stories of Keller – the untouchable man ruling half of Dublin's criminal underworld. He carried out Tole's orders with his own personal army.

'I'm intrigued by your visit, Mr O'Neill. After hiding for so long, why would you…' Tole waved his hand, taking in the whole room.

Ed held his eye. Willed his voice to stay strong. 'I've come to offer you the opportunity to do the right thing.'

He could hear a pin drop in the room.

'About what?'

‘About Tolacaine.’

Tole’s face did not move.

‘Professor Wyndham has told me everything. Are you willing to do the right thing?’

A thin smile broke out across Tole’s face.

‘I presume you’ve been studying me for long enough to know that’s *not* going to happen.’

Ed nodded. ‘I just wanted to give you one last chance to … voluntarily make amends.’

Tole held his gaze. His eyes locked on him. Then he took one step forward and Ed felt a chill ripple through his spine.

‘Do you still have nightmares, Sean?’

In a soft voice, with no preamble, Tole had gone straight for the jugular. Ed knew it would happen. Had tried to prepare himself, but the words had a visceral effect.

‘I heard your parents squealed like pigs when my men questioned them.’

Ed didn’t respond. His hands clenching.

‘The forensic report didn’t give all the information. Bullets to the knees and head. I’m sure you’ve read that … They didn’t mention the … persuasive tactics used.’

Ed looked down. He couldn’t hold Tole’s eye any longer and couldn’t respond now, even if he wanted to. His mind unable to stop the dark visions.

‘I gather your mother was especially vocal. But they didn’t give you up. Either of them. I admire that. I always liked Prudence. A strong woman.’

His mother's name on Tole’s lips sickened him. These were his dreams. Wondering. Imagining what happened as his parents were murdered. Always ending with the fire that burnt their house to the ground. He pulled his head back up to face dark, sadistic eyes. Hatred and rage burned inside him. It took all he had not to jump forward and attempt to claw the life out of Paul Arthur Tole. But he knew he wouldn't have got within six feet of him.

Struggling to take even breaths, he felt a gentle hand touch his own, circling the clenched fists behind his back.

Jamie.

Her touch grounded him. Focused him back on his task.

'Let's skip any more pleasantries, shall we,' Tole said, stepping back. 'I have something – someone – you want. You have things I want. Things which belong to me. It's time to return them.' Tole nodded towards Keller and the top television screen next to the door came to life.

Ed turned as he heard Jamie gasp beside him. His father was on screen. Tied to a chair. Hunched over. A gag across his mouth. His face swollen. His eyes black and bruised. A man standing on each side of him.

What had he said to Jamie? *Whatever it costs.* Could he carry through those words? His mind was already imploding. It was a blessing his father couldn't see him. Couldn't see any of this. Then he realised he could. His father's eyes had widened. Tears on his damaged face.

'It's time to trade.' Tole's voice brought him back.

As Ed turned and pulled his eyes away from his father, he steadied himself. 'I uploaded the files to your Charter portal thirty minutes ago.'

For the first time, Tole looked unsettled. He glanced at Keller, who signalled to the man behind the laptop.

One minute passed. The man perched on a chair, computer on his knees, looked up and nodded.

'You need better security.' Ed said. 'Your new server is vulnerable.'

The man at the computer looked terrified.

Tole's mask slipped for the first time. Anger visible on the surface.

Ed glanced at the analogue clocks on the wall. 8:55 p.m. Then he looked back at Tole.

'And the copies and your own research?' Tole's eyes were laser focused and back on him.

'It's in my interest to keep those.'

Tole paused. 'Isn't losing one father enough, Sean?'

Ed saw a slight nod of the head from Tole. Watched as Keller whispered into a bluetooth earpiece. And with no more warning, one of the men on screen held his father's arm and the other wielded bolt cutters. In one swift move he severed his father's right little finger. The sound was ear-piercing. The audio so loud and so long it echoed around the room. He watched in horror as the blood poured from his father's hand. The man beside him began roughly binding it up.

He felt Jamie sway beside him. He glanced at her. Her face in shock. He looked to his left at Conor. Saw him struggling to keep his mask in place, his hands clenched by his side. He thought of the Professor. That broken man who had put his family before the world. He saw how easy it would be to give in. But he knew there was no point. Documents or not. Copies or not. If he gave way now, none of them would survive this visit and his father would not live through the night. There was no bargain to be made with a man like Paul Arthur Tole.

Ed glanced at the clocks on the wall. 8:56 p.m.

'I'd like to speak to my father.'

Tole considered this and nodded.

The torturer on screen pulled down his father's gag.

'Ed?'

The soft, questioning voice almost broke him in half.

'Is that really you?'

'It is Dad. I'm … so sorry. Sorry for all of this.'

'Jamie?'

‘I’m fine Dad. Everything’s going to be OK. You’re going to be alright. We’ll be with you soon. I love you.’

Ed heard her shaking voice. Saw her forced smile. Trying to reassure their father.

‘It’s up to you, Sean.’ Tole said.

He turned back to face him.

‘We can make it quick. We can make it slow. The choice is yours.’

‘Either would be a mistake.’ Ed said. Tensing his body.

For the first time, Tole looked surprised. An unguarded expression.

He gave that almost imperceptible nod and his father’s scream filled the room again. Watching it was worse than he could have ever imagined. Sickness rose from his stomach. Hot anger burned in his brain. His beloved, wholly innocent father, was now being used as a weapon against him. Just as he’d read in his years of research from Tole’s other victims. He knew why they’d all given in to his demands. Said what they were told to say. Did what they were told to do. The pain, the guilt, watching his father suffer, was unbearable.

As he watched his father gain his breath from the searing pain, he saw that something else was wrong. One bandaged hand was moving upwards. Clutching his chest. His face contorting. He looked at Jamie, at the horror on her face. Then he watched her step towards the screen, moving forwards, as though this would somehow get her closer to their father.

Ed saw a nod from Tole and the video closed down.

87

Ed watched Jamie spin around from the television screen.

'Put the video back on!' she shouted at Tole. 'Get him an ambulance!' Breathless, she looked around at the faces in the room. Searching for help. But no one was listening.

One of Tole's men moved towards her. Ed pulled her back, gripping her hand, holding her close beside him. He could feel her whole body shaking.

'Maybe we should look closer to home.' Tole gave a sickening smile. His eyes shifting to Jamie.

Ed could feel sweat running down his back.

8:59 p.m.

He needed to stay focused. Any second now.

Ed took a step forward, towards Paul Arthur Tole. 'You must find it hard to understand someone who's willing to sacrifice everything for the good of people they don't even know.'

Tole's eyes narrowed. 'I understand altruism is for fools. Let's see how much you're *actually* willing to sacrifice.'

Tole nodded to the man on his left. He moved towards Jamie.

She fought him off. He came at her again. Held her

tighter. Ed looked at Jamie. *Trust me,* his eyes said to her. She stopped fighting.

9:00 p.m.

Ed took another step nearer to Tole. Keller stiffened and reached towards his chest. Ed put up a hand. 'Don't worry, Mr Keller. I just have a question for Mr Tole. I wondered if all his … colleagues … workers,' he waved his hand around the room, 'know what this is all about.'

'They don't need to know,' Tole snapped. His voice ice cold.

'Really? I think they do need to know. I think they'd be interested. Very interested. If they knew the secret you've been hiding.'

'Don't say another word!' Tole shouted.

Ed could see barely contained rage brimming closer to the surface. And he could feel a shift in the room.

'I've wondered something else, too,' Ed said.

Tole held his eye.

'How much money is enough for you?'

'It's never enough.' Tole reacted instantly. And Ed saw the terrible darkness in those near black eyes as Tole turned to Keller. His patience spent. 'Bring in Albescu,' he ordered.

The blood chilled in Ed's veins. He had heard, read, and seen the 'work' of Vadim Albescu.

Ed checked the clock. 9:01 p.m. He glanced at the man sitting at the laptop. Something should have happened by now. Had he made a mistake? He needed to keep talking.

'I believe, if you all…'

There was a knock at the door.

One of the men moved to answer it. Holding the door ajar, a man entered the room. The gaunt figure of Vadim Albescu came forward. Like a dead man walking, he carried a small, silver suitcase in his left hand. The tools of his trade. He walked to Keller and spoke with him in whispered tones.

Then he began to move towards Jamie. Ed turned to her and saw terrified eyes locked on him.

9:02 p.m.

Ed went to speak as he saw Michael Keller move. Pull his phone from his trouser pocket and scan the screen. His face creased. Puzzled. Then Keller's eyes moved back up and looked directly at him. Relief flooded through Ed. It was starting. And in that look, he realised something which surprised him. Keller had not known the truth.

'As I was saying,' Ed repeated. His voice louder, stronger now. The torturer, Albescu, within four feet of Jamie. 'If you all knew what this was—'

Hammering at the door drowned out Ed's words. Keller moved across to silence the sound, but as he opened the door two men burst in. Keller could not contain them.

'Sir. Mr Keller.'

'Get out of here!' Tole bellowed.

'You must … you must see this, sir.'

One man reached for a remote control, pointed it at the screens on the wall, and pushed the buttons.

Ed looked at Jamie.

Looked across at Paul Arthur Tole.

And waited for the explosion.

88

Jamie watched the bottom television screen come to life. The picture changed to RTÉ Nine O'Clock News. She saw Conor and all the men turn towards the sound. The strip in white running along the bottom of the picture repeated statements on a loop.

Breaking news.

Valocaine. A miracle cure for chronic pain found by Tole Pharmaceuticals.

Off patent.

Paul Arthur Tole reports – We've found the Holy Grail.

The men were silent. All eyes on the screen. She saw the recognition in Tole's eyes as the words scrolled by. He pieced it together fast. Then came the rage.

'Turn it off!' Tole yelled out. But the other men in the room remained transfixed. Including Keller.

The female presenter was in mid conversation with a man on a video screen.

'Did you ever think this day would come, Dr Balfour?'

'Mary, I honestly didn't. I hoped. We have all worked on this for decades, and we can't believe someone has finally put all the pieces together. That it's finally happened. It's early days, obviously, but if these claims turn out to be true then this will be a game-changer. We've already been very impressed by the success of Tolacaine, this … well, this will make those successes pale into insignificance. An end to chronic pain. It's miraculous!'

'And it says it will be "off patent". What does that actually mean?'

'Mary, it means the formula will be available for any company to manufacture it without restrictions. It's unheard of with a new drug. It could be as cheap as paracetamol. This could change millions of lives. Change the world!'

'Turn it off!' Tole exploded. His calm facade gone. Eyes like a madman. Grabbing the handset from the man who had burst in. Shoving him aside. Hammering at button after button to turn it off. Only succeeding in muting the audio.

Jamie felt a palpable shift in the room. The men looked at Tole. At Keller. At each other. Trying to understand what they'd seen. What was happening.

She focused back on Tole. His face burning red, his body taut but shaking with rage. Looking at Ed with vicious hatred.

She turned to her husband. There was no victory on his face. No gloating. No sign his plan had trumped anything Tole had in mind.

She looked for Conor. He'd moved. He was closer to Keller now. His eyes fixed on Tole.

'You really think you can beat me? Don't you know who I am?' Tole's shout reverberated off the walls of the room.

'I know exactly who you are.' Ed's voice was quiet and measured. 'Here is my deal. You leave us alone and no one else will ever know who you truly are. What you did. If something happens to either of us, or the Professor and his family, if you come after any of us, I will release all the files and all of my research. Everyone will know that you deliberately hid this cure from the world for two decades. And that you murdered and destroyed lives to cover it up. It will be the biggest mistake you ever make. It will ruin you.' Ed paused. 'Be thankful. This way you get to be a hero. It's more than you deserve. It's over now. It's done.'

This enraged Tole even more.

'I'll say when it's over!' He roared into the room. 'I'll say when we're done!'

Keller moved across in front of Tole, attempted a calming gesture. But Tole shook him off. Pushing him to the side. He was past hearing reason.

'You think you can take me down? You think you can blackmail me? You think…' He was breathless. Gesticulating wildly. Like a raging animal, he'd lost any semblance of control. 'You think you're getting out of here alive?'

Then he moved towards Keller. Pulled his gun from its holster. And Jamie screamed.

89

Ed saw it in slow motion.

Tole turning to the side.

Reaching for Keller's gun.

Aiming it at him.

Jamie crying out.

Conor flashing across his line of vision.

Wrestling Tole.

The mighty crack.

Conor falling.

Crashing to the ground.

Keller grabbing the gun from Tole's hands.

Moving between him and Conor.

Holding Tole back.

Jamie was on her knees beside Conor before Ed had even moved. He dropped next to her and looked on helpless.

'Conor.'

She touched his face.

'Stay with me, Conor.'

'Jay … J…'

His words a whisper. Face contorted with pain. Already turning white.

Her hand pulled up his shirt. Ed saw the wound in the middle of Conor's chest. Blood pumping out, soaking everything.

She covered it back up. Didn't attempt any intervention. It was clear, Conor wasn't coming back from this.

She placed her hands on Conor's face. His eyes wide open. Trying to talk.

'Sor…'

She put her finger to his lips. 'It's OK. It's OK. I understand.'

She stroked his cheeks. Kissed him on the forehead. Feathered kisses on his cheeks.

She put her lips to his ear. 'I'm here. I'll always be here.'

Tears were falling from her eyes. A lone tear travelled down Conor's cheek. His hand tried to lift to her face and she bent her head towards it. She grasped the hand and kissed his fingers one by one with such tenderness. Such love.

'I love you.' She said as she looked back into his eyes, stroking his cheek. 'I love you.' And Ed watched as she bent her head forwards and put her lips on his.

And in that moment, Ed realised that she'd always known. Always known how Conor felt.

He watched the bliss in Conor's eyes. For seconds. Fleeting moments close to ecstasy.

Then nothingness.

Conor was gone.

She stayed there. Motionless. Then slowly lifted her lips from Conor. Lifted her head. Pushed up on her arms with such effort he could see the whites on her knuckles. Her body weighed down. It took every inch of her strength to pull away from him.

She brushed her fingertips across Conor's face. Tracing every part of it. Put her hand up to his eyes and closed the lids. Held her hand there, speaking silent words as she bent over him.

Ed wanted to reach out to her, but he couldn't move. The entire room was like a scene paused on a film. All except her.

Ed glanced across at Tole. Even he was still. In shock. He wasn't used to doing his own dirty work. Giving a kill order was one thing. Pulling the trigger himself was something else entirely. For the first time, Tole looked shaken.

Ed looked back at Jamie. Finally, she rose from Conor's lifeless body. Blood saturated her clothes, her hands. Her eyes moved to his and looked straight through him. She brushed a hand across her face, pushing at the tears. The blood now streaked across her cheeks. She looked like a tiger after a kill.

And as she stood to her full height, and looked around at each man, he saw something he'd never seen before. He didn't recognise her, the look on her face. The look in her eyes.

And Ed was sure, that in the terrible silence, he felt the room tremble.

90

Jamie could taste Conor. His last breath between her lips. Feel the last touch of his hand. See the last look in those slate-blue eyes she had loved for so long. Just not in the way he had loved her.

She floated as she moved. As though in a dream. But this was not a dream. This was a reckoning.

She had seen each face around the room. And she moved towards the one who mattered most. Standing in front of his employer. Still guarding him. In charge of the rest.

She locked eyes with Michael Keller.

'I need you to let me pass.'

He did not move.

His bulk alone a barrier. The shirt taut, showing the definition of his muscular frame. A Glock held in his hand. The gun that had killed Conor. But she did not fear him. She felt she had the strength of ten men.

'You didn't know, did you? I saw you watching the screen.'

Keller held her eye.

'You didn't know what he stole from the world. For over two decades. The lives lost and ruined. The suffering he could have prevented. You didn't know what you were protecting.'

Her voice quiet. Controlled. Holding Keller's eyes.

He still didn't react.

'You didn't ask. You did his bidding. You didn't think it affected you. Didn't think it touched you.' She paused. 'Who do you have in your life, Mr Keller, that this drug could have helped, could have saved?' She took a step nearer to him. Just inches between them. 'A mother, a daughter, a brother.' She saw his eyes flicker.

'A brother.' She waited. 'What's his name?'

Keller still did not speak, but she saw him swallow. The bulge on his Adam's apple betraying him.

'Did you know you were helping to deny him hope? To deny a world full of people relief from agony and despair?'

She scanned the room. Held each man's eye. They looked away from her. Unable to stand her penetrating stare.

'With Valocaine, he can start living his life again. And so can millions of others.' Her eyes fixed again on Keller. She saw him open his mouth.

'It's too late.'

Finally, he had spoken. A rasp in his voice. A glisten in his cold, grey eyes.

She nodded her head. Grief and rage fighting inside her. And emptiness. Too late for Conor. Too late for so many.

Her eyes still fixed on Keller. 'Will you stand aside now?'

An electric charge crackled around the room.

Michael Keller held her gaze. His eyes unreadable. Then his weight shifted. And he took one step to his right. Leaving her prey exposed.

91

Jamie stepped forward in one swift move. Tole backed up. Hitting the wall behind him. Nowhere left to go.

Jamie felt the cold steel in her pocket. Conor's flick knife. Taken from his dead body. She pulled it out, hit the button, and exposed the long blade. It was at Tole's throat before anyone could blink.

She saw the terror in his eyes and relished it. She wanted to end him where he stood. Wanted to shout the condemnation for the millions who couldn't. But the words stayed in her throat.

She thought of Conor. Her beautiful, brave Conor. Cruelly manipulated. Forced to choose between a living death and betraying the person he loved most in the world. Conor, who had just given his life to save Ed. She would not waste words on this man who had just ended Conor's life and broken a piece of her own. He was irredeemable.

She traced the blade down his throat. His chest. Positioned the point directly on his beating heart. And she started to move. To press forward with all her might.

'Jamie! Stop!'

Was it Ed's voice? Was it even real?

‘We need him! Jamie! We need him!’

The screaming voice was real. She stopped in her tracks. Pulled back the knife. Blood trickled down the blade where she had pierced his skin.

Wiping the blade on the bespoke pinstripe jacket which covered Paul Arthur Tole’s chest, she held the knife up in front of his eyes. Clicked the switch. And the blade retracted.

92

Jamie saw it instantly. Tole's face changed. He rallied. As the knife blade retracted something shifted in his eyes. The fear disappeared and the menacing eyes were back.

'I'll give you one last chance.' Tole said. 'Hand over the copies and your research.'

His gaze was focused to the right of her. Looking at Ed.

'Nothing will make us do that,' Ed said. 'You're done. It's over.'

Tole reached into his top jacket pocket and pulled out his phone. Tapped the screen and turned it around.

A photo.

A colourful tiger.

Freya's tiger.

Jamie felt the beat in her chest stop, her stomach drop. He was dialling a number.

'Yes, sir.'

Jamie recognised the voice on speakerphone immediately. Chief Inspector Denis O'Malley.

'Where are you?' Tole said.

'Teams are outside the house. Front and back.'

She looked towards Ed. His face now ashen.

'Give me your files.' Tole's voice was even more menacing as he focused his eyes back on Ed.

Jamie's heartbeat pounded. She felt Ed shift beside her. She put her hand on his arm. If Ed gave up that information, they would soon be lying next to Conor. But much worse than that, she didn't trust Tole to get this drug out into the world.

Whatever it costs.

She saw beautiful Freya. Colourful cupcakes on a shiny plate. Hayley, her rock. How they had kept her alive in the last two dark years. Was this how she repaid them? Abandoning them. Sacrificing them. She didn't know how she was going to live with herself afterwards, but she knew what she had to do.

'Tell me!' Tole's words were louder this time. His commanding voice back, resounding into the room. Believing he was in control again.

Tole's eyes flicked between them. Watching as they both contemplated the worst decision of their lives. The worst decision they would ever have to make. Sacrifice two people they loved for a world of people they didn't even know.

Jamie looked at Ed. His eyes hollow. Empty. It took everything she had. She shook her head. And they both turned back to Paul Arthur Tole.

As Tole brought the phone to his lips, she thought she would fall where she stood. And Ed would not be far behind her.

'O'Malley…'

The word hung in the air.

Jamie held Tole's eyes. She would not move from them. She had made the choice. She would face this darkness and live with it. But as she saw Tole's mouth open to speak, a hand reached across the space. Grabbed the phone and spoke into the handset.

'Stand down, O'Malley. I repeat … Stand down.'

Michael Keller's voice.

THREE DAYS LATER

93

Mountains of Mourne, Northern Ireland - 11th April 2024

Ed and Jamie stood in front of Conor's farmhouse, in the shadow of the Mountains of Mourne. Michael Keller opened the passenger door of the black hearse and walked towards them.

He'd promised to bring Conor home. He'd done just that. And sorted out all the paperwork. The death certificate confirmed Conor had died of a heart attack. There'd be no inquest. No further enquiries. Such was Keller's power and influence.

Four men, dressed in black mourning suits, stepped out and carefully placed the oak coffin on steel legs. Jamie walked forward. Touched the lid. And touched the engraved bronze plate.

Sergeant Conor Daly
8thApril 2024
Aged 35 Years
At Peace

She looked at Michael Keller and nodded.

He dipped his head.

Ed turned and watched as they walked. Jamie led the small group at the front. The men followed, wheeling the coffin over the uneven flagstones. They moved slowly towards the open door where their father stood, leaning for support on the door jamb, his head bowed, both hands heavily bandaged.

Ed turned back to Keller and put out his hand. 'Thank you for bringing him home.'

Keller nodded as he took Ed's hand in a firm grip then dropped it. 'He was a good man.' He looked to the ground, then back up at Ed.

'I have a ring of steel around you. No-one in Ireland will touch you. But it won't last. Tole will come for you. It'll be a while, but he'll use outside sources to get to you.'

It's what Ed feared. It would never end. He'd continued to monitor Tole's networks and Keller had confirmed what he already knew. But he couldn't track everything. He needed as much information as he could get.

Keller continued. 'Tole won't allow anyone to blackmail him, as he sees it.' Keller paused. 'He won't rest until you're gone.'

'Gone?'

'In the ground.' Keller looked towards the house. 'And your family.'

Ed took in a breath. Pulled his jacket around him. It was more than the chill of the wind which was cutting through to his bones.

'You're sure?'

'Information is leaking like a sieve around him. I'm sure.'

'He knows where we are?'

Keller nodded. 'He does. When I hear something, I'll be in touch.'

'We appreciate it.'

'You're not going to run? To hide?' Keller said.

Ed held his eye. 'I've run enough.'

'Do you need anything? Weapons or—'

'We have a garage full.' Ed pointed behind him.

Keller paused. Looking him in the eye. 'My men could handle this, we—'

Ed shook his head and held up his hand. He was already in Keller's debt. At the moment, Ed needed him. Needed his information. But he didn't forget who the man in front of him was. What he was capable of. He had no desire to get any deeper into an alliance with him or be beholden to him. He had no idea how long this period of goodwill would last before Keller asked for favours in return.

'Thank you,' Ed said. 'But I'll deal with it. I'll keep my family safe.'

Keller held his eye. He went to speak but seemed to think better of it. He nodded, turned and moved towards the car. The other men who had carried Conor inside passed beside Ed, their heads bowed, not meeting his eye. Keller gave a final, solemn nod as the car drove off down the rough track.

Ed turned towards the farmhouse and felt his phone vibrate. He pulled it from his pocket and read a text message from George. He replied quickly.

Conor home. It's not over. Stay hidden. Talk later.

Then he walked across the flagstone path, towards the house. Towards Jamie.

Inside the front room, his father was sitting on an upright chair, looking pale and drawn, and Jamie was standing beside the open coffin. He walked forward slowly. Not making a sound.

What he saw caught his breath.

Conor. Dressed in full uniform, top to toe. Looking

strong. Sleeping. As if he would open his eyes and sit up at any moment.

He couldn't find the words to comfort Jamie, to comfort himself. Whichever way he looked at it, this chain of events started with him and Conor was a casualty of it. Because of him, there was a hole in Jamie's soul. He stepped closer to her. Moved to take the hand now hanging at her side, wondering if she'd let him. She grasped and held it fast.

Then they both stood there together. Side by side. In silence. Watching Conor. Watching the stillness of a life now gone.

TWO MONTHS LATER

94

Killiney Bay, Ireland - 3rd June 2024

Sitting in the latest emergency board meeting, Paul Arthur Tole allowed his mind to wander.

For the last two months, he had been a hero throughout the world. Although he usually cared little for peoples' opinions, this adulation had been pleasing. He'd watched it all unfold and found himself glorying in his quasi god-like status.

Global news headlines afforded him more fame. *Saviour of the World ... An end to pain in our lifetime ... Generous benefactor saves a world from pain ... Valocaine and the impact on global economies.*

Engagements had been coming in for an international speaking tour which would make him millions and even further enhance his reputation. Then there were prestigious awards being created in his name. And even whispers of a Nobel Prize which would give him a place in history.

But closer to hand, he had more immediate problems. His business, Tole Pharmaceuticals, was in free-fall. Many of his pain-relieving drugs would soon be obsolete. The moment the news report had announced the discovery of Valocaine – that loathsome name would forever haunt him – prices had plummeted as people offloaded shares. Added to that, his new drug was going to be without a patent. This would cost him billions in revenue. At every turn, he was taking a massive hit to his bottom line.

Tole pulled himself back and focused on his heir. His oldest son.

'We need to pivot and pivot fast.' Lincoln said. 'I already have a list of drugs to invest in. It's package C in your binders.'

The board members flipped through their folders.

'How quickly can you implement this?' Tole said, scanning the contents.

'Immediately.' His son answered. A mirror image of him in character but with his mother's handsome features.

It was as Tole expected. There were plenty of drugs out there and ongoing research. There was always money to be made in pharmaceuticals. And with his newfound fame, companies would be keen to work with him. This financial crisis would be short-lived. Those shareholders who jumped ship would rue the day. Tole Pharmaceuticals would come back stronger.

His bigger problem did not lay in the boardroom, but with his security and protection. Keller had proved to be a great disappointment. Normally he would deal with such treachery, but Keller was not someone even he could dispose of without serious repercussions, he had far too much power and influence. Keller had even managed to put an embargo on him. No-one would work for him in this country. He'd had to draft in security from outside of Ireland.

Then there was Sean O'Neill. The man who never left his thoughts, day or night. Who caused him to burn with barely containable rage. Along with his wife, the one who had drawn his blood. And the Professor who had betrayed him.

Knowing documents were out there, in the hands of others, which could expose his secrets, was intolerable. He had to get this situation back under control.

To that end, he'd been making plans. Making connections. Preparing to deal with this situation once and for all. To find the Professor and his family. And watch as Sean O'Neill begged for his wife's life. Then begged to die.

95

Mountains of Mourne, Northern Ireland – 5th June 2024

Standing at the kitchen table, looking at Jamie, Ed hung up the phone.

He took in a deep breath.

'It's confirmed. They're coming from Eastern Europe. Via the UK. They'll be here in the next few days. Keller will let us know when they land in Dublin.'

He watched Jamie grip the worktop.

'He's never going to stop, Ed.'

'I know.'

If he was honest with himself, he'd always thought it would come to this. He'd created a plan where they could all survive this terrible nightmare. But it had always been dependant on Tole. On him letting things rest. But nothing had changed. Ed heard the words echoing inside his head. *Find and kill Sean O'Neill.* Tole was never going to let things lie. Let him live. And now it wasn't just him, it was his family. And the Professor's family. People he'd promised to protect.

'It's not enough that he's fêted around the world,' Jamie

shouted, 'that we don't look for justice for Conor, for your parents, for everyone he's…' She broke off. He could see the pulse at her neck throbbing. 'He still can't let us live.' Fire burned in her eyes. Her anger and grief raw and exposed.

He watched her rapid breathing as she tried to control her rage. And he thought of all those years when rage for his own parents had burned him alive. How he'd forced Jamie to hold back her own anger, hold back justice, when Conor lay dead on the floor. All for the greater good. To make sure this drug would reach the world. That the legal documents would be in place to ensure it would be available for all companies to manufacture.

He'd worked hard to put a fence around those emotions. To cut them off and count his blessings. He was alive, with Jamie. His father was safe, recovering well from his ordeal at the hands of Tole's men. It didn't get any better than that for him. And he was finding a way to live with Tole's face as the hero across the globe, with only a handful of people knowing the truth of his real evil.

But if Paul Arthur Tole was coming for them, then that was a different matter. He could allow himself to vent that rage. Not for vengeance – even though he ached for it. Not for justice – even though he longed for it. But in self-defence. He *would* act to keep his family safe and defend those he loved.

Jamie looked him in the eye. 'What do you want to do?'

He returned her look. 'We do what we have to do.'

She took his hand. 'Let me. I've already—'

'No.' He took her hands in his. 'It began with me. It ends with me.'

He paused and put his hand up to her cheek. How he loved her. It took his breath away every single day. He didn't want her carrying that burden, she already had more than enough to bear. He looked into the distance, then back at Jamie. ‘Scorched earth?’

Her time to nod now. ‘It’s our only choice.’

Ed took in a deep breath and stayed a few more moments in the warmth and safety of her embrace. Then he left Jamie where she stood and moved towards his office. To prepare for the end of it all.

96

Dublin, Ireland – 7th June 2024

Jamie watched the television screen as Paul Arthur Tole walked into the entrance of The Douglas Conference Centre, offering a wave to the waiting press. Her stomach turned over.

The picture moved to an empty table with four microphones and a podium to the left. The camera panned around the space to the packed press corps – the noise of chattering voices audible through the screen.

On the dot of seven o'clock, the host, RTÉ news anchor Meredith Hall, stepped up to the podium. The room hushed. The Press Conference was about to begin.

Jamie glanced at Ed beside her. His face was fixed on the screen.

'I'd like to welcome everyone here today to witness this historic event. Let's welcome our four special guests,' Meredith Hall announced, her arm outstretched. 'Susan Wright from *People Against Pain*. Dr Helma Ramesh, a Pain Management Consultant from St James's Hospital. Dr George

Yale, Professor of Economics at Trinity College Dublin. And, of course, Mr Paul Arthur Tole, whose company, Tole Pharmaceuticals, discovered the miracle drug, Valocaine.'

A burst of flashlights went off as the four guests walked into shot, smiles wide across each of their faces. Tole led the group and took up his position closest to the podium.

The camera moved back to Meredith Hall and zoomed in.

'We're all here today to bear witness to a momentous event. After two months of intensive legal work, we have made it. Valocaine has now begun its final trials and when it's ready to release, it will be off patent. An open-source drug with no restrictions on manufacture.'

Clapping engulfed the room as Meredith Hall stood and smiled. Stepping back herself, she joined in the applause, her hands vigorously slapping together. After the applause subsided, she moved forward again to speak.

'Before I hand over to questions from the eager press,' she smiled, as a ripple of laughter travelled around the room, 'I want to ask Mr Tole a couple of questions, if I may.' She took a pause and continued.

'We're especially fortunate to have you with us today, Mr Tole. I know you're not one for the limelight, so we all appreciate it. Can I ask how you're feeling?'

'Meredith, it's a wonderful day.' He beamed at the camera. 'I couldn't be happier.'

'It's a moment of such generosity. I imagine a less altruistic person could have made billions from this drug,' she said.

Jamie was sure she saw Tole's jaw tighten. He hadn't yet learned to hide all of his body cues.

'I'm just happy that everyone will be able to benefit from our groundbreaking discovery.'

'And one last thing. The name, Valocaine. I read it was called after a family member. Such a lovely tribute.'

Tole's eyes narrowed, then quickly adjusted. A smile across his face. 'Yes. That's right.'

Meredith waited for more, but no more words were forthcoming.

'Wonderful. Just wonderful,' she said, covering the awkward silence.

Then she turned back to the waiting press. The camera view shifted to show the press pack, crammed into the space in front of the guests, then moved back to focus on the podium.

'So … who'd like to ask the first question?'

Meredith Hall glanced across the sea of hands and pointed.

'Thank you, Meredith. Susan Wright from *The Sunday World.* Mr Tole, there's already talk of you being awarded the Nobel Prize for Medicine. Do you have any thoughts on that?'

Tole dipped his head in fake humility.

'Susan, none of these things are necessary. I'm just happy that suffering will be relieved for so many people around the world.'

Jamie could barely watch. It was despicable. He was despicable. She could feel and hear Ed's leg tapping up and down. His whole body taut, on alert.

Meredith pointed again.

'Ben Jones from *The Irish Medical Times.* Dr Ramesh, can you give us some timeline for when Valocaine will be available and the importance of this new drug?'

'Ben, we estimate Valocaine will come out of its final fast-tracked trials in two years. Tolacaine will fill the gap until then. And as for the importance. Well, Ben, it's incalculable. Physically, mentally and personally. The level of physical and mental suffering from pain is enormous. This is not just a life-enhancing drug, but a life-saving drug. I'm sure everyone here has been affected in some way by pain. Conservatively, figures show twenty percent of people globally endure some form of long-standing, persistent pain. Personally, the improvement in quality of life for those with many illnesses will be vast. And for us as doctors, to see the end of so much suffering, it's beyond what any of us could dream of. Our appointment lists will also be lighter.' She smiled and a ripple of laughter travelled around the room. 'We are all just so thankful to Mr Tole for his generosity.'

Jamie felt Ed's hand reach for hers and hold it tight. She saw him glance at his watch then back at the screen.

Meredith pointed again.

'Kelvin Black, *The Economist.* Professor Yale, can you give some insight into the effect Valocaine will have on the world's markets.'

'We predict it will be extraordinary. It will ease pressure on health services across the world, reduce pressure on welfare systems, and give a massive boost to the global economy as more people get back to work. It's going to have a huge impact. Unprecedented.'

With the camera back on Meredith, she spoke. 'Can we go to…' She took a pause. The camera panned again across the media. As the voices clamoured to speak, hundreds of beeps and noises went off around the room. All the hands went down. A hush spread across the room. Every one of them had their heads down, buried in their phones. Muttering between each other. Then the hands were back up again. A sea of waving arms.

Meredith pointed. 'Thank you, Sara.'

'Sara Feeney from *The Irish Independent.* Mr Tole, when did your company first discover Valocaine?'

'It was during our work on Tolacaine. Our researchers identified the elements of the miracle drug we now have, and we've been working on it ever since.'

'As a follow up, if I may. I'm confused. I have paperwork in front of me showing the chemical formula of the drug we now know as Valocaine, signed, dated and authorised in 1998. Over two decades ago.'

Tole shifted in his seat. He looked down into his hands. Jamie glanced at Ed. His eyes had not moved from the screen.

Tole rallied quickly. Looked up. Focused on the waiting journalist and gave her a tight smile. 'Ms Feeney, you have been given the wrong information.' Tole glanced at the host and waved his hand for her to move on.

'Trevor Night from *The Guardian.* A question for Mr Tole. Do you know a Professor Wyndham?'

Tole held his gaze steady. 'I don't think so.'

'What about Sean O'Neill?'

Tole shook his head. 'I've heard the name, but I'm afraid I don't know him either.' A grimace more than a smile settled on his face.

Jamie could see it happening in front of her. He was rattled. His confidence ebbing. He could see the car crash coming.

'Fay Dunlow from *The Irish Times.* Mr Tole, isn't it true that Professor Jeremy Wyndham actually discovered the miracle drug called Valocaine in the late 1990s? That the drug trials you released to us just two months ago were actually conducted more than twenty years ago? And that you've been hiding this drug from the world since then?'

Meredith Hall looked uncomfortable, glancing at the panel.

The camera zoomed in close on Tole.

'That's complete and utter nonsense.' His voice was ice cold.

'Isn't it also true that you deliberately released Tolacaine, a less effective version of that miracle drug, for financial gain?' Fay Dunlow carried on.

Camera flashes were going off. A sheen of sweat was now visible at Tole's hairline. The camera panned across the other members of the panel looking around at each other, mystified.

Fay Dunlow didn't wait for an answer. She wasn't stopping. Jamie recognised her name from the article she'd read on the ferry about Ed's parents.

'And isn't it true, Mr Tole, that it was whistleblower Sean O'Neill who released the formula for the miracle drug Valocaine? The same Sean O'Neill, who has been in hiding after his parents were brutally murdered in the summer of 2005. Murders which shook Rathgar to its core. Murders which you ordered.'

Tole's face was now empty. No emotion across it. But the camera zoomed in so close his twitching eye betrayed him. As the camera pulled back, Jamie saw his body was rigid. His hands balled into fists. His eyes full of hatred. She had last seen that look moments before he'd killed Conor. He looked as though he could murder them all as they sat.

'This is slander.' His voice held no emotion. Chilling to its core. 'My lawyers will be in contact with you.' His eyes pierced through the screen. 'You'll never work again, Ms Dunlow.'

The camera panned back to Fay Dunlow. The journalist, still standing, roving microphone in her hand, did not flinch.

'Mr Tole, Mr Tole—'

Cameras were flashing. Competing voices fighting to get their questions heard and answered.

But Paul Arthur Tole was out of his chair and up on his feet. Without a glance back to the audience, he calmly walked from the studio and left the clamouring crowd in his wake.

Jamie looked at Ed. 'It's over.'

He looked back at her.

'Almost.'

97

Killiney Bay, Ireland – 8th June 2024

Tole stood in his study. Enraged.

The very foundations of his world were shaking. The roof was cracking and the four walls were crashing in on top of him. A fall from grace of such epic proportions that it had no parallel in living memory.

The humiliation at the press conference yesterday made him burn inside. He felt like the cowering child whose father had used him for boxing practice. Powerless, pitiful and weak. But he would turn it around. The way he'd done all of his life. He'd turn it into hate and rage.

The news of his shame was wall-to-wall. Every detail mulled over, debated and explained. Families coming forward of people he didn't even remember, telling stories of his evil deeds. His phone ringing off the hook.

His wife had sat watching it all. Transfixed to the screen.

'Is this all true?'

He couldn't be bothered to lie. She was a trophy wife

who'd given him what he needed – children with her good looks and his brains. He had no need of her now.

'Yes.'

He ignored the disgust on her face as she turned and left the room.

Lincoln had been on the phone the moment the press conference had ended. 'We need to limit the damage.'

'We will. But first, I need to leave the country,' Tole said.

'I'm dealing with it. I'm preparing a private plane for you.'

'Good. Make sure it's ready by noon tomorrow.'

His other children had not rung. Choosing silence as their weapon. He realised that he didn't care. The disgust of his family barely touched him. It was the burning effigies of his face in some countries, with crowds baying and chanting, "Death to Tole", which disturbed him more. It finally tipped him over the edge. The rage inside him exploding. His humiliation was complete and public. It was everywhere.

A trailer came across the television screen in his office.

'Tonight, *Unmasked,* a news special, will reveal the truth, the real truth, behind the drug Valocaine. We'll share the story of how Paul Arthur Tole, the man who came from the slums of Dublin, deceived the world and deliberately allowed decades of global suffering to continue in order to build his pharmaceutical empire. We will be hearing from Paul Arthur Tole's parents and other family members. Also, Professor Jeremy Wyndham, who discovered Valocaine in 1998. He will tell us the extraordinary story, going back two decades, of a missing boy whose parents were brutally murdered in Rathgar, near Dublin. Police are already reviewing leaked documents and interviewing witnesses. They have begun their own investigations into fraud, money laundering, blackmail, threats of violence and incitement to murder. All with alleged connections to Mr Tole.'

For the first time in his life, Tole could not speak. His lawyers would tie the legal system in knots but the idea that he could end up on trial, even more publicly humiliated, was incomprehensible to him. And his parents appearing on screen. Talking about him. It was the last straw. He picked up a paperweight from his desk and hurled it at the TV screen, relishing the sound of glass smashing. The pieces shattering and scattering across the deep pile carpet.

He pulled out his phone. Scrolled and hit the screen. He issued no greeting when the phone was answered.

'Where are you?'

'We are approaching the port in Belfast.' The cool voice had an Eastern European accent.

Tole was pacing the room. How long did it take to get a job done? They'd meandered their way here to avoid detection. That wasn't his problem. He just wanted it done. Now even more than before. He was going to wipe Sean O'Neill, and those he loved, from the face of the earth. But not before watching them all suffer. Watching the breath go from each of their bodies. The man he was speaking to, and his crew, were carefully selected for that job. Known for their abilities in the dark arts of persuasion. And they were almost on these shores.

'What time will you get to them?' Tole said.

A pause on the line.

'We can be there in under three hours. We await payment before we proceed.'

'Payment has been sent.'

'We have not received it, Mr Tole.'

I can assure you, payment has been sent.'

'We have not received it.' The cool, accented voice repeated.

'Hold the line,' Tole said abruptly, exasperated. He moved across to his computer.

He clicked and scanned the screen. The details were there. He pulled up a browser window to check his bank account. His password was not recognised. He attempted to reset the password, but the authentication code was not going to a phone number he recognised. He tried another account. Repeated the process. The same problem. Anger mounting, he tried a third account. The same result. He couldn't access any of his accounts. He was completely locked out.

His heart began to beat a little faster.

He moved to his Cayman Island accounts. After several security measures, he logged in and what he saw horrified him. He scrambled. Clicking buttons. Checking each screen. There was nothing there. The accounts were all empty. It had to be Keller. No-one else knew about these accounts.

His email app pinged. He clicked and scrolled. There were hundreds and hundreds of unopened messages. He scanned down. *Thank you for your donation to The Irish Chronic Pain Association ... Thank you for your donation to Burning Nights CRPS ... Thank you for your donation to People Against Pain.* The list went on and on. This was not Keller. It was Sean O'Neill and his pathetic altruism. He hadn't just ruined his reputation – he'd bankrupted him. Rage coursed through his body. Did O'Neill really think he could beat him?

He heard the buzz of his phone. Glanced at it. A text message from Garda Byrne from the local Dun Laoghaire Station.

Gardaí en route. They have search warrants and arrest warrants. Thirty minutes out.

He still had a few friends in law enforcement. People he had influence over. Blackmail was one word for it. Influence was the one he chose.

He went back to his phone call, to the man waiting on the line.

'Just do the job now and I'll pay you double.'

'Payment in advance. This was agreed,' the voice said.

'I'll pay you triple. I'm good for it. You know that.'

'Mr Tole, we are fully up to date with global news.' The man paused. 'We insist on payment before proceeding.'

Tole gripped the edge of his solid oak desk. Knuckles white. Slammed his fist down and felt the pain shoot across his hand and up through his arm. He stopped himself from crying out.

'Wait for my call.'

He hung up the phone.

His heart rate had never been this high. He undid the button at the top of his shirt and pulled the tie loose. He was struggling to breathe. Nothing would stop him getting these men to Sean O'Neill's house.

He texted Lincoln. *Need funds urgently. 100,000 Euro. Find a way.*

He moved across to his safe and transferred the contents into his briefcase – cash, diamonds, his wife's jewellery and his personal documents. He strode towards his garage, took the key for his SUV from the hook on the wall and jumped inside.

He checked the time. It was close to noon. The private plane would be waiting to take him to his property in the Maldives. The government scheme he'd heavily invested in, plus the compromising information he'd amassed on various officials, ensured he would be tolerated there. With no extradition to Ireland, he could live there in comfort. It would take time, but he would rise from the ashes.

As he turned the steering wheel to exit his garage, an alert sounded on his phone.

He checked the text message from Lincoln.

No plane. Accounts all empty or frozen. No money to pay for it.

This sent Tole spiralling.

The next message beeped.

New plan. Go to Coliemore Bay. Boat waiting. I'll figure out the extra funds.

Tole exited his garage and travelled up the drive. As the electric gates opened camera flashes went off. Press surrounded his vehicle. His security men tried to hold them back, but there were too many of them. He revved his accelerator and moved forward, driving through the pack, deliberately scattering them.

He sped up on the winding road, took a left onto Killiney Hill and left again onto Military Road.

Without warning, the lights on his console started flashing and his dashcam came to life. Tole turned the dial to switch it off, but it didn't respond. The visible screen now showed the road ahead.

He picked up speed, his heart pounding in his ears, his hand hitting the wheel in frustration. Imagining it was Sean O'Neill's head. What he felt was beyond hatred. The man had humiliated him in front of the world. Had destroyed all he'd worked for. He would not rest until he was dead in the ground.

He felt sweat pooling on his back. He swiped his forehead. He was burning hot, beads of sweat creeping down his cheeks. The seat beneath him and the air around him was suffocating. He tapped button after button but the aircon continued blasting heat. His right hand touched the button on his driver door, but the electric window did not open. He banged on the steering wheel again, raging at the world and this overpriced, useless technology.

His phone beeped. Lincoln. He slowed the car, glancing at the words.

'Have accessed Moira's accounts. Where do you want the money?'

Tole hit the call button. Pulled a card from his top pocket.

Lincoln answered. 'What do you—'

'Send it now as a bank transfer. Account AL643—'

His phone cut off.

Tole thumped the dashboard. Hit the call icon. There was no dial tone.

He was now on the Vico Road, a cliff-edge route along Killiney Bay, known for its stunning beauty. But Tole saw none of that. His eyes were on his phone and the tarmac. Going as fast as he could. Braking dangerously at each curve of the road. The images of burning effigies seared into his mind.

He moved to try his phone again when a flashing alert hit his dashboard. *Airbag disabled.* Distracted, touching buttons, he almost hit a braking car ahead of him.

He pulled again at his shirt. He had to get his jacket off – his body was soaking wet. Sweat dripped onto his shirt collar.

As he took the next curve, he glimpsed the white, clifftop terrace of Sorrento Point in the distance. He was so close now.

A bend in the road came towards him. He braked to take the curve, but the car did not turn. His heart pounded even harder. His knuckles were white, gripping the wheel. He pressed the pedal again and it responded. The car turned. He took a deep breath in. He continued on, the speed dial nudging back up.

Another bend in the road was up ahead. He needed to slow to take the curve left at Coliemore Road. He was just two minutes from the boat which would take him to safety. He hit his brake. The car did not respond. Panic began to rise. His head pulsed.

As he approached the white terraced houses of Millionaires Row on his right, he hit the brake again and turned the wheel. But his car did not slow. And his steering wheel did not turn. Instead, the car accelerated. Straight on. Picking up speed at an alarming rate.

It was only then that Paul Arthur Tole realised he was not in control of his vehicle.

He desperately pulled at the emergency brake and pumped the brake pedal, but he was still speeding forward. He tried frantically to open the door as he ploughed into the iron gates of the last house on the row. His car hurtled across the forecourt and crashed into the low wall ahead of him. Somersaulted over it. Throwing him forward.

Then he was screaming.

And falling.

Falling onto the rocks below.

98

Disgraced Pharmaceutical Tycoon, Paul Arthur Tole, Dead

By Fay Dunlow, *The Irish Times*
Published 8 June 2024 –17:35.
Breaking News.

Earlier today, disgraced pharmaceutical tycoon Paul Arthur Tole, aged 64, died in a car crash close to his home in Killiney Bay. Following the extraordinary revelations at the Douglas Press Conference yesterday, Mr Tole has rapidly become a pariah around the world. Our sources confirm that multiple warrants were out for his arrest for murder, conspiracy to murder, fraud and other charges. Eyewitnesses at the scene reported that Mr Tole's car accelerated past the prestigious white terraced houses, known as Millionaires Row, and piled into the iron gates of number one Sorrento Terrace, the most famous house in Killiney Bay. Crossing the forecourt, his SUV then hit the wall at more than seventy miles an hour, flipped over, and plunged onto the rocks of Sorrento Point. Mr Tole's body has been recovered from the scene. Gardaí are not currently treating his death as suspicious and are not looking for anyone else in relation to this incident. Mr Tole is survived by his wife, two sons, a daughter, and seven grandchildren.

FOUR YEARS LATER

EPILOGUE

West Cork, Ireland – 7th February 2028

They walked at a steady pace. Haversacks on their back. The three side-by-side. Hand-in-hand.

'Swing me! Swing me!'

They looked across at each other and smiled. Then they started to swing the small three-year-old boy between them.

'Higher! Higher!'

They swung him until their arms ached and they were nearly home.

Now at the rocky pathway, the darkness was coming in fast. As they got to the cottage gate, Ed unlatched it. Jamie watched him turn back around, as he always did, to look across the dark fields, the low-lying scrub and around to the cliff edge holding back the Atlantic Ocean. He scanned the whole area.

All was still. All was quiet.

Jamie passed him, walking up the gravel path. Opened the door and tugged the boy's arm.

'Come on, Conor, let's get inside.'

She held the child's hand as he made it up the large step, landing on the mat in the hallway.

'Where's my jar? I need my jar! Want to show Grandpa.'

The boy was hopping from one foot to the other.

'OK. Hold on a second.'

Jamie burrowed into his little backpack covered in dinosaurs. Passed the jar to him and watched as he walked towards the sitting room with his treasure carefully held between his hands.

Moments later, the child barrelled back and Ed swung him up into his arms.

'What did Grandpa think of your caterpillar?'

Conor looked at him and shrugged. 'He's asleep.'

'Never mind. You can show him later.'

The child smiled and Ed started to unbutton his coat.

Taking off her shoes, Jamie padded along the corridor, her thick woollen socks making no sound on the oak floor. She turned the corner and moved towards their father, sitting peacefully in the chair, his head lolling to the right as it always did. Hands resting on his knees, glasses perched on his nose, his sudoku on his lap. She heard the sound of gentle snoring and the wheeze of his chest as he inhaled. The caterpillar, in its clear jar, sat on the table next to him, perched on top of *The Irish Times* with the headline:

How Valocaine Changed The World

She looked up. Ed was at the door, watching her. She met his eyes. He moved towards her as Conor ran between them.

'Shhh,' Jamie said, crouching down. 'We don't want to wake Grandpa.'

But it was too late. Grandpa was already stirring, and the boy was at his knees, pointing at the jar.

'Look, Grandpa. Look!' he said, as he clambered up and

began chatting and waving his arms. Telling him about his find.

She stood back up and leaned towards Ed. His arm came around her back. His other arm bent to pick up the newspaper. She saw him scanning the words.

On the two-year anniversary of the release of Valocaine, we reflect on how this miracle drug has changed the world.

A world changed because of the Professor. And because of her husband. Because of his relentless search for truth and justice.

Ed looked at her. And for a moment, she couldn't breathe. His eyes spoke.

It's us against the world.

And it finally was.

'Mummy!'

She turned towards her beautiful boy. As he looked back at her, eyes wide with laughter, she glimpsed the picture on the mantelpiece.

Afghanistan 2013.

Her heart gave another lurch. The tender place that never left her. The person she would always carry with her. And as she looked again at the smiling faces of her own family, she said more silent thanks to him. To Conor. The one who sacrificed everything for her to have this life.

To have this joy.

MORE FROM RUTH:
DEAD LIAR EXTRAS

* If you enjoyed *Dead Liar,* get Free Exclusive Bonus Scenes from Jamie, Ed and Conor, the inspiration behind this story and more: **https://ruthninawelsh.com/books/dead-liar-extras**

* If you'd just like to know when my next thriller is out, then you can sign up here: **https://ruthninawelsh.com/books/next-thriller-release**

AUTHOR'S NOTE

Major spoilers ahead.
Please don't read if you haven't completed Dead Liar!

Over the years, I've written a lot of words – in song lyrics, in non-fiction and in other thrillers I'm working on. Never have I wanted a story to be as true as this one. I've spent two years writing it, inhabited the world so deeply, I can almost believe Valocaine is real. And how I want it to be real.

My own life is deeply affected by chronic illness and pain.

In 1982, when I was eighteen, I had a virus which I didn't recover from. Myalgic Encephalomyelitis left me unable to walk, in constant pain, with bone-shattering exhaustion, severe and complex allergies and that was just the beginning. It began a forty-year battle with multiple chronic illnesses which have now left me housebound and living from my bed. In Conor, I wanted to shine a light on some aspects of my own life. He'll forever have a piece of my heart.

For those who know what pain, chronic illness and disability is like, or who care for someone who is ill, my heart is with you. We can dream that one day there will be a Valocaine.

With love,

Ruth.

January 2025

ALSO FROM RUTH

BOOKS

Self-Help: Live A Happier, More Fulfilling & Meaningful Life

MUSIC

Introducing Ruth Nina Welsh (EP)
Breathe (Album)
Somehow (Album)
Heartland (Album)
Misfits (Album)
The Acoustic Covers Collection (Album)

ABOUT RUTH

Ruth Nina Welsh is a musician turned thriller writer. She has travelled through life as a singer-songwriter, counsellor and coach, freelance self-help writer and now novelist. *Dead Liar,* her high-stakes debut thriller, is out now. Ruth lives in Northamptonshire, in the UK, surrounded by music, books and an ever-growing mountain of craft supplies.

Visit Ruth's website for more details and to join her monthly newsletter:

https://ruthninawelsh.com

Shop

https://rnwstore.com/

Follow Ruth on Facebook:

https://www.facebook.com/RuthNinaWelshWriter

Follow Ruth on Instagram

https://www.instagram.com/RuthNinaWelshMusicBooks

ACKNOWLEDGEMENTS

Many thanks to my editors – Richard Welsh, Virginia King and Steph Warren. To Richard, my brother and first reader – I couldn't have written this book without you. To Virginia, my friend and writing mentor – your support is invaluable to me. And to Steph – your story insights were important. Thanks also to my Beta Readers and ARC Team for your encouragement and help as I launch my first novel – I appreciate you all so much.

To those who have answered questions related to this book – thank you. Any mistakes left are my own.

A big thank you also goes to the rest of my family and friends who always support me. I am blessed to be so loved.

My final thanks go to *you.* Thank you for reading my book. By turning these pages, you have made one of my dreams come true.

Printed in Dunstable, United Kingdom

77337352R00265